A Reckless Witch

Debora Geary

Copyright © 2011 Debora Geary
Fireweed Publishing
Print Edition

ISBN: 978-1-937041-11-3

To all those who seek a home—
and to the wonderful readers who
find one, however temporary,
in the pages of my books.

Chapter 1

Sierra looked up and down the beach carefully before she walked out into the water. She didn't want any stray tourists freaking out about her little swim.

Not that there were a lot of tourists on Oregon beaches in December. She tossed a light trickle of power up to the Heceta Head lighthouse. It was foggy enough today that she wouldn't be able to see it from out in the water. This way she'd be able to come back—if she wanted to.

Maybe Momma just hadn't wanted to come back.

Her ankles were freezing. Sierra activated the small spell that kept her warm even in the frigid winter ocean waters.

"I call on Air, I call on Fire,
Molecules dance and heat inspire.
Coat my skin with fire-warmed air,
Warmest summer waters wear.
A child of the ocean, swimming free
As I will, so mote it be."

Her ankles warmed nicely, thanks to her magical wetsuit. Momma had shown her this trick when she was a little girl and even the much-warmer ocean waters of Hawaii turned her into a Popsicle.

She missed Hawaii almost as much as she missed Momma.

Gathering power one more time, Sierra dove into the surf and swam out into the ocean with long, sure strokes. In less than a minute, she'd cleared the protected waters of the Heceta Head bay and felt the playful pull of the riptide currents.

Careful, she murmured to the water. *Not just yet. Let me get out past the rocks first.*

She continued kicking out to sea in a steady freestyle. The riptides were strong today. They often were in midwinter—just one more reason to brave the chill waters.

Bubbles of laughter blew out of her lungs when she crossed the shoreline riptide and swam into the much larger one that would pull her out to sea. *Want to play today, do you?*

Excellent. She was in the mood to wrestle, and the heavy mists would hide them from prying eyes onshore.

She rolled onto her back, power streaming through her outstretched hands.

"*I call on Water, friend to me
Curve and swirl, a tempest be.
I call on Air, sister of mine
Dip and whirl, a twisted line.
A storm of fun, we playful three
As I will, so mote it be.*"

Swells of water rose and fell under her back as energy gathered. Sierra opened her eyes just in time to see the ten-foot wave about to crash on her head. With a flip of her feet, she twisted and dove under the base of the wave, giggling. *Play nice!*

Surfacing, she threw a bolt of power at the backside of the wave, splitting it in two, and pulled nimbly onto her feet, surfing on the surge of water that charged up the middle.

Energy crackled from both the clouds overhead and her sizzling fingers. She toyed with making a real storm for a moment, and then dropped back into the water. Real storms required a decent breakfast if she didn't want to run out of fuel and freeze on her swim back to shore.

She dove into another swell, spied a funnel of air and water forming to her left, and swam up into the tail. It was like riding a washing machine, round and round, a solid wall of water at her back. Sierra laid her head back and reveled in the speed.

Blood pounding in her ears, she reached out more gently now. The funnel slowed. Catching her bearings, she sent out a seeking finger of power, heading southwest. Hawaii wasn't the closest source of warm-water currents, but the Gulf waters didn't carry the same feel of welcome.

Her heart ached as the first trickles of Maui water came, bringing sunshine and time-faded memories. Foster-care budgets didn't extend to plane tickets to Hawaii, no matter how often she asked.

If she found a job, maybe she could earn enough.

That was a big "if." There weren't a lot of jobs on the Oregon Coast in winter, and DHS only paid for her to go somewhere else if she already had a job.

Yeah—because people handed those out all the time to eighteen-year-old kids they didn't know. Here, cuddled by the ocean waters of her birth, she could let loose some of her seething frustration with a system of unbending rules and soul-stealing piles of paper.

For the first twelve years of her life, she'd lived a life of utter freedom, being exactly the Sierra Brighton she'd wanted to be.

For the last six, she'd lived numb and dead, dumped into a world where no one cared who Sierra Brighton really was.

Oh, Momma, what happened to you?

Sierra let her tears wash away with the waves. Today wasn't for crying, either. She needed a plan.

Four days. On December fourteenth, she would age out of foster care—but if she didn't have a job and a place to live by then, they wouldn't let her go. She'd end up living under the court-ordered "transitional plan," whatever that was.

She'd refused to read it. She had no intention of being there.

With a last good-bye to her playmates, she flipped onto her front and started swimming toward shore.

In four days, Sierra Brighton would be free. She just needed to find a job. And breakfast. She'd stayed out too long—her toes were getting cold.

~ ~ ~

Govin frowned at the flashing orange alert on his computer screen. "Hey, Teej—that Hawaii anomaly's back."

"Lemme look." His long-time best friend ambled over to his desk, a beer in one hand, bowl of chips in the other. Most people would have bet TJ Hamblin was a truck driver, not one of the world's best meteorologists.

Or as the bumper sticker on his desk chair said, "Weather Genius." TJ wasn't exactly humble.

And it was a bad sign he was eating chips for breakfast. "Doreen didn't feed you?"

"She kicked me out. Said she's tired of living with a slob."

"She's got some grounds for complaint." Govin looked pointedly at the mountain of chaos on TJ's desk. He wasn't terribly upset to see Doreen go. Maybe next time, his buddy would raise his standards. He could always hope. He sighed—friendship probably required a little more than a shrug here. "Want some scrambled eggs?"

TJ brightened. "Sausages, too? She kicked me out before dinner last night—I'm starving."

Govin rolled his eyes. TJ was clueless about at least half the life skills required to be an adult.

His mom often said that's why the two of them had been matched up—that he'd been born with an extra dose of TJ's missing common sense. As a mathematician, he appreciated her sense of humor. As a guy with a brilliant, but often clueless friend, it wasn't always quite so funny.

He pulled out a carton of eggs and discovered that the package of breakfast sausages only contained one sad little link. Which wouldn't even put a minor dent in TJ's appetite.

Grabbing his cell phone, he called their personal rescue service. Nell always had extra food lying around. They'd had a deal in college, when the three of them had lived together—if the guys weren't total pigs, she'd occasionally feed them. He looked around the room and winced. They weren't exactly keeping up their end of the bargain.

Nell was laughing when she answered the phone. "What do you need?"

"I'm wounded. I don't always need something when I call you." Govin hoped that was true.

"It is when you call before noon. Until then, you're usually too deep into your data to talk to an actual human being."

"Mornings are busy." Weather never stood still, and he had to catch up on what he'd missed while he slept.

He could hear rummaging on the other end of the phone. "I've got bacon and sausages, and pumpkin pancakes in a few minutes. No more eggs, though. Aervyn's growing again."

"Just some sausages would be great." He peered at the contents of his fridge. "I have some extra eggs I can send back with your delivery boy."

She laughed. "What's the expiration date?"

He sighed. Nell had lived with him and TJ for two years, so she had plenty of data driving such suspicions. "Probably not within your tolerances."

She was still chuckling when she ended the call. A package of sausages, well within their expiry date, thunked onto his counter moments later. Govin saluted in the general direction of Nell's house. "Thanks, little dude." Aervyn was a good witchling to have around.

Taking a minute to get breakfast underway, he walked back to his laptop. "Learn anything new?" They'd been trying to understand this particular Hawaii anomaly for two years now—one of their private projects. Their funders didn't like to pay for the weather version of ghostbusting.

TJ scowled. "Not really. Just that it's getting stronger."

Govin looked at the new plots. Same story as always—an errant currant of warm water would appear and run from Hawaii to the Oregon Coast. Less than an hour later, it would disappear, violating all laws of logic and mathematics. It was driving the two of them crazy trying to figure out the source.

He leaned a little closer, and then clicked a few keys, pulling complex displays up on their three oversized monitor screens. "Yeesh, Teej. That's getting awfully close to tipping point."

"Yeah." TJ finished the last of his beer. "It's still about twenty percent below the threshold, but at the rate it's been growing, we've got three or four months before we have some serious weather perturbations on our hands."

In weather speak, three or four months meant it was time to stop watching this anomaly and start doing something about it instead. It was what the two of them did—smooth small bumps in the weather patterns where they could so disasters didn't develop.

It wasn't very sexy work—but if TJ's data modeling was correct, they'd saved almost half a million lives in the last ten years. Plus or minus 15.7 percent.

He went back to staring at the readings. "We need to figure out the source." Magic couldn't fix what it couldn't see.

TJ raised an eyebrow. "What do you suggest—camping out on the Oregon Coast and watching for warm-water magnets?"

Govin sighed. "I'll dig into the geo-oceanic data again." That was the most likely source of their problem, but damned if he could find it.

TJ just stared at his computer monitor. "This isn't geo, bro. I don't know what it is yet, but it doesn't smell like anything natural."

Govin chuckled, knowing exactly where this conversation was headed. "No alien conspiracy theories before breakfast. Come on, the sausage smells ready."

The aliens—or whatever was causing their anomaly—could wait half an hour.

~ ~ ~

<u>Sophie</u>: Is Nat going stir-crazy yet?

<u>Nell</u>: Does she ever? I swear, by the time my due date rolled around, I was ready to reach in there and yank the baby out myself, but she just folds up into lotus and meditates. It's eerie.

<u>Moira</u>: Well, you didn't exactly have easy pregnancies to wait out, Nell. The triplets were a bellyful, to be sure, and Aervyn wasn't patient in those last weeks.

<u>Nell</u>: That would be an understatement. Nat and Jamie's baby has been playing with power streams for so long that we expected something similar from her, but she's been really quiet. Lauren says her mind is pretty content in there.

<u>Sophie</u>: Jamie's going to pop Nat into Realm tomorrow so we can all check out her belly.

<u>Nell</u>: That will make Ginia feel better.

<u>Sophie</u>: She's been doing a beautiful job of monitoring Nat. This is just to spoil me and Aunt Moira.

<u>Moira</u>: At my age, I deserve to be spoiled. And Sophie, are you sure we can't meet in our Realm room now? This typing is still so hard for my poor fingers.

<u>Sophie</u>: Which is exactly why we're doing this the old-fashioned way. You know the deal—one typed chat a week. It's good physical therapy. Besides, we can't fetch some poor new witch

into Realm without any warning. Pulling them into a chat room with no warning is tricky enough.

Nell: You're sure you want to be fetching more newbies right now? We have births, Winter Solstice, and the big push on the WitchNet library.

Moira: My Elorie's a splendid organizer. She tells me WitchNet is coming along very nicely.

Sophie: She is indeed, and she's got Jamie and his team hopping. Nell, we can wait if you want—but with all these babies on the way, I figured it was going to stay busy for a while. Maybe we can just look for actively practicing witches for the moment, though, and keep building our community that way. I'm not sure we have the energy to handle another Lauren or Elorie right now.

Nell: Okay, I'll set it up. One day, though, I'm going to retire and sit on the beach and drink mimosas all day long.

Moira: Good luck with that, my dear. Just when you think that day's arrived, some sprightly young witch will show up and tell you she needs you to help with her new project.

Sophie: Witches' Chat wouldn't be the same without you, Aunt Moira. And you don't even like mimosas.

Moira: The sitting-on-the-beach part sounded lovely, though.

Nell: Just tell us what beach you'd like to visit. Aervyn's getting pretty talented at schlepping people through Realm to wherever they need to go.

Moira: Ah, my soaking pool takes good care of me. I don't really need to be anywhere else.

Sophie: Way to call her bluff, Nell :-). We've been trying to send her to the beach for weeks now. Some warm-water swimming would be good for her.

<u>Moira</u>: All these healers are trying to turn me back into a twenty-one-year-old instead of an old lady. Not everything works perfectly when you're my age.

<u>Nell</u>: Ha. That's already true for me, and I'm half your age. All right. I've turned on the fetching spell, and Moira can entertain us with her grumpy-patient routine while we wait.

~ ~ ~

Sierra sat down at the library computer and looked around furtively before grabbing another bite of the bagel in her hoodie pocket. She always needed tons of carbs after a winter swim.

Not as badly as she needed a job, however. And if there weren't any on the Oregon Coast, then she needed to start looking further away. Maybe California. She had vague memories of a couple of fun days riding the streetcars in San Francisco with Momma. It cost a lot to live in California, though.

She logged into her Monster job-search account and widened the search parameters to include every city she could find that was on the coast in California. A quick scroll showed the same brain-numbing jobs that were available in Oregon—but at least there were a lot more of them.

Taking the lucky red dice out of her pocket, she shook them and rolled a seven. She counted down to the seventh job listed—poodle-grooming assistant. Didn't sound very likely, but she clicked anyhow. Momma had always said some of the best decisions in her life had been made with the lucky red dice.

This didn't look like one of those times, however. A job where unhappy dogs tried to bite you all day long needed to pay better than eight dollars an hour.

The next job listing was for a Spanish translator. Her Spanish was pretty decent. She clicked on that one—all good until the part about a university degree and translator certification. Ugh.

Stunt double. Ick. Shower scenes were not stunts.

Then she spied one that sounded pretty cool. Indie-film gopher. But crap, they just wanted people willing to work for lunch and possible future fame. That didn't pay the rent.

Frustrated, she started clicking at random—and suddenly got a rainbow swirl on her screen, followed by a chat interface. What the heck?

Sophie: Hi, Sierra—we'd like to welcome you to Witches' Chat. Thank you for joining us!

Sierra: I'm where?

Sophie: Nell, Moira, and I are the three founding members of an online chat group for witches. It looks like our fetching spell found you.

Sierra: Fetching spell? You're doing magic online? Seriously?

Sophie: Just a small spell to locate people who actively use magic. You're free to stay or go, but we'd love to chat with you for a bit.

Sierra: You can tell I'm a witch? That's really cool. Do you have any spells that could fetch me a job?

Nell: Hi, Sierra. Looks like you were running a job search when we found you. What kind of job do you want?

Sierra: Anything close to the ocean that pays well enough to get an apartment. Oh, and where nobody bites, requires a university degree, or wants me to get naked.

Moira: That last bit sounds rather shady, my dear—surely we can find you something better than that.

Sierra: Doubt it. I've been looking for months now, and I've only got four days left.

Moira: Ah, rather an emergency then. Perhaps there's a reason our spell fetched you today.

Sophie: Can you tell us a little about yourself? Nothing too personal, but maybe some of your skills?

Sierra: I don't know. I'm eighteen, I speak bits of a lot of languages, and I learn pretty fast.

Moira: Eighteen? Sweetheart, don't you have family who can help you out?

Sierra: No. And that's all I want to say about that.

Nell: Smart. How are you at herding cats?

Sierra: I don't have much experience with animals.

Nell: Sorry, I was trying to be cute and didn't do a very good job. I might be able to find you a job. My brother and I run a gaming website called Enchanter's Realm, and—

Sierra: OMG. You're Nell Walker. You made Realm.

Nell: With my brother, yeah. You play?

Sierra: Can't anymore. The library computers block your site. But I used to play while we traveled. It kept me from being too bored in the train stations and stuff.

Nell: Were you any good?

Sierra: I got to the third witch-only level. But I was twelve, so I could probably do better now.

Nell: That's pretty fancy. Only my daughter has made it any further that so young. So—you need a job that pays enough to cover your living expenses, you're open to learning new things, and you're a pretty good gamer.

Moira: And she needs it in four days, dear. It sounds rather urgent.

Nell: Let me talk to Jamie. Sierra, is there some way I can reach you?

Sierra: Yeah. GirlWhoNeedsAJob@gmail.com. Are you serious about this?

Nell: Yup. I'll get back to you later today—can you get access to a computer after dinner tonight?

<u>Sierra:</u> Um, wow. Yeah, and thanks. I gotta go, I only had half an hour on the computer and my time's up.

Sierra backed away from the monitor, really glad to see the screen go blank. Most of the librarians already thought she was totally weird. Chatting with witches would probably get her library card taken away or something.

And not just any witches. Nell Walker. When Momma told all her stories about famous witches, Nell had always been one of Sierra's favorites. Really rich, a totally awesome gamer, and the first woman to ever spellcast a class-one spell. She must have such an exciting life—parties and famous people and lots of cool magic.

As she waited in line to book another slot on the library computers, Sierra shook the lucky red dice in her pocket. Maybe they'd worked after all.

Chapter 2

Nell deposited the last of the morning's dishes on the counter and turned to call her youngest. "Hey, Aervyn. Let's go visit Uncle Jamie and Auntie Nat."

He arrived wearing a black cape and carrying her kitchen broom. "Mama, I need a pointy hat."

"Really. And why's that?"

"Cuz Harry has one, and I'm trying to fly like him."

Her older kids had seen the latest Harry Potter movie and laughed it off as cool, but totally fake. Her baby, a week short of his fifth birthday, was still gullible. "You know real witches don't fly on brooms, right? Most witches can't fly at all."

Aervyn rolled his eyes. "I *know*, Mama. It's just pretend. But I still want a pointy hat."

Well, it probably wasn't that much different from his superhero fixation. "Maybe your Auntie Nat can help you with that—she's got a pretty good imagination." And a lot of tolerance for little boys with oddball requests.

He grinned and grabbed her hands. "Wanna port?"

She'd planned to walk, but given his current garb and the fact that his feet kept levitating off the ground, maybe teleporting was a good idea. "Sure, munchkin. Just let me grab my bag." It thunked into her hands a moment later, and Nell barely grabbed the strap before it landed on the floor. She sighed. And they wondered why she'd needed three new laptops already this year.

13

A grin from her son, and they landed in her brother's living room. Aervyn immediately took off running, broom between his legs—and crashed into the wall when he tried to navigate the turn down the hallway.

Jamie got to him first, with a kiss for the dinged elbow and a hug for the bruised ego. "Brooms don't fit through doorways very well, little dude."

Aervyn sniffled. "Harry Potter does it. He can fly anywhere."

That last part concerned Nell. Unfortunately, in the movie, Harry had jumped on his damn broom and flown like a maniac first time out. Her son hadn't seen the movie, but he'd quizzed his siblings until he might as well have. "Real witches have to practice a lot of flying low to the ground nice and slow before they try the fancy stuff."

Jamie kissed the top of her son's head and stood him back up. "How about we go to Ocean's Reach tomorrow and try some flying?" He glanced at Nell. "Really close to the ground, so we don't get hurt if we fall."

Aervyn's eyes brightened. "Can I bring my broom?"

"Absolutely, superboy. And if you go ask Nat, maybe she knows where you can find a broom for me too."

Her son took off, witchling on a mission. Nell wondered if anyone had a handy spell for fixing holes in walls. "You're really going to fly on a broomstick?"

Jamie grinned. "Tell me you don't want to try it too."

"Not on your life." She didn't have enough air power, or the teleportation skills to avoid the inevitable crashes.

He snorted. "Liar."

She gave in. "Yeah." They walked into the living room laughing.

A RECKLESS WITCH

Nell ignored the loud thud from the kitchen. By now Auntie Nat was an old hand with minor witchling mishaps. "So, could we use another set of hands for Realm?"

Her brother raised an eyebrow. "That sounds like a loaded question—what's up?"

She sighed. "We fetched another witch this morning. She needs a job."

"And you think we should give her one?" He slouched into a really ugly relic of an armchair. "Gotta be a story there. Keep talking."

"I don't know a lot about her. She's eighteen, and her IP address is from a library on the Oregon Coast. She needs a job in four days."

He frowned. "Or what?"

"She didn't say." Nell pulled out her trump card. "But she used to play Realm when she was younger. Said she hit the third witch-only level."

That got her brother's attention. He grabbed his computer. "Seriously? How much younger?"

"When she was twelve, so six years ago." They kept meticulous records of their gamers, particularly the witches and underage ones. Realm was as safe for kids as humans and magic could make it.

"I don't see her." Jamie typed on his keyboard a few moments longer, and then sucked in his breath. "Wait, maybe I do. I have one account that reached level three, active until six years ago. It's not a child account, though." He looked up, eyes wide. "Registered to Amelia Brighton. You found Amelia?"

Nell just stared, trying to connect all the crazy dots. "I don't think so. Her name was Sierra, and she knew who I was, but not like Amelia would have. She sounded young, Jamie."

Amelia Brighton was the wild hippy witch of the eighties. A decade older than Nell, she'd been adventurous, rebellious, and a world traveler. She'd been famous for showing up unannounced and then taking off a couple of days later, equally unannounced. Then she'd drifted further away, occasionally sending tales and emails from far-flung lands. And then about six years ago, they'd stopped hearing from her altogether.

Jamie tapped idly on his computer keys. "You think she had a kid? And nobody knew?"

"Dunno." Nell shrugged. "But if we're talking about Amelia, anything's possible."

"Yeah." He shook his head as if trying to clear a clog. "So what do we do now?"

That much she knew the answer to. "We offer Sierra a job, and we get her down here."

Jamie nodded. "Okay. I could use some extra help with all the WitchNet work. Elorie's got us hopping."

"It's a smart idea she has, hooking other witch projects in so everyone can coordinate."

Jamie grinned. "Yup. And she might just pull it off, too. But my nine-year-old staff could use some assistance—herding witches isn't easy. Sierra could help with that. It sounds like she's got some coding skills."

"They might be a little rusty after six years out of the game."

He shrugged. "Then we'll find something else for her to do."

She'd known her brother would come through. "Thanks. I owe you one."

"No big. We take care of our own." He grinned, eyes sparkling. "But if you want to be in my debt, you can go grab Matt and Devin at the airport tomorrow."

She was pretty sure that had been on her job list anyhow. Her brothers were coming home for the long and rowdy family celebration that ran between Winter Solstice and the New Year. The terrible threesome would ride again. "They're cutting it kind of close. Nat could pop any minute."

He shrugged. "She says not yet. And maybe our baby's not going to need a big circle—she's not playing with power much these days."

"You'll have a huge circle just because no one wants to miss it." Nell grinned. "Besides, it's usually the dads who need the most help."

She caught the pillow just before it beaned her in the head. Some things never changed.

~ ~ ~

The power flows were practically crackling, just waiting for her to shape them. Sierra stood on a small outcropping north of the Heceta Head lighthouse, well out of view of normal tourist trails, and reached for more.

It was time for a storm.

Patience had never been something she was any good at, and waiting for Nell Walker to maybe offer her a job was driving her crazy. The last six years had taught her a lot about living in a life that sucked. She'd learned to turn to the storms for comfort.

Magic was her birthright, her destiny, and her way of kicking a big hole through the crap of foster care and caseworkers and people who didn't truly care about Sierra Brighton.

She reached her fingers to the sky, feeling the storm that was already brewing. It wasn't hard to find one on the Oregon Coast in winter. She just planned to make it a little bigger.

"I call on Air, warm and light
Rise, a sheet of narrow flight.
I call on Water, dewdrops cold

Catch a ride, with friends of old.
I call on Fire, give heat to rise
Energies three, toward the skies.
Lift a storm up from the sea,
As I will, so mote it be."

Her heart soared as wind and water raged, lifting a current of warm, wet air into the waiting storm above. Power kicked and drove heat into the clouds of ice and snow. Sierra backed off just a stitch. Lightning tended to draw too much attention, at least in the middle of the afternoon.

She laughed as a tail of air spun her in a circle. *Wanna play, do you?* Her left hand circled, drawing the air closest to the ground into a funnel. Her right hand circled the other direction, keeping the funnel short. Hurricanes also tended to attract attention, even baby ones.

Then she leaned back into the whipping wind of the funnel, spinning around, hands out as far as she could reach. Funnel dancing had been one of Momma's favorite things. Sierra closed her eyes and imagined, just for a moment, that she didn't dance alone.

And then she reached for the sky one more time, pulling down the torrent of rain that wouldn't attract any notice at all as it washed away her tears.

~ ~ ~

"Holy crap!" Govin spun his chair around and yanked TJ's earphones off his head. "We have a bloody hurricane brewing up in Oregon, and it came out of nowhere."

"Weather does that." His partner took one look at the blinking orange alert and turned back to his own workstation, pulling up multiple screens on their bank of big monitors.

Govin watched, power itching to be let free. However, he knew his limits. Unless TJ could figure out exactly where to act, he didn't have enough magic to make a difference from this far away. When a flea wanted to turn an elephant, it had to hit precisely the right spot.

The muttering from their resident math genius increased to a dull roar. And then went totally silent, except for the insane clacking of the keyboard. Silent was TJ in genius mode.

Then he jumped up, grabbed a sheet of paper from the printer, and headed for the barn at a dead run. Govin knew better than to ask. He just ran.

As the helicopter took off, heading out to sea, TJ handed over the piece of paper. Govin jammed his headset down. "What do we need?"

"A bolus of heat to those coordinates. And don't miss."

Which was mathematician-speak for "this is a tricky bugger of a storm." Govin looked at the data points. They were at the far end of his reach—not exactly the best range for accuracy. "People in the vicinity?"

TJ shook his head. "It's a really small storm, very localized, but strong. If you're going to miss, do it on the high side. That way we don't get a full-blown funnel, just some big wave action. We'll be over the right ley line in about ninety seconds."

Govin readied his spell as he hung his feet over the edge of the helicopter, doing his best imitation of a special-forces weather witch.

"I call on Fire, a tinder blast
A white-hot shield, flat and fast.
I call on Air, a package to blow
Vectoring north on ley line flow.
Carry heat into the storm
Letting loose, disperse the form.
Just wind and rain, no funnels see,
As I will, so mote it be."

At TJ's 3-2-1-mark, Govin released his spell—a stingray-shaped fire shield, wrapped in a layer of air to minimize impact on weather between here and its destination. It should trigger when it met with the storm flow. TJ's job was to pick a ley line that connected here and there without any other weather obstacles along the way. Most of the time, he got it right.

Slight tremors of spell kickback signaled that the fire shield had released and done its job of heating a layer of air. It had either dispersed the funnel, or made it worse.

TJ scowled at the tablet computer plugged in by his copter dash. "No funnel, but weird readings. Dunno what's going on. We need to get back to headquarters to figure it out." The tablet was cool, but it lacked the power of their main computer stations. Even TJ couldn't jam a supercomputer into a digital toy.

No funnel was probably good news. Govin leaned back against his seat. Weather witches had to live with uncertainty, even in this day and age of satellite feeds and monster computing power. It was the nature of the beast. "Nice job finding a free ley line."

TJ shrugged. "Hopefully that part will get a lot easier when we get set up with WitchNet."

They both hoped so. In the last fifteen years, they'd learned a lot about how to dampen a storm or adjust an ocean current, but it all hinged on having a witch in the right place at the right time.

Or at least, a witch's spell in the right place at the right time. Elorie's WitchNet project was showing a lot of promise for being able to do exactly that—deliver magic exactly where it was needed.

Govin adjusted his headgear. It never sat quite right. "Could make things a lot more complicated, too." It was a conversation they'd had about a million times in the last three months. "You're sure you don't want to act as liaison with them?"

TJ snorted. "You're the witch, buddy. I'm just the math geek. I'll predict the weather—you organize the response team."

Team. That was a strange and scary thought. It had always been just the two of them. When you played with planetary weather systems, you needed lots of brains, lots of patience, and unconditional trust. Adding more people was going to make all of that really complicated.

It was either going to save a lot of lives, or drive him batshit crazy. Possibly both.

He sat contemplating those eventualities until TJ landed the chopper. His partner laid his headgear on the seat and waved in the general direction of the house. "Let's check the computer readouts first—then we can come back out and do the pre-flight." They always left the helicopter in flight-ready condition.

Govin hopped down and hurried after TJ. For a guy fueled on potato chips and beer, he could really hustle—especially when data called.

It took less than thirty seconds before the weather genius had an answer. Unfortunately, it headed toward the batshit-crazy end of the spectrum. "Gotta be aliens." TJ slammed his hand down on the desk, causing a cascade of paper and weird desk crud. "No way this is a natural weather pattern."

"Any theories that don't require little green men?"

TJ snorted. "Rogue witches?"

Govin groaned. He'd walked right into that one. His old college roomie had swallowed the idea of magic and witches with ease. Unfortunately, that same mental flexibility wrapped around UFO sightings, Area 51 conspiracies, and alien spies running for the Berkeley city council. "There are only a dozen witches in the world strong enough to mess with planetary weather patterns, and none of them are anywhere near Oregon." And none of them would play fast and loose with the weather, either. Which TJ already knew. "Just give me the data for now. What do you see?"

"The funnel formed about ten minutes before you hit it. Smaller than it should have been, and it disappeared before you did anything."

"I threw magic at a regular storm?" Govin winced. There were a lot of ways that could end badly. "Anything we need to go back and fix?"

TJ clicked a few more keys and shook his head. "Nope. Whatever was there totally dissipated about five minutes before we got into position. You probably just warmed a few fish."

Awesome. Mom would be so proud. "How'd it disappear?"

"No freaking clue. Aliens, witches, or unexplained phenomena—take your pick." TJ leaned in closer to his screen. "Whatever it is, though, it's connected to our Hawaii anomaly. That warm-water current from this morning ran right up to the same damn beach that just tried to grow a hurricane."

Govin frowned. "The warm water caused the hurricane?"

"Nope. No relation. Just a happy locational coincidence."

Yeah. As a mathematician, he had to acknowledge that possibility. As a witch, this was starting to smell. Witches didn't like coincidences.

~ ~ ~

Sierra waited impatiently at the library check-in desk. She'd booked a slot for 6 p.m., and there weren't any open terminals. She was antsy and cold—too much magic and not enough food. Her foster family's food budget didn't really stretch to witch portions, and they got really grumpy when she ate too much.

Sticking her hands in her pockets, she lit a couple of small fireglobes. She'd pay for the magic use later, but hungry was better than cold.

A woman stepped up beside her and grinned. "You must be Sierra. I'm Nell Walker."

"Get out!" Sierra lowered her voice as half the library turned to look. "I didn't know you were going to come here." Wow, Nell totally didn't look like what she expected. No fancy clothes, no big-shot attitude. She looked like somebody's mom.

"It wasn't the original plan, but I thought it might be easier to chat in person." Nell turned and walked a little way from the library desk, clearly looking for some privacy.

Sierra motioned to the back of the library. "There are a couple of language-learning stations back there. It's okay to talk, but they're not very soundproof."

Nell grinned. "We can fix that."

They stepped inside the small room, and Sierra watched in fascination as Nell set a spell in place. "Air layering? How'd you get it to stop bouncing?" Air spells were notoriously unstable because air molecules preferred to be in constant motion.

"You can see what I did?" Nell raised an eyebrow. "What powers do you work with?"

"Mostly air and water. A little fire." Sierra eyed the walls again. Her feet got cold all the time when the layers in her magical wetsuit spell got too wobbly. She needed to figure this out. Carefully, she traced the lines of Nell's spell. "Oh, cool. You're not trying to hold the layers still—they're looping. The air's like—running around on a track or something."

"Yeah, pretty much."

Oh, man—she was in a room with a totally famous witch and being a complete geek. "Sorry. You probably didn't come here so I could watch you do magic." Although that sounded pretty awesome.

"No worries." Nell looked at her for a moment, and then turned off the spell. "Why don't you give it a try? Easiest way to learn."

Sierra called to power and mumbled under her breath. No point letting Nell hear her dorky rhymes. The joining part was a bit tricky, but a few moments later, she had the air currents flowing in three layers around the room.

"Dang." Nell grinned. "Nice—you've got some good training."

"Momma taught me." Sierra cursed as tears filled her eyes. "She said I was a natural."

"Aw, sweetie. Come here." Strong arms pulled her in for a hug. Nell kissed the top of her head, and then led them both to a couple of chairs. "Tell me about your mom. She was Amelia Brighton, wasn't she—you have her eyes."

"You knew my mom?" Her nose sniffles were threatening to turn into a torrent.

Nell handed over a Kleenex. "We all did. I didn't know her well—she was older than I was, and she did a lot of traveling." She paused a moment, and then spoke gently. "We didn't know about you, Sierra. I'm so sorry about that. We would hear from your mom sometimes, and then that stopped about six years ago."

Yeah. Six years ago. Sierra stood up, arms wrapped around her waist, and started walking around the edges of the tiny little room. "We were in New Orleans for Mardi Gras. We'd just come from the Carnival in Venice—Momma loved any place with a really big party, but she loved those two best. Said it was like the planet's birthday bash for a few weeks every February."

Nell chuckled. "That sounds like Amelia."

"One night I was really tired, so she dropped me off in our hotel room and went out to dance some more."

"She left you alone?"

Sierra shrugged. "Sure. I was twelve, and I was just going to sleep." She frowned, wanting Nell to understand and stop looking at her with those serious eyes. "She was a good mom. I was really responsible."

"Okay. So she left you to get some sleep..."

There was a spider working busily in the top corner of the room. Sierra stared hard at the strands of the web. "She never came back. They said she must have abandoned me." She spun around. "But Momma wouldn't have done that. Something bad must have happened to her."

Something inside her eased when Nell's eyes didn't show any doubt. "I'm so sorry, sweetie. That must have been awful."

It had been. Six years of awful.

"I didn't really know how to find any of Momma's friends." A fact that still troubled her deep in the night. "So they put me in foster care. I ran away a couple of times, but..." She shrugged. "The streets suck. This sucks too, but not as much. I like being near the ocean, so when I got placed here, I didn't run again."

Now Nell just looked mad.

"It really isn't that bad." Sierra tripped over words, trying to be completely honest. Some kids in foster care had it way worse. "The family I live with is okay. They're just used to having lots of kids come and go." She shrugged. "More like a cheap motel than a family."

Nell nodded slowly. "And what happens in four days?"

"I turn eighteen." Sierra turned around, remembering she desperately needed Nell's help. "If I have a job, I can leave. Otherwise, I have to go into the transitional program. Halfway-house hell." Help. Please.

It was amazing to watch Nell's face change. Suddenly she didn't look like a mom at all. She looked like an avenging warrior. "You have a job and anything else you need." She looked straight at Sierra, eyes glistening bright. "You've found your mama's friends, sweetie. I'm so sorry we didn't know about you six years ago, but we know about you now."

Light slammed into Sierra's soul and jackhammered six years of loneliness. She gasped for air, hardly able to stand it. Nell took two steps and swept her back into those strong arms. It was the first time in six years Sierra had felt someone hold her tight and whisper meaningless words in her hair. Her tears came in a torrent.

Chapter 3

"Morning, everyone." Sophie landed in the Realm meeting room, a tray of still-warm cinnamon buns in her hands. Judging by the kicks in her belly, even the baby could smell them. "Aaron had extras, or so he said."

"Ha." Moira reached out to take the tray. The handoff was a little tippy, but she managed to get it down to the coffee table. "He knows I can't resist them, and someone must have told him licking my fingers afterward is good therapy."

Sophie blushed, and Jamie laughed as he grabbed a cinnamon bun. "You're so busted."

Moira giggled. "Never try to fool an old healer, my dear."

It was very satisfying to hear her clear and easy speech. Five months after her stroke, Aunt Moira still had some difficulty with fine-motor skills, but her mind and her speech were almost entirely back to normal. It had taken hundreds of hours of healing—and they'd had to fight off offers of more help.

"I learned everything I know from an old healer." Sophie patted her belly, letting Seedling know food was on the way. "Including how to manage grumpy patients."

Moira nodded, a twinkle in her eye. "I had to make sure Lizzie and Ginia got enough practice, didn't I?"

Ha. The two girls were frighteningly competent healers now.

Nell laughed. "Aervyn had a sore throat last week, and he had no idea what hit him. Ginia had him in bed under a poultice in about ten seconds flat. Nat gives her a little more grief, though."

Jamie grinned. "Someday people are going to figure out that my nice, sweet wife isn't a pushover."

It was Moira who got control of her giggles first. "None of us has ever believed that, my dear boy. Your Natalia is about as easy to push over as a small mountain." She began the somewhat laborious process of licking cinnamon-y goodness off her fingers. "And we should send you back to her fairly soon—I don't like a woman left alone this close to her birthing time."

Sophie nodded. Time to get this meeting underway. "Nell, why don't you tell us more about Sierra. Is she Amelia's daughter?"

"She is." Nell's voice saddened. "And she's pretty sure her mother must be dead."

Sophie heard Moira's sharp intake of breath, matching the dread in her own heart. "She doesn't know for sure?"

"No. Amelia left Sierra alone in a hotel room during Mardi Gras and went back out to join the party." Nell shook her head, eyes fiery. "I don't understand how a mother could do that. I'm trying not to judge, but Sierra was just twelve." Her voice cracked. "Can you imagine waking up alone in a strange hotel room and not knowing where your mama was?"

Sophie tried not to shudder as a bolt of fear shot through her. "Amelia never came back?"

Nell shook her head mutely.

"Something must have happened to her, then." Moira's voice was soft and sad, but she didn't seem surprised. "Amelia was rash and took far too many risks, but I can't believe she'd abandon her own daughter."

Nell looked surprised. "Did you know her well?"

Moira shrugged. "As a girl, yes. She came to witch school for several summers, along with her older brother. He had a stitch of earth power, but little else. She was a moderately talented weather witch."

All Sophie could remember was a laughing older girl her first year of witch school.

Sighing, Moira reached for a second cinnamon bun. "As you know, I'm a firm believer in being cautious with magic, and we try to impart that to all our witchlings. We were singularly unsuccessful with Amelia. She did magic on a tightrope, no net in sight."

Taking unnecessary risks with magic was anathema to most witches. "Was she dangerous?"

"Not intentionally." Moira's eyes were sad again. "But accidentally—yes. She was reckless, and she could easily have brought harm to herself or others. We'd hoped that would temper over time. I rarely saw her after her teenage years, but I never got the sense her recklessness had waned."

Sophie closed her eyes and tried not to judge. It was exceedingly hard, especially if a child had been left orphaned as a result.

"Amelia was a weather witch?" Nell sounded pensive. "Sierra might be as well. Given her desire to live by the ocean, I assume she's a water witch. She's definitely got air talents—she duplicated my soundproofing spell with impressive ease."

Jamie frowned. "Your layering one? That's pretty tricky spellcasting, sister mine."

The room was silent as the implications sank in. Sophie winced and shifted as a foot poked up under her ribs. "It sounds like we need to assess her, no? And figure out where her training is at?"

"Aye." Moira leaned forward, every inch the witch matriarch. "If she's been taught by Amelia's hand, we need to know how much power she has, and how much respect for doing magic safely."

Nell shook her head. "I don't mean to disagree with you—I think that's important. I don't want a dangerous witch on the loose any more than you do. But first we have a lonely teenager who needs a job and a place to go in three days. Let's get her down here. Then we can worry about any holes in her training."

Every head in the room was nodding when she finished.

"A job's not a problem." Jamie shrugged. "With regular Realm stuff and WitchNet, we'll find her something to do. If she might be a weather witch, and she's a decent coder..." he trailed off, clearly thinking the next steps through. "Maybe we should hook her up with Govin. He could use some help on the basic weather-spells library, and that might give us a good sense of her skills without being too intrusive."

Sophie nodded. Govin was a very smart witch, and one of the nicest guys she knew.

Nell snorted as Jamie looked her way. "What—I suppose you want *me* to tell him he's getting a teenage apprentice?"

"You were his college roomie." Jamie held up half his cinnamon bun. "I offer compensation."

Nell grabbed the tray, still holding half a dozen of the sticky treats. "It's him we need to bribe, brother mine. Not me."

Sophie was feeling a bit like a fifth wheel. "Is there any way we can help?"

Nell started to shake her head, and then stopped. "Yeah, actually. Sierra's going to need a place to live. She can stay with us for as long as she wants, but I'm guessing she's going to want her own space. Eighteen and finally free of foster care and her caseworker..."

She needed a nest. Sophie grinned. "Can Lauren find her an apartment? I'll head up the decorating team."

"I have three assistants for you." Nell stood up, getting ready to transport back home. "Keep her warm. Water witches get chilly during our cool nights here."

"She'll be needing a nice throw, then." Moira nodded happily. "Elorie brought me some lovely blue yarn from Halifax last week. I'll get right to work."

Sophie tried very hard to keep a straight face as Nell's wink sailed right over Moira's head. Knitting was excellent physical therapy, and she'd been trying to get Aunt Moira to pick up her needles for months now. Nell Walker was a very sneaky witch.

~ ~ ~

Devin looked out the car window as they reached Nell's neighborhood. He always thought of home as wherever his feet were, but there was an easy familiarity to these streets he appreciated. "Still no neighbors freaking out over Aervyn's magic tricks?"

"Nope." Nell shrugged. "People really do see what they want to see. Although if he gets this broomstick-flying thing down, we might have to have a little chat about daytime displays of magic."

He tried to picture his nephew flying down the street on Nell's kitchen broom and chuckled. "They'd probably just think they were having Harry Potter flashbacks or something."

"We can always hope. So what held Matt up?"

His overgrown sense of responsibility. "He's got a couple of teenagers in labor. We weren't expecting them, and his relief doc doesn't know a whole lot about delivering babies in the rain forest, so he'll stay until they're done and come in with Mom and Dad."

Nell frowned. "Mom can deliver babies in her sleep."

"Yup. But Matt was worried she might have to leave soon, if Ginia says Nat's gonna pop."

"Trust me, nothing about Natalia Sullivan is going to pop, even when she gives birth."

Devin shrugged. He liked Nat, but he had no idea how his brother had hooked up with someone so... calm. "They still doing okay?" Marriage was a rocky road for some, and they'd gotten married in kind of a hurry.

"Not everyone is as allergic to marriage as you are." Nell put a hand on his arm, and her voice lost the teasing tone. "They're awesome together. Jamie's really happy, Dev."

He nodded. "Good to know." It really was—he wanted only the best for his brother, even if it seriously cut into their cross-country motorcycle trips.

Nell pulled her car up to the curb. "Prepare to be mobbed."

He grinned. "Prepare to be invaded."

He almost made it out of the car before three nieces landed in his lap. "Uncle Devin!"

"Aren't you guys supposed to be in school or something?"

Mia giggled. "It's Saturday, silly. We're supposed to be coding, but Uncle Jamie let us escape long enough to drag you down to help."

He wiggled his fingers. "Master coder, ready for action. Lead on, minions." Laughing hands tugged him toward the house. Time to shake the rust off his coding skills, preferably before his nieces figured out he was badly out of practice.

Given what he'd seen of Ginia in Realm lately, he was probably in trouble.

Jamie stopped their small herd at the bottom of the basement stairs and gave Devin a quick hug. "Shh, guys. Aervyn and Lauren are working on something a bit tricky, so let's not disturb their concentration, okay?"

Hey, Devin. Good to see you again. Lauren's cheery mental voice didn't sound overly occupied. *Aervyn's doing all the heavy lifting—I'm just holding things steady for him. We'll be done in a minute.*

The last time he'd seen her, she'd been Nat's maid of honor, and Matt had won the coin toss to escort her down the aisle. He'd assumed the slight itch he'd felt all that day had been related to the wedding. As he watched her doing magic with his nephew, it was pretty clear he'd been wrong.

The itch was back. And his brother's wife's best friend was way out of bounds for his usual love-'em-and-leave-'em routine.

Jamie punched him in the shoulder. *Way out, dude. She's not your type, anyhow. Boobs are too small, brains are too big.*

You might want to save your discussion of my boobs until there are less people listening, sent Lauren dryly. *Aervyn's education on that front could stand to wait a few years.*

Jamie winced. *Sorry, I forgot I was monitoring the two of you.*

Really. Lauren rolled her eyes and Aervyn shook with giggles, but they managed to close off the spell before totally falling apart.

Devin picked up his giggly nephew for a big bear hug. He also kept his eyes way, way off Lauren's chest. "How's it going, superboy?"

"I'm good, and I'm learning to fly on a broom." Aervyn's hearing aids flashed visible for a moment, a clear sign he was trying to whisper. "And I think Lauren's boobs are pretty nice."

Terrific. Now his three nieces joined Lauren in the puddle of laughter on the floor. Jamie sighed. "You're not helping us out here, cutie. It's not really nice manners to talk about that kind of stuff."

Aervyn nodded solemnly. "It's guy stuff, right? For just inside our heads."

Devin, well used to being in hot water, caught Nell's well-aimed pillow just before it pinged Jamie in the head. His sister still had her MVP pitching arm.

She'd stopped partway down the stairs. "Brownies in the kitchen for all people with boobs, and all boys too young to know any better. You big boys are out of luck."

Aervyn debated which category he wanted to be in for a moment, but the lure of chocolate was strong. Jamie grinned at Devin as they were abandoned for sweeter pastures. "Welcome home."

Man. In trouble in less than five minutes. It wasn't a record, but it came pretty close. Devin grinned back. "Port us some of those brownies, and then you can fill me in on babies and Net power and whatever else I've missed."

~ ~ ~

Sierra stared at the box on her bed, heart in her throat. It was about twice as big as a shoebox and wrapped in plain brown paper with *Care Package—From Nell* written on the top. It had landed on her bed about thirty seconds ago, like it had beamed in from outer space.

And it smelled like heaven.

She grinned and ripped off the paper. Whatever it was, her belly wanted some.

A whole plate of cookies sat right on top. Sierra had three of them down before she realized the box contained plenty of other stuff. Moving more slowly now, she lifted up the plate and contemplated the contents underneath. Four neatly wrapped packages and a big envelope that said *Read This First*. It was like Christmas.

The packages were seriously tempting, but she took another cookie and opened the envelope. A bus ticket, a hundred dollars, and a letter. She got up and quickly tucked the money in her tampon box, the one totally safe hiding place in her life. Then she opened the letter.

Dear Sierra,

If you're like my daughters, you're halfway through the plate of cookies, and you've opened the other packages already. No big deal—but it might all make more sense once you read this.

We have a job for you, working for WitchNet. That's a Realm-related project you probably haven't heard of yet, but it involves lots of spellcoding and working with other witches. We have a couple ideas of things you can help with, but we can talk about that more when you get here. There's lots of work to be done, and my brother Jamie will appreciate the help.

My good friend Lauren is a real estate agent (and a witch). She's found you a nice one-bedroom apartment about four blocks from the beach. You can stay with us until that's ready for you in a few days. It's a bit crazy here, but there's lots of company and lots of food. You don't need to move to the apartment at all if you don't want to, but the choice is there if you want it. We thought you might enjoy your own space. Your salary at WitchNet should be enough to pay rent and live comfortably on your own.

There's a second letter attached with an official job offer. I sent a copy to your caseworker, so hopefully that will take care of the paperwork. Let me know if we need to do anything else to bust you loose—one of the presents in the box will make contacting us easier :-).

You should also have couple of tickets in this envelope—for tomorrow, just like you asked. Take the bus to Eugene and then the train to San Francisco. Someone will pick you up at the train station. If you pack up your things and leave them by the side of your bed tonight, my teleporting witchling will grab those for you so you don't need to lug them on the train. The money is to keep you fed until you get here.

I hope I haven't forgotten anything important. We're really looking forward to your arrival—there are a lot of people waiting to say hello.

See you tomorrow,

Nell

Sierra stared hard at the letter for a final moment, and then danced crazily around the room. Very quietly, so no one came to find out what all the noise was about. She kissed the tickets and tried to figure out where to put them—they were too big for her tampon box. Hmm.

But wait—there were more presents too. She dove for the box on the bed, yanking lime-green paper off the first package. Holy cats. She touched the iPhone with reverence. No freaking way. Foster-parent budgets had never extended to a cell phone, and this was the coolest phone ever.

The next package was a little bigger and contained a small photo album. Sierra opened it, puzzled, and found a picture of three identical girls, with a note written in purple, glittery pen. *Dear Sierra—here are pictures of some of the people you'll meet in Berkeley. You don't have to remember who we all are, but we just wanted to say hi! Love Mia, Ginia, and Shay.* She flipped the pages slowly. More than twenty pictures, and each had a little handwritten note saying hello.

Swallowing a lump, she turned to the last two packages. The first held a pair of beautiful wool gloves, knit in intricate patterns of blue and green. Sierra slipped her fingers into their cozy warmth. She didn't know why, but they felt like the ocean. She opened the piece of paper sitting under the gloves and squinted, trying to decipher the crooked handwriting. *Lovely Sierra—I hear that, like me, you're a water witch, and I know my hands are always a bit chilled in the winter. I hope these will keep you warm. Much love from Nova Scotia, Moira.* It was hard for her to take the gloves off to open the last package. Her hands *were* always cold.

The last package was small and light and smelled faintly of herbs. When Sierra took the lid off the small box inside, she found an ugly orange plastic frog hanging from a beautiful silver chain. Weird. She looked around for a note that might explain this last gift and found it written on the inside of the wrapping paper. Which was a serious bummer, because she'd pretty much torn the paper to shreds.

Carefully, she pieced the wrapping paper back together. This time, when she read the message, tears fell. *Sweet Sierra. One day, when I was about eight and at witchling school for the summer, some of the older kids drove us all into Halifax for ice cream. Your mom was one of them—it was my first year at Aunt Moira's, and Amelia's last. I vividly remember the big gumball machine that dispensed treats and small plastic toys for a nickel. Your mom bought one for each of us. This little frog was mine—it's been sitting in my jewelry box for a long time now. I thought you might like to have it. Love, Sophie.*

Sierra's hands shook as she clasped the little frog tightly. Oh, Momma.

Chapter 4

Govin looked at the contents of the grocery bag he'd just unpacked. Potato salad, TJ's favorite beer, two jars of Jamie's world-famous spaghetti sauce, and three different kinds of cookies. Ooooh, boy.

He looked at Nell. "Awfully big bribe—what do you want?"

She grinned. "I come bearing an offer of help and assistance."

"Sure you do," he said dryly, taking a cookie. If TJ caught sight of them, they'd be gone before dinner. "Do you need me to give Aervyn weather lessons again?" Their last lesson had gone fine—until Aervyn had made a pet thunderstorm that followed him everywhere for a couple of weeks. Nell had not been impressed, and Govin hadn't been able to reverse the spell. He could come close to matching superboy's talents with fire, but his water and air talents were puny by comparison.

Nell rolled her eyes. "Not just yet, thanks. My house has finally dried out, and I think I'd like to keep it that way for a while."

He waited patiently. Mothers of five couldn't beat around the bush forever—they had too much to do.

"We've fetched a new witch. We'd like to assign her to work with you on the weather-spells library for WitchNet."

"That sounds like you'd be doing me a favor." He eyed the cookies. "What's the catch?"

She sighed. "She's eighteen and just coming out of foster care. Her name is Sierra. We don't know much about her, but she's Amelia Brighton's daughter. And we suspect she's a weather witch like her mama."

That name sounded very familiar. Govin cast back in time, trying to make the connection. "The weather witch who ran off in the eighties? Claimed magic needed to be free? Disappeared a few years ago?"

Nell nodded. "Yeah. And according to Moira, the one who didn't use enough safeguards in her spells and took lots of unnecessary risks."

Govin winced. Those were scary qualities in a weather witch. "Was she any good?"

"Moira says she wasn't strong enough to influence anything beyond very local weather patterns, so perhaps they didn't work hard enough to convince her of the folly of her ways."

He snorted. "Anyone who hangs out with Moira for a summer and still practices magic recklessly is irredeemable." He had enormous respect and love for the woman who had been the driving force behind several generations of very well-trained witches. "We don't know what happened to Amelia?"

"We didn't even know she had a daughter." Nell's eyes were fierce, a mama bear on the prowl. "Putting aside for a moment how mad that makes me, she also likely taught her daughter magic."

Now they were getting to the reason for the cookies. "And?"

She shrugged. "No one's evaluated her yet, but her air talents are strong, and she insists on living near the ocean."

Which practically guaranteed she worked with water, as well. And air plus water talents was the classic recipe for a weather witch. Govin spun around a jar of spaghetti sauce and thought for a minute. "So you want to assign me an intern for basic weather-spell work. An intern who's motherless, powerful, and possibly dangerous."

"Yup." Nell didn't say anything else, just held his gaze quietly. "You're the best one to evaluate her, Govin. And if she has the power we suspect, the best one to help keep her and the rest of us safe."

She'd once called him a weenie, cautious witch. Today that was apparently a good quality. "Can she spellcode?"

"Six years ago, when she was twelve, she reached the third witch-only level in Realm." His old college roommate's eyes held hints of pleading now.

He had no idea why—he'd have done it just because she asked, and they both knew it. "Well, that's something. Another spellcoder would be handy. When does she start?"

Nell handed him a cookie. "She comes in on the train tomorrow. Why don't you and TJ come over for dinner, and we'll introduce you."

Anyone who volunteered to feed TJ was a true friend. "We'll be there."

~ ~ ~

Devin shook his head. "Nell's going to kill you, bro."

Jamie grinned, watching the flight test in progress down the valley at Ocean's Reach. "Nope. She gave us her blessing before we left. Aervyn's been putting way too many holes in her walls with the end of his broomstick. At least out here, there's not so much to run into."

"Except for a big-ass rock."

His brother winced. "He's pretty good at porting out of the way. And hopefully the bike helmet will keep his head from getting too dented."

It had taken a fair amount of discussion and an illusion spell to convince their nephew that real witches needed to wear bike helmets when they rode broomsticks. The pointy-hat illusion hadn't survived high-speed flying, but Aervyn didn't seem to care anymore.

He was too busy.

Hey, dude—slow down a little, okay? Jamie's mental voice sounded a bit worried. *It's just like a bike—you have to be able to stop, too.*

Aervyn turned and headed straight for them, cape flying. *I can stop. Watch!*

It was a serious act of uncle courage for Devin to hold still while a broomstick flew at his head at forty miles an hour. And basic survival instinct to get out of the way when his nephew's brakes lacked a little in the way of precision.

"Oops, sorry." Aervyn giggled and held his broom out. "You want to try, Uncle Devin?"

Oh, man, did he ever. However, he lacked the right kinds of power. Aervyn was basically flying by slingshotting himself against a complicated mix of air updrafts and gravity pulls. "I don't think water magic's much good for flying, superdude."

That caused a moment of silence, and then the offer of the broom again. "I can fly you, I think. Just don't lean over too far—that makes it kinda tippy."

Who could refuse an offer like that? Devin swung his leg over the broom. "Start low and slow, okay?" There was adventurous, and then there was suicidal.

The next few minutes considerably lifted his respect for both big-ass rocks and Aervyn's magical talent. He leaned over the broom as it winged across the valley toward the ocean, wind whipping his hair and power streams calling to his magic. *This* was living—small-boy dreams wrapped up in big-boy speed.

He pulled up on the front of the broom. This thing had to be able to do a loop-de-loop. It started out well—and then he felt the broom break.

When shit happened and you only had one kind of magic, you used it. Hard. Even if it was totally sucky for the job at hand. Devin grabbed powerful lines of water magic from deep in the ocean and *pulled*. The mighty energies of the ocean pulled back, arrowing him the hundred feet forward he needed to hurtle over the edge of the cliff.

He curled into a ball, readying for a hard water landing—and felt his butt thunk onto hard rock instead.

Jamie rubbed his nephew's head and snickered. "Nice catch, kiddo. I say you should have let him land in the ocean first, though."

"That would've been kind of cold." Aervyn looked sadly at the two pieces of broom in his hand. "We better get Mama a new one, I think."

Devin felt about two inches tall. Nothing like breaking a kid's favorite new toy to make you feel like the world's lousiest uncle. He pondered for a minute. Water power sucked for fixing things, but there had to be a way...

He took the two pieces of broom and twisted them together until he found a tight fit. "Hey, hot stuff—I have a picture in my head of how to fix this. Can you take a look?"

Aervyn nodded, and Devin felt the incoming click of mindlink. Two clicks—obviously his brother was looking too. Their matching grins suggested the idea was a decent one. Which was good, since Devin had none of the magic required to actually get the job done. The two of them should be able to do it, though.

You've been gone too long, Jamie sent. *He'll get it done all on his own.*

That rocked Devin. He knew his nephew was very talented—they all did. But this kind of cellular weaving was a spell that would normally require a full circle.

Watch and learn.

Devin bootstrapped onto Jamie's mind connection—a trick they'd figured out as small boys—and watched his nephew build a spell. In ten seconds, he was impressed. In thirty, he felt something akin to awe. Aervyn wove delicate streams of earth power into a very tight funnel, and then stretched down into the earth and tapped a small aluminum deposit.

When he tied off the spell and opened his eyes, the broom was sheathed in a very thin, very strong layer of metal. Devin had seen the metal strands lace right into the wood of the broom. It would handle loop-de-loops—and probably a flight to the moon, too. It was now one very over-engineered broom.

Aervyn stroked the shiny metal and grinned. "Thanks, Uncle Devin. That was the awesomest idea. Wanna try flying again?"

Yeesh. Break the kid's broom and he still wanted to give you the next turn. "You go first, superboy. And watch out for the air currents near the water. I probably stirred them up a little trying to avoid my crash landing."

A huge grin, and then one silver broom was off in flight, with one very loud and happy witchling holding on for dear life.

Jamie shook his head. "I don't think he even needs the broom."

"He's got some incredible control. Real finesse, and not just on the flying. You've done an amazing job of training him."

"When you've got that kind of power, control matters."

Devin nodded, suddenly aware of exactly how much responsibility lay on his brother's shoulders. "So does finding some freedom."

Jamie grinned and ducked as Aervyn streaked by. "Yup. And the best things give him both."

Devin laughed and clapped an arm around his brother's shoulders. "You've got to give it a try when he gets back. It's way better than a motorbike."

A RECKLESS WITCH

"That's heresy, dude." Jamie's eyes looked a little wistful as he watched Aervyn shoot back up the valley, cape streaming. "I think I'd better stay off the broom. Karma says I'd crack my head open, Nat would go into labor, and Mom would show up just in time to kill me."

There was more than one responsibility lying on his brother's shoulders. "More turns for me, then."

Jamie punched his arm. "Next time, I'm letting him drop you in the ocean."

~ ~ ~

Nell looked around their Realm hangout and grinned at Moira. "I feel really old."

Moira grinned back. "It is feeling rather fertile in here, isn't it?"

She looked over at the couches where Elorie, Sophie, and Nat sat with their feet up. Ginia was running through the basic prenatal checkup for each of them, her hands currently resting gently on Sophie's belly. Her girl was growing up. "Ginia's so excited to be part of the healer team for Nat's birth."

"She's got a very steady mind for such a young witch. It won't be too long before she could handle a birth on her own, if need arose."

Nell was very grateful that would probably never be necessary. "With our new ability to shuttle healers through Realm, our witchlings won't have to grow up quite so fast." Healing talent came with heavy responsibilities, not all of them pleasant.

Moira reached for her hand. "She has so many people who love her. Whatever comes her way, you've rooted her well. She has a deep and generous heart, and a lovely sense of competence."

"I know." Nell smiled. "But it never hurts to hear it again."

"You have wonderful instincts with your little ones." Moira glanced at the couch again. "And Nat watches you carefully. I believe she knows what's coming, at least as well as any non-witch can."

"She's not exactly getting an easy first baby."

Moira chuckled. "A fire witchling who's clearly coming into her power early? No, she certainly isn't. But she also has many people who love her, and she knows how to nurture her own roots as well as anyone I know."

"It's changing Jamie." And it was an odd experience, watching your baby brother take those steps.

"As it should. But he's a man who knows exactly who he is. I don't expect it will change him all that much."

Nell grinned, oddly comforted. "He's out giving broom-flying lessons to Aervyn."

Lauren laughed behind them, having just beamed in. "I think it's the other way around—Aervyn's schooling Jamie and Devin. And if Aervyn's mind-glee is any indication, they're having a very good time."

Nell raised an eyebrow. "You can hear them all the way from Ocean's Reach?" She was a little envious.

Lauren pulled over a chair and shrugged. "Evidently so. The more circle work we do together, the further away I can hear him, at least when he's got his barriers down. I think he's been flying Devin around."

Oy. "Only an idiot gets on a broom magically driven by a four-year-old."

Moira giggled. "Devin's always had the soul of an adventurer, dear."

That was one way to put it. "You weren't his big sister."

"Don't you worry." Moira patted her hand. "One day soon, he'll find himself a nice girl and settle down."

Porky pink pigs would fly first. Nell wiggled an eyebrow at Lauren. "You interested? He's tall, dark, handsome, and rich."

Damn. Was Lauren actually blushing?

Moira's eyes sparkled. "You'd make beautiful babies together."

Lauren's laughter bounced off the walls of Realm. "I think there are enough babies in the works at the moment, don't you?"

Something odd tripped in Nell, just for a moment. Whatever it was got interrupted by Ginia's call. "Mama, I think Auntie Nat's baby is playing with fire again—can you come check?"

That was interesting—the baby had been very quiet lately, and her daughter didn't have fire talent. "How can you tell?"

Ginia shook her head. "I don't know, exactly. It just feels like something is shifting, kind of."

That got everyone's attention. Sophie moved over to sit beside Nat as well, laying her hands gently beside Ginia's. A moment later, she looked up, frowning. "I can feel it too, but I don't know what it is." She looked at their apprentice healer with respect. "It's really subtle—I'm impressed your scan is picking that up."

Nell and Moira both moved in. Nat looked up at Lauren and grinned. "You might as well come too. My belly has plenty of real estate these days." It wasn't the easiest thing in the world to position five set of hands on one baby, but they managed.

Nell shook her head first. "I don't feel anything." She laughed as the belly under her hands rippled. "Well, besides the kicks. Whatever it is, she's not playing with elemental magics."

Moira tilted her head. "I don't feel it either, but my healing scans aren't nearly as strong as Sophie's." She patted Ginia's hand. "Or yours either, apparently. You do me very proud, sweet girl."

The glow on her daughter's face made Nell's heart tilt a little.

Lauren's breath of awe shifted all their attention. "She's mindreading. I can hear your feelings echoed in her mind." She frowned. "I've never noticed that before. And her head hurts, a lot."

"Emergence headache." Sophie leaned forward again, eyes intent. "That's what you were feeling, Ginia. Help me clear her channels."

Nell took her hands off Nat's belly. Time to let the trained healers fix things. She spoke very quietly to Lauren. "The baby's got mind powers?" Even Aervyn hadn't come into mind magics that young.

"I think so." Lauren nodded slowly. "And she's picking up a lot. Too much, I think—my head would hurt if I was taking in so many other thoughts and feelings. Nat's mind is most prominent, and that's really soothing for her, but..."

Moira nodded. "You'll need to teach her to barrier, then."

Lauren frowned. "Nat?"

"No, sweetheart. Our newest little mind witch."

"I'm supposed to give magic lessons to an unborn baby?"

Nell tried to stifle her giggles—Lauren looked totally gobsmacked. "Ask Jamie for ideas. He worked with Aervyn on some basic control over his elemental powers before he was born." Not that it had worked all that well...

"We should have her channels cleared now." Sophie looked up at Nat. "Ginia will be able to take care of that for you moving forward, and Jamie could probably do it in an emergency. It would be good to do at least once a day, at least until she's born." She grinned. "Or until Lauren teaches her how to barrier."

Nat laughed and looked at her best friend. "I guess you're starting your aunt duties early."

Lauren still looked dazed. Nell snickered and leaned over toward Moira. "I guess that means we know at least one member of the birthing circle, then."

Moira nodded sagely. "It's a wise choice." She patted Lauren's hand. "You'll do very well, my dear."

Now Lauren looked utterly panicked. "Me? That's insane. I've never had a baby. I've never even seen a baby born."

Nat took her hand, highly amused. "Breathe deeply. I hear it's supposed to help."

~ ~ ~

It was always the same dream. Sierra yanked on power lines, fought the thick-as-water air that slowed her down. Faster. Her heart slammed in terror and the exertion of trying to move faster than the wind.

Fear. Awful, tearing fear. She wouldn't get there in time. Hurtling over the ocean, skimming the swells, every cell in her body straining to reach the small rock in the middle of the water.

The tiny magical rock island where her mother stood, arms in the air, reveling in the storm building over her head. Playing with the lines of water and air, dancing in the heart of power unleashed.

And blind to the killing wave barreling in behind her.

Sierra raced the wave. She pleaded and begged and offered the wave her life in trade.

And she lost. She always lost.

Oh, Momma. I'm so sorry.

Chapter 5

Sierra stared out the window, exhausted and numb, as the train chugged through the outlying areas of San Francisco. It had been a really long day of traveling after a short and crappy night's sleep. She'd woken up hiding under the bed again, and like always, she couldn't remember why—just a dragging tiredness, and the sense she'd been crying.

She hated waking up under the bed. And she'd learned to do it quietly, so her creep of a younger foster brother didn't tease her for being a weenie crybaby who missed her momma.

Then she'd had to say good-bye to her foster parents and pretend it mattered. Saying good-bye to her favorite librarian had been harder. Her placement family had been decent, but they'd been taking in kids for long enough to avoid getting too attached. Not that she'd been looking for attachments. It had been a place to sleep and almost enough to eat.

Her caseworker had driven her to the bus station, proud of her graduate. In the files, Sierra knew she was a success story. Finished high school, stayed out of trouble, rode off to a rosy future employed and not yet pregnant.

The bar for success was set pretty low.

She'd waited for this day for six years. It didn't feel like she'd always thought it would. She'd imagined it would be like riding a funnel—full of joy and speed and freedom. Instead, she was tired, cranky, and missing Momma.

Missing her beach a little, too. She wouldn't miss much from Oregon—but the beach had kept her sane.

Maybe it was the train ride. She and Momma had ridden a lot of trains together, always looking out the window in excitement as they arrived at a new place, a new adventure.

Sierra looked out the window and tried to get a sense of her new home. Lots of fog—it reminded her of Momma's ghost stories of Londinium and the friendly beings who lived in the fog and helped you find your way. These days, when Sierra wandered on a foggy beach, she hoped Momma was there, reaching out to touch her face or tickle her toes. Or maybe one of the ghosts of Londinium, traveled across the sea to the wilds of the New World. There had been lots of stories of the New World on the trains as well.

In another time, Momma would have been one of those storytellers that sat by the fire at night, telling long tales of lifetimes past. Or maybe a bard—she'd been a pretty good singer, too.

And then the next morning, she would have strapped on her sword and rucksack and gone off on another big adventure. Momma could never sit still for very long.

Sierra remembered a set of shiny silver swords she'd gotten for her eighth birthday. She and Momma had strapped them on and danced around on a castle drawbridge in Ireland, laughing as all the tourists took their pictures.

She'd give anything to have a couple of those pictures now.

The fog was clearing a bit as they came into the downtown train station. People started shuffling around, getting their belongings together. A small boy dashed down the aisle, clearly ready to be off the train. He tripped over the corner of someone's bag, and Sierra caught him just before his nose crashed into the arm of her seat.

"Thanks!" he said. "My name's Joey, and I'm not supposed to talk to strangers, but if you catched me, maybe you're not a stranger."

Sierra had always thought that was a really dumb rule. How boring would life be if you never talked to anyone new? She remembered many happy train rides talking to her fellow passengers. "Have you ever been to San Francisco before?"

Joey shook his head, eyes gleaming. "Nope. Mommy says we're gonna go see a big bridge and ride a streetcar and everything!"

She grinned. Riding the streetcar had always been one of her favorites too. "If you stick your head out just a little bit, you'll be able to feel the wind fairies playing in your hair."

His eyes were huge. "There's fairies in the wind?"

"Of course. Who else do you think does all that blowing?" She pulled just the lightest touch of air magic and tickled his curls.

Joey giggled and ran back down the aisle. "Mommy! We hafta go play with the wind fairies!"

Sierra danced the tiny wind through her own hair. The fairies and ghosts would be there to keep her company, just like always. Time for a new adventure.

~ ~ ~

Nell drove up to the house, trying to page her youngest. Or her brother. Or any mind witch in the vicinity. She had an exhausted and shell-shocked passenger—not what they'd been expecting—and she wanted the party waiting inside to calm to a dull roar.

You called? Lauren's mental voice landed in her head.

Yeah. Nell cast a worried glance at Sierra. *I have a girl here who looks ready for food and bed, not a welcoming celebration. I thought having her ride the train down here would give her some time to transition, but maybe I should've just had Aervyn port her. See if you can simmer things down in there a bit?*

Oh, sure. Give me the easy jobs. Now Lauren sounded a tad worried too. *I'll see what I can do.*

Nell felt Sierra's muddled surprise as they parked in front of the house and wondered what the girl found strange. Judging from the racket she could hear out the car window, a warning was in order. "There are a lot of people inside waiting to meet you. If it's too much, just let me know, okay? The party can always wait until tomorrow."

The effect of the word "party" was astonishing. Sierra's eyes sparkled, and she jumped out of the car with the eagerness of a small child. She beat Nell to the front door, nearly colliding with the herd of children who rushed out.

Lauren followed close behind, apology on her face. *Sorry—I don't have your noise-management skills.*

Nell looked at Sierra and shrugged. *She seems to be rolling with it.*

Lauren frowned. *She's got images of castles and people in evening gowns in her head. What gives?*

No idea. By now, the under-ten crowd had shepherded their new arrival into the house, and Nell followed at the back of the parade. In under two minutes, they had Sierra sitting in the middle of the couch, pink and glittery crown on her head, brownie in her hand, and one of Aunt Jennie's purple-haired grandsons on her lap. *Welcome to Witch Central, girl.*

Jamie slid up beside Nell, bearing extra brownies. "She doing okay?"

She shrugged. "Seems to be now. She was running on fumes when I picked her up, but..." They both looked over at the mob of kids.

Someone had started a game of Hot Potato with a brownie. Probably Leo of the purple hair—he finally had enough control over his earth magic to play, and it was his current favorite game.

A RECKLESS WITCH

The kids were slowly backing up into a large circle. The adults were more quickly backing up out of the line of fire.

Jamie laughed. "Wimps. I remember way messier choices for the hot potato than a brownie."

"You aren't the one that usually got hit with them." Nell was pretty convinced her spellcasting abilities had evolved as a consequence of losing one too many hot-potato matches with her brothers.

He shrugged. "We had to do something with all that green slime Devin kept making."

"Just you wait. If there's any karma in the world, your daughter's going to be a supremely good mess-maker."

Jamie tried to look innocent and failed hopelessly. "I have no idea what you're talking about." He turned back to the game. "Sierra's holding her own."

Nell watched more carefully. He was right. Leo wasn't much competition, but Aervyn was. And Ginia... "Holy crap. When did Ginia figure out how to arm her sisters?" Splitting power streams was complicated. Giving control over a power stream to a non-witch was even trickier. That Ginia could do both and still dodge the flying brownie was very impressive.

"She's not the only one." Jamie spoke quietly, but he was intently focused on the game now. "Sierra's splitting streams, too—she's helping Leo out."

He was right. She was using primarily air power to push the brownie around herself, but she was feeding small amounts of fire magic to Leo to speed up his earth power flows. Which was probably good, because slow magics didn't survive at Hot Potato for long.

Sierra sent the brownie on a swift rolling loop, and then laughed and assisted as Leo tried to copy it. Nell snorted. "Who baked the brownies?"

Jamie grinned. "Aunt Jennie. It'll survive a while longer."

Yup. Aunt Jennie was a sweetheart, but her brownies were on the dense side. Nell kept watching, fascinated. It was one of the most complex games of Hot Potato she'd seen in a long time. Ginia feeding power to her sisters, Sierra helping Leo, and Aervyn doing... "What's my punk witchling up to?"

Jamie shook his head. "Not sure. Some kind of dividing spell."

Nell watched, mystified, and then grinned in pride as the brownie broke into four pieces. Not a big magic trick for her son, but good witchcraft was as much about brains as talent. Training a four-year-old with fairly unlimited power to use both wasn't always easy.

The game had shifted sharply now. Four flying objects were three too many for most of the players, and they sat down, laughing. Ginia lasted a few seconds longer and then giggled and dove for the floor as brownie chunks dive-bombed each of her ears.

Jamie leaned in as Sierra and Aervyn faced off, the only two left standing. "Now we'll really see what she can do."

They weren't the only ones paying attention, either. Govin watched intently from across the circle, his eyes entirely on Sierra.

And no wonder. Aervyn had four separate energy streams directing four brownies. He jumped from one to the next, redirecting one chunk at a time. Sierra had a dancing whirlwind of air that was juggling all four chunks at once. Every time Aervyn pushed on one brownie piece, she tossed all three others at him.

Her son was fast, precise, and strong. And he was barely holding on.

Then Aervyn switched tactics, and Jamie grinned. "He's learning. He's trying to do what she's doing."

With your average four-year-old, learning was a bit of a process. With her son, a couple of wobbly pushes and he was air-juggling brownies almost as well as Sierra. Nell saw their new arrival's eyebrows wing up. "She's just figured that out."

"Does she know she's facing the baddest witchling in the west?"

Nell snickered as two brownies collided in mid-air and crumbled. "She will now." With only two chunks left in play, Aervyn's four-year-old-boy disadvantages were going to evaporate.

In a bet, she would have given Sierra thirty seconds, max. And been very impressed if the girl lasted that long.

Two minutes later, Sierra was still standing and had earned the serious respect of everyone watching. *He's stronger, but not by much. And she's got better control.* Jamie was probably the most impressed witch in the room—he'd faced off with Aervyn in training more than everyone else combined.

Nell watched as Sierra tugged and shaped power lines on the fly. Lots of witches could toss power around. To do it with that kind of precision took countless hours of practice. Maybe Amelia had trained her daughter more responsibly than they'd all assumed.

In a lightning-quick move, Sierra grabbed a trickle of firepower and superheated her air currents, spinning them into a funnel. Nell winced—even Aunt Jennie's brownies weren't going to make it through a mini tornado. Aervyn and Sierra busted up laughing as brownie crumbs flew everywhere.

Most of the adults joined the mirth, well used to the messes that were the usual price to pay for witchling antics.

Except for one. Govin's face was awash with concern. And he'd lived through plenty of hot-potato messes—something else was up.

~ ~ ~

Govin thunked into the Realm meeting room, grateful he landed on a couch. Even being a gamer for as long as he could remember, it was still a very odd sensation to actually land in-game.

He laughed at the balloon-festooned sign hanging over his head. "What's up with the new name?"

Jamie grinned. "Our child-labor force has decided that 'Realm meeting room' isn't a cool enough name for our hangout here. I vetoed several choices. Apparently this one is boring, but acceptable."

Govin wasn't sure how "Witches' Lounge" in gold-glittered letters qualified as boring, but he was definitely not the expert on nine-year-old girls. "Nell said to come at three o'clock—am I early?"

"Not at all, dear boy," said Moira, freshly landed on the couch beside him, cup of tea in her hand. Govin was impressed—no way was he comfortable transporting while holding hot liquids. He kissed her cheek and settled in, figuring Nell and Sophie weren't far behind.

They were three of his favorite women. And he was only beginning to understand the depths of the mess they'd thrown him in.

Nell beamed in, a big plate in her hands. "Quesadillas—I know it's dinner time for some of you."

"Seedling thanks you." Sophie laughed, rubbing her belly.

Jamie reached for the plate. "It's never too early for dinner. Hang on, and I'll ping Ginia to send us some drinks."

A tray materialized on the coffee table in front of him. Drinks, apples, and napkins. Nell grinned. "Do you really think I'd miss a detail like that?"

He lifted an eyebrow. "No cookies?"

"Time-delayed transport." Nell rolled her eyes. "Ginia's brainstorm. She has this weird idea we should eat our veggies first."

Jamie laughed and bit into his quesadilla. "Since when is cheese a vegetable?"

"It's what I hide in the cheese." The whole room laughed as Jamie looked at his dinner in not entirely faked horror.

Govin chuckled and handed Moira an apple and a plate. He'd run tame in the Sullivan house growing up. He knew that bickering was a sign of love, Jamie really was fairly allergic to vegetables, and Nell did most of her serious negotiating over food. He bit into a quesadilla and waited.

"How is our Sierra doing?" Moira asked. "I was surprised you wanted to meet so soon after the wee girl arrived."

Nell passed out napkins. "She's sound asleep on Aervyn's top bunk. The kids were playing hide-and-seek after the Great Brownie Cleanup, and she conked out waiting for someone to find her."

Her brother grinned. "She's an extrovert. They gain energy from being with other people. As soon as the kids abandoned her, boom. Out like a light."

Everyone in the room shook their head, amused. Jamie had taken a recent interest in trying to find patterns in witch talents and personality traits. As a result, they'd all been filling out a lot of multiple-choice tests.

Govin smiled. He was a bigger fan of data than most, but clearly not everyone was in love with Jamie's latest venture.

Nell handed her brother another quesadilla wedge. "You might be right. She was barely sitting up on the car ride back from the train station, but our mob of kiddos turned that right around."

"That's interesting." Sophie tilted her head. "Sierra's eighteen, but it sounds like she was more attracted to the young ones than the adults."

That hadn't failed to escape Govin's notice, either. On its own—no big deal. Coupled with what else he'd noticed, and he was nervous. It was why he'd asked Nell to call a meeting.

Jamie shrugged. "Well, the kids kind of swooped down on her. But if I remember correctly, Amelia spent a lot of time playing with us when she came to visit, too. Maybe Sierra inherited her mother's love of kids?"

"For Amelia, it was more than that." Moira sipped her tea pensively. "In many ways, she was forever a child—she shared their joy in laughter and a life of fun and games." She looked over at Govin. "And their lack of concern for the consequences of their actions. You've seen something of her mother in our Sierra, I think."

Moira had always been a very perceptive witch. He nodded slowly, not sure where to begin. "She was playing Hot Potato with the other kids just after she arrived."

Jamie reached for more food. "She held Aervyn to a stand-off. That was some pretty impressive control she had."

Nell tossed an apple hand-to-hand and looked at Govin. "Tell them what you told me."

"She did have impressive control." He laid down his plate. "She was essentially using storm magic to control the flying brownie chunks. The little funnel at the end? Make that a hundred times bigger, and your house would have been doing a pretty good imitation of Dorothy and Toto in *The Wizard of Oz*."

Sophie blinked. "You think she's that strong?"

"No idea." He shook his head. "Or at least, no quantifiable data. But unless she played an awful lot of Hot Potato with her mother, she had to develop those skills somehow. And they're easier to learn moving bigger streams of power." It was one of the ironies of magic that small spells were often more difficult than large ones.

Jamie was frowning now. "You think she learned on house-sized funnels?"

"I suspect so." Govin nodded. That wasn't the part that had him most concerned, but it was a start. "At the very least, it's a strong possibility—and she controlled three power streams at a time like it was child's play." For her, it had been exactly that.

Moira sat up straighter. "That kind of power might be enough to disturb planetary weather patterns."

Exactly. They all sat silent for a moment as Moira's words sank in. Most witches could only impact very local weather. The few with more power than that had to be extremely careful. A butterfly flapping its wings in Berkeley might not really be able to create a hurricane in the Gulf—but a witch with enough power could. Govin had thought he was aware of everyone who had that kind of talent. He made it his mission in life to find them.

"You're the best one to test her." Jamie nodded at Govin, distracted by a plate of cookies landing on the table. "Do you want help?"

Govin shook his head, ignoring the cookies for a moment. "It's not the testing that concerns me. It's figuring out what to do if she does have that kind of power."

Sophie frowned. "I feel like I'm still missing something. It sounds like she has excellent control, so her training must be pretty solid, no? Wouldn't another strong weather witch be an asset?"

Govin looked down at his hands for a minute. "Yes. She's a skilled witch, likely just reaching the peak of her power." The rest was pure conjecture, which didn't sit well with his data-based mind—but it was really bothering him. "And she didn't ground."

Jamie looked blank. "Didn't ground what?"

"Her power streams. She played Hot Potato with no grounding."

Now he had everyone's full attention. There were basic precautions every witch with decent power learned—and one of those was running a groundline to deal with power flashes and kickbacks. It was as automatic as breathing.

Nell tapped her fingers on the arm of the couch. "To play devil's advocate for a minute, it's possible she just wasn't grounding for Hot Potato. It was tricky magic, but the power flows weren't big enough to require a ground." She looked at Govin. "But that's not what you think."

He shrugged. "I'm a pretty cautious guy, so this might just be my inner scaredy-witch talking."

She scowled at him. "No one gets to call you that but me. You're right—every witch I know with any decent power grounds every time they do magic."

Jamie nodded. "That's how we teach it, so it's habit." He paused. "Maybe Sierra wasn't taught the same way—maybe she only grounds when it's really necessary."

"Maybe." But that wasn't the possibility that had put the lead weight in Govin's stomach. "And maybe she was never trained to ground."

He turned to Moira, who was looking pale. "I assume you taught Amelia the way you teach every witch."

"We did." She nodded slowly. "But she got hit with power backlash at least twice that I know of. We never could get a good read on whether it was accidental or intentional, but she didn't take magical safety nearly seriously enough. Whether she'd have been foolhardy enough to skip that step teaching her child, I can't say."

Sophie rubbed her belly, eyes deeply concerned. "So we're saying it's possible that Sierra was trained to do magic without the proper safeguards in place—and she might have enough power to mess with planetary weather?"

Govin shrugged helplessly as the worry levels in the room went up substantially. "I hope not, but I think we'd better find out quickly." He had a very bad feeling about this.

~ ~ ~

Sierra stared at the ceiling, disoriented and cranky, as she blinked awake from her nap.

She was always cranky when she hadn't had enough to eat. Should have eaten the brownie instead of making a big mess in Nell's house.

Not that Nell's home was anything like she'd expected. Momma's stories had made it sound like Nell was a rich movie-star witch. Ha. She was a mom with five kids, a messy living room, and socks that didn't match.

Movie stars didn't even wear socks.

She froze as the door squeaked open. "See, she's awake. I told you."

Aervyn. Well, he wasn't a movie star, but he was kind of cute. She sat up—and discovered her witchling visitor wasn't alone.

"Hi, I'm Lauren." The stranger smiled and held up a tray. "We got sent to see if you were hungry."

Aervyn scrambled up the ladder and plopped himself at Sierra's feet. Then he waved his fingers, and the tray in Lauren's hands vanished and reappeared on the bed.

Wow. "You can really teleport?" Porting had been in Momma's stories too.

Lauren grinned. "Just be glad he ported the food up, instead of you down." She put a hand on the ladder. "Okay if I come up?"

He could port people? Sierra stared at Aervyn, wide-eyed—then realized she was being totally rude. She looked back over at Lauren, apology in her eyes. "Sure—sorry. Come on up."

"No worries. I remember my first few days here in Witch Central. It's a lot to take in."

Sierra took a bite of the cheesy-pasta goodness on her plate and nearly groaned in delight. Who needed rich movie stars?

Aervyn giggled. "Caro's not a movie star, but she's a really good cook."

Sierra had no idea who Caro was. "Are there lots of witches who live here?" Momma had made it sound like a whole city, but she was beginning to think Momma might have exaggerated a little.

"Uh, huh. Well, not all in this house." He giggled, eyeing her pasta. "They wouldn't all fit."

She held out a forkful, knowing exactly how magic could make your belly gnaw.

Lauren snorted. "He had three platefuls while we were in the kitchen." She sobered and spoke more quietly. "There's always enough food for a witch in this house. If you want more, just ask."

Sierra blushed—and then realized she hadn't been talking out loud. "You're a mind witch?"

"Yup." Aervyn nodded, eyeing her noodles again. "She's a new one, though. Caro says she's still freshly hatched." He grinned at Lauren. "Maybe you'll grow up to be a rooster one day."

"Roosters are boys, silly." She tweaked his nose, laughing. "Maybe you can go ask Caro for another plate of noodles, since you're obviously growing."

Sierra tried not to stare as he ported himself off the bed to the floor and raced out the door. "How does he do that?"

Lauren laughed again. "I have no idea. But you get used to it. Mostly. He ported into my kitchen the other day and scared the living daylights out of me."

As pasta warmed her tummy, Sierra's curiosity was coming online. "So you're really a new witch?"

"I am." Lauren smiled. "You know the spell they used to find you? I was the first witch they ever fetched, about nine months ago. The only problem was, I didn't know I was a witch."

Sierra blinked. "How could you not know?"

Lauren leaned back against the wall. "It's a long story..." One she was clearly prepared to tell.

Sierra ate and listened to the tale of a grown woman who had no idea she had power. And thought that maybe life in Witch Central was pretty interesting after all. Even without the movie stars.

DEBORA GEARY

Chapter 6

Jamie pulled into the parking lot at Ocean's Reach and turned to his team. "Remember, guys—we want to see what Sierra can do, but we don't want to make her nervous. We're just going to try some test weather spells for encoding into the WitchNet library."

Devin met his eye, but didn't say anything. He didn't need to—skepticism was written all over his face.

Aervyn was more easily convinced. "How come we came *here*? Are we trying to make really big spells for Elorie?"

Jamie grinned. Elorie was finding it a challenge to convince certain witchlings that she wanted mostly small, everyday spells for WitchNet. "We'll start with some little ones, but maybe we'll try a couple of bigger ones, too."

His nephew's eyes gleamed. "Can we make a storm? Pretty please? Govin says I'm almost safe enough now to make him happy."

"That's good to hear, hot stuff." Devin rolled his eyes at Jamie and spoke in an undertone. "I bet a four-year-old weather witch is the answer to all Govin's dreams."

"Not exactly." Govin—for good reason—found it extremely hard to balance Aervyn's natural exuberance and need to play with the very real possibility that if he sneezed mid-spell, a tsunami could hit a beach in India. Weather patterns were seriously tricky, and any witch who could affect them kept Govin up at night.

Especially four-year-olds, even ones with superlative training.

Govin waved as he pulled into the parking lot, Sierra sitting in the seat beside him. Nell had hoped the drive up might give them time to get to know each other a little. Judging from the body language, that hadn't happened yet.

Jamie hoped his sister knew what she was doing, matching up a thirty-something math geek with an eighteen-year-old kid who liked to play Hot Potato. Govin was an awesome guy, but teenage girls were way outside his normal world.

Aervyn headed across the parking lot and grabbed Sierra's hand, dragging her in the direction of the path to the valley where they typically worked.

Jamie smiled at Govin in welcome as the rest of the crew followed. "TJ stayed home?"

Govin reached into his pocket and pulled out a gizmo. "Yup, but he sent a monitoring device so we can record the energy readings."

TJ funded their partnership's more magical work by doing some fancy weather modeling for government agencies. Watching energy shifts during spellwork gave him insights into weather patterns that agency types paid big money for. He and his gadgets were often present during training sessions.

It didn't take them long to get to the valley of Ocean's Reach, one of Jamie's favorite places for group magic lessons. Even fairly weak witches could access decent power here, and the group today wasn't weak. He felt the familiar thrum of anticipation and grinned at his brother. "Ready to play with some weather?"

"Do we get to make a really big storm?" Devin was an excellent mimic, sounding exactly like his young nephew.

Aervyn laughed. Sierra just looked excited—and Jamie could feel the concern building in Govin's mind. It wasn't good when the trainer was tense. *Start small, Gov. And if it gets out of hand, you have lots of talent available. Use us.*

A RECKLESS WITCH

Govin grinned ruefully. "Is that a nice way of calling me a scaredy-witch?"

Jamie tried to look innocent. Since even Aervyn was giggling, he clearly wasn't doing a very good job. Time to point the conversation somewhere else. "So, what's our first test spell?"

Govin consulted a list. "A warm-air current."

Aervyn's face scrunched up in disappointment. "That's it?"

Govin crouched down. "Most weather happens when warm air and cooler air hit. So if a witch sets off a warm-air-current spell in just the right place, what do you think happens?"

Superboy's eyes gleamed. "A storm?"

"Right. And we want this to be a safe spell for people to use, so we need to do a couple of tricky things."

"Keep it small." Superboy knew his weather rules.

"Right." Govin nodded. "And we need to make it smart enough to pick the right temperature to be. We want it to be about ten degrees cooler than whatever air it ends up next to—otherwise you might get snow in July, or something crazy like that."

Aervyn obviously thought summer snow was a fairly cool possibility, but he nodded solemnly. Then his forehead wrinkled. "How exactly do we do that? Air's not very smart."

Jamie grinned. That was one of Govin's favorite lines.

The guy in question tapped his temple. "We need to think hard. I want everyone to try their own spell first, so we see how many different ways we can think of to try to make our air smarter. Then we'll pick the best couple to work on together."

Not bad for a guy who didn't usually do much training. Aervyn had all kinds of power, but sorting out the best way to build a spell was a work-in-progress. This was a way for him to develop that skill, and learn from others, without making the coaching obvious.

Aervyn looked thoughtful. Devin waited with breezy confidence. And Sierra was already in motion.

> "I call on Air, friend to me
> Split a layer, one times three,
> Each slower than the one inside
> Cooler air giving warm a ride.
> I call on Fire, sister of mine
> Heat the core, one plus nine
> Subtract two layers on word from me
> As I will, so mote it be."

She looked up at the group, grinning, a spellshape on her palm. "This should work."

Jamie gaped. Holy shit. If he'd followed her spellsetting right, she'd come up with a smart design that split air layers from the existing air currents, solving the relative-temperature challenge Govin had posed. It had a built-in trigger, which he hadn't even asked for. And she'd done it all with less than ten seconds of thought.

Aervyn was still trying to catch up, and Devin was all kinds of impressed. With good reason—it was a heck of a spell on short notice.

It was also a spell that spoke of deep familiarity with air currents. And that would be why Govin's mind was spewing uneasiness.

Jamie hadn't been made Aervyn's trainer because he was afraid to take a risk. He glanced at Govin, doubled his own groundline, mind-messaged Aervyn and Devin to do the same, and then nodded to Sierra. "Let it loose."

A quick finger wave, and a category-three storm broke loose—in a perfect circle ringing their small group. Another finger wave, and it turned off.

Well, hell. Jamie looked grimly at Govin. The spell, and the way Sierra had made it dance, confirmed they had a weather witch with serious power and mad skills.

It had also confirmed that she did major magic with no net—even with a small child standing two feet away. She'd done no grounding, no training circle, no layering, no failsafes. Backlash from a storm that size could easily have killed Aervyn if he weren't taking his own precautions.

And the witch who'd caused it all stood looking at them with an expectant grin on her face.

~ ~ ~

It was so cool to do magic and not have to hide on the beach to do it. Sierra looked down at Aervyn, who watched her, puzzled. Maybe the spell had been too complicated for him to follow. She crouched down. "Wanna try it? I can do it slower so you can see all the parts."

That's how Momma had taught her.

He frowned. "How come you don't use a groundline?"

A what? She looked toward at the others for explanation—and realized no one was smiling. Govin was looking at her like she had a booger dripping out of her nose or something. The other two just looked worried. Really worried. Cripes. Maybe she wasn't supposed to be teaching anyone magic. She stood up, feeling the last echoes of the energy streams she'd called for the baby storm leaking away.

First day of her new job, and she'd somehow already screwed up. Nice one, Sierra.

Jamie's eyes looked the friendliest, so she focused on him. "Sorry. Whatever I did wrong, just tell me, so I don't do it again." Rules, she could live with. Most of the time. Rules she didn't know about sucked.

He just stared at her, not saying anything.

She jumped as a small hand slid into hers. "Don't be mad, Uncle Jamie. Maybe she doesn't know how to use a groundline. I can teach her."

It felt good to have someone on her team, even if he was only three-and-a-half feet tall.

Devin nodded and ruffled Aervyn's hair. "You're totally right, buddy." He turned to Sierra. "Most witches use an extra line when they cast a spell—one that they tie off somewhere safe. Kind of like an overflow valve, in case there's backlash or you pull more power than you expected."

Sierra had no idea what he was talking about. "Isn't it better just to pull the right amount in the first place?"

He shrugged. "Sure, but with your kind of power, if you judge wrong, a groundline gives you a safety net. So you don't hurt yourself or anyone around you."

Now she was really confused. "But that was just a baby spell. How could I hurt anyone with that?"

Devin blinked twice. Hard. "That was a baby spell for you?"

Aervyn grinned. "You must be a super-awesome weather witch."

She nodded slowly, more worried about what she saw in Devin's eyes. "That was just a class-three storm. It wouldn't hurt anyone." Especially not while she was standing right there.

Govin's sharp intake of breath had everyone's head turning. His eyes lasered in on hers. "How big a storm can you build?"

She had no idea. "I made a little hurricane once, but Momma said not to make a bigger one." She smiled at the memory. "We had fun dancing in the funnel, though."

Aervyn's eyes were as big as plates. "You danced with a hurricane?"

She was about to offer to take him funnel dancing, and then she looked at the faces around her again. Maybe not. "Only once. Mostly we just played in smaller funnels. No bigger than a house." Maybe that would get her out of whatever mess she'd stepped in. Maybe witches in California didn't like to play.

Govin's eyes were still glued to hers. "You made a hurricane without any groundlines?"

Sierra's temper suddenly flared. It was time for all these people to stop dissing her magic. "I do magic exactly the way Momma taught me." She grabbed for power, ready to show them exactly what she could do with it. And ran into a brick wall.

One with a very determined four-year-old holding the reins. "You can't do that, Sierra. It's dangerous. Just lemme show you a groundline, please? You're a good witch—I bet it's totally easy for you."

Holy cats. He'd stopped her magic in its tracks.

Jamie smiled grimly. "He can stop mine cold too, if that makes you feel any better."

Aervyn nodded solemnly. "That's why they call me superboy."

He was so danged cute. Sierra crouched down again, temper leaving as easily as it had come. "So show me how to be supergirl, then. What's this grounding stuff?"

Two minutes later, she looked up at the trio of guys watching. Grounding was dirt easy. "That's it?"

Jamie nodded. "It's not hard. It's usually one of the first things I teach my trainees. But it's important—it keeps everyone safer."

That was the part she really didn't get. "But I've never been seriously hurt by my magic." Banged up a little, but she'd been hurt worse riding her bike.

Govin spoke softly, but with a force that nearly knocked her to her knees. "That little storm you just made had enough power to kill a small child if it wasn't handled properly."

It had just been a plaything. Not even a funnel. "I'd never hurt anyone. I know how to control my magic."

His eyes sparked. "No one can control their magic all the time. What happens when you screw up, or the energy lines aren't clean, or you catch a bad bounce?"

That happened to weather witches all the time. "You catch it. You clean it up." She wasn't stupid.

"And if you fail?" The words came hard, almost mean. Just like her foster brother, only more grown up. Sierra fought back the tears.

"Cut her a break, Gov." Devin stepped forward, touching her shoulder. "Grounding matters—can you just trust us that far for now? It keeps us all safer, and it's a pretty easy thing to add to all your spells."

It was like he'd taken this huge ball of tension and made it vanish. Sierra took a deep breath, thankful the squeezing pressure on her ribs had stopped. She liked Devin. "I can do that—I promise." She'd done way dumber things in her life to keep people happy.

"Good." Then he grinned, and it reminded her so much of Momma, just before something really fun happened. "Now let's go build a funnel. You can show us all how to dance with one."

~ ~ ~

Devin crashed into a seat at his brother's table. He'd had one of the most fun mornings of his entire life, and he was hungry enough to eat the table. Unfortunately, breakfast was waiting on the other guest of honor.

Nat grinned at him. "Lauren's on her way, honest. And I'll even let you into the food line before me." She patted her belly. "Our girl here doesn't let me eat much anymore."

"My brother would beat me up if I didn't let his pregnant wife eat first."

She winked. "You can take him."

Devin had been fairly skeptical that Nat was the paragon of perfectness for Jamie that everyone had claimed. Their wedding hadn't done a whole lot to dispel that—probably because weddings in general made him twitchy.

His skepticism hadn't made it two hours in the same house with Nat. She was every kind of awesome.

He stretched out and tried to convince his ravenous belly to take a quick nap or something. "Not after this morning. Funnel riding is the coolest thing I've done in a really long time, but we didn't carb-load enough before we left." He rolled his eyes. "I thought we were making little weather spells for Elorie's library. I should have known better."

Jamie came around the corner from the kitchen and laughed. "Don't blame that one on me—you're the one who wanted funnel-riding lessons."

Devin grinned. "Yeah. Govin nearly blew a gasket. But they were properly grounded, all seven of them." It had been better than the Zero-G rotor ride at the state fair. Way better, and that had been their favorite ride ever since they'd been the required four feet tall to ride it.

Nat shook her head, highly amused. "I can't believe you took a small boy spinning in a hurricane."

He snorted. "The small boy made at least three of them. And they weren't big enough funnels to be a hurricane." He thought. Govin was the weather expert.

Jamie grinned. "You can help our nephew with his latest brainstorm. He wants to spellcode a small funnel for Realm so he can take Moira for a ride."

"A ride on what?" Lauren walked into the room, bearing a huge basket of strawberries. "Sorry I'm late. Clients who couldn't make up their minds."

"No prob." Nat reached for the strawberries. "Especially when you bring fresh berries in December. Aervyn wants to take Moira for a ride on a hurricane funnel."

Lauren laughed. Then she stared at Jamie. "For real?"

He nodded. "Yup. Sierra showed him how. I bet you can have a ride if you want one, too."

She lifted an eyebrow. "Exactly how far off the ground would my feet get?"

Jamie and Devin looked at each other and shrugged. That was one of those unanswerable "mom" questions. Heck, their feet hadn't even been pointing down the whole time. Devin grinned, remembering one particularly funny moment when the funnel had peeled Aervyn's pants off as he whirled upside down.

Nat laughed and handed Lauren a plate. "I'm guessing that if you have to ask, you probably don't want a ride."

"We'll see." Lauren's eyes twinkled. "I'll wait and see if Moira looks green after she's done."

Devin grabbed the platter of waffles. "Somebody should warn Aervyn that if he makes Moira puke, she has some devilish ways of getting even." And scrubbing her cauldron was the least of it.

"Idiot." Jamie shook his head. "Do you really think it's the four-year-old who will get in trouble if Moira gets sick on his funnel ride?"

"Point." But it would be worth it. The Sullivan name would carry on in infamy—even if his nephew wasn't technically a Sullivan.

~ ~ ~

Lauren poured maple syrup over her waffle and listened to the two Sullivan brothers, amused. Identical faces, but such different minds.

Well, not entirely different. They shared family loyalty and an easy generosity toward everyone who swam into their pond. But after that... Jamie was the cool gamer, patient trainer, devoted husband. Devin was the guy you'd want at your back in a gunfight.

Nat laughed as Devin reached over to wipe a smudge of whipped cream off her belly, making a much bigger mess in the process. "I don't think you're helping."

He grinned. "I'd be doing better if my niece in there wasn't kicking from the other side."

It was an easy goofiness Lauren was really happy to see. Devin had been fairly skeptical of Nat the first time he'd seen her. Then again, that had been the day she'd been getting married to his brother, and weddings seemed to give Devin mental hives. Still. Anyone who dissed her best friend, even in his head, started off on Lauren's bad side.

"So, Aervyn wants to come cliff jumping with you." Jamie waved a bite of waffle at his brother. "Next time you send pictures, it would be good if you showed the landing-in-water part."

"Come again?" Devin raised an eyebrow.

"You sent pictures of the cliffs, and the nice waterfall, and the leaping into the air like a nut. But you didn't send any that show you landing in the water."

Lauren was as confused as Devin. "What does superboy think you land in?"

"He doesn't much care," said Jamie dryly. "This is the kid who can teleport, remember? Nell, on the other hand, would rather he didn't go jumping off too many dry cliffs, just in case he misses on the porting spell."

"He wouldn't seriously try that, would he?" Devin's mental devil-may-care attitude vanished hard enough that it rocked Lauren's head.

"Relax, bro." Jamie handed over more waffles. "This is the kid who wants to be a superhero. I told him long ago that one of the rules of being a little Sullivan is that he has to ask a grown-up Sullivan before he goes leaping off tall buildings. I just told him the same rules apply to cliffs and pretty waterfalls."

"Smart." Devin snagged the bowl of berries, looking totally relaxed. Lauren wondered if anyone else could see the caped man jumping off buildings running through his mind.

That would be the other really big difference between Jamie and his brother. Devin still thought most of Aervyn's harebrained ideas sounded like fun.

Nat rubbed her belly. "It *was* a really pretty waterfall. Maybe we can come visit one day soon." She grinned at Lauren. "With an aunt in tow to babysit while I go cliff jumping."

Lauren snorted. "Or not." After ten years, it wasn't hard to spot one of Nat's attempts to add a little spice to her life. She wasn't chicken—she just preferred to have both feet firmly planted on the ground. The risks she took were the calculated kind, not the kind that left you splattered all over some hard surface.

Devin grinned. "There's a baby pool you can jump in. That cliff's only fifteen feet or so."

Oh, God. That was a two-story building. "How high is the big one?"

Jamie clamped a hand over his brother's mouth. "A little bigger."

~ ~ ~

Devin sat quietly, wondering how any woman as timid as Lauren managed to channel for his nephew.

Shut up, bro. She's a lot braver than you think. Dev caught the hint of something more serious in his brother's mental voice.

Jamie raised an eyebrow at this wife. "You still sure he's the one you want?"

Nat smiled, with a look in her eyes that had Devin's belly flipping over. His Spidey senses were tingling. Something was up. A glance at Lauren told him two things. Her suspicions were up as well—and she didn't know what was going on either. He'd played a lot of family poker—he never bet against the instincts of a good mind witch. Whatever this was, they were both involved.

A lifetime of practice told him the best strategy when trouble lurked was teammates. He passed Lauren the bowl of whipped cream. "Aim for his eyes. It makes it harder for him to retaliate."

It took a second for her to understand—and then her laugh was pure, appreciative mirth. Which for some unknown reason, did nothing to settle his belly. "You want me to start a food fight with a witch who can teleport?"

Devin took a spoonful of the whipped cream and dropped it onto his waffle with a meaningful glance at his brother. "He can't teleport what he can't see. That's why you have to hit his eyes first." He shrugged. "It works better with the stuff you can squirt from a can, though."

Lauren snickered. "I bet."

"We'll be sure," said Nat dryly, "not to have any whipped cream at the birth."

Devin froze, all food-fight tactical advice evaporating from his brain. Long experience in reading his brother's eyes told him the serious topic for the day had just hit the table. Lauren caught on almost as quickly. Mindreading was a handy talent.

Jamie took Nat's hand. "We'd like to ask the two of you to lead the birthing circle."

Devin tried to get his jangling thoughts in line. "I appreciate the thought, but wouldn't Matt be the better choice? He's a doctor and all."

"Hardly a qualification for leading the circle, Dev. And he might arrive late or leave early if duty calls back in Costa Rica." His brother was serious enough to make him squirm. "Besides, you're really the one we need. Nobody's better under fire."

Devin blanched. With his tiny fire-witchling niece on the way, that could be all too literal. "I guess a water witch makes sense."

Lauren frowned. "What exactly does the birthing circle do?"

Jamie sighed. "Sorry—sometimes I forget you're still new to all this." He paused, collecting his thoughts. "It's a little bit like a full circle. Everyone gathered will be part of the outer circle, and then eleven witches form the inner circle."

"Eleven?" Lauren still looked puzzled, but clearly she caught on fast—normally circles had fourteen.

Nat smiled softly. "The other three are Jamie and me and our baby."

Lauren's face melted into happiness. "You'll be in the circle?"

Devin found himself strangely caught by the obvious depth of their bond. There were very few times a non-witch could be at the center of magic. Giving birth was one of those times. Jamie clearly wasn't the only witch who would treasure the chance to share magic with Nat.

"The birthing circle is often more about ritual and love than anything else," said Jamie, touching his wife's belly. "It's a way for the witching community to welcome the new arrival, and support the brave mamas and terrified dads."

Devin snorted. At the most spectacular witchling birth of memory, it had been Daniel, non-witch and very brave man, who had held the circle together and kept Nell and Aervyn safe. There were few magics more powerful than the love of a father waiting to meet his child.

Lauren tilted her head. "This one isn't just a ritual, is it." It wasn't a question.

Jamie shook his head. "No. The circle also keeps everyone safe. With a babe already playing with power flows, things can get fairly exciting."

Lauren nodded slowly. "I've heard some of the stories of Aervyn's birth."

The stories couldn't possibly touch the memory of the most insane few hours of Devin's life. And he hadn't been leading that particular circle.

Jamie shrugged. "Our baby's been pretty quiet lately." He kissed his wife. "If her mama has any influence, she might make a nice, mellow entrance."

Nat laughed. "If she doesn't, you can't blame it on me."

Jamie's eyes were back to serious. "If she doesn't, we want two of the people we trust most in the world working to keep her safe." He looked at them both. "You'll have a circle behind you, but it's the two of you who will decide how best to handle whatever happens."

Nat reached out for their hands. "It's a big thing we're asking of you. Take some time and think about it, if you want."

Devin looked at Lauren and saw his answer mirrored in her eyes. They were both absolutely terrified. And they'd both do it. They loved far too much to do anything else.

DEBORA GEARY

Chapter 7

Her new life rocked. Magic tricks in the morning and cool computer games after lunch. Sierra clicked a few more keys, compiling the spellcode like Ginia had shown her. Realm was way different than when she'd played six years ago. "Okay, I think I have this storm spell set."

Ginia grinned. "Awesome. Gandalf will never know what hit him."

Apparently some old-fart gamer dude had raided Ginia's spell stash, and she wanted revenge. Sierra was more than happy to help, especially since it would gain her access to level four in Realm. Still three to go to get to the top level where all the real fun happened, but adding unique spells to the library was a fast way to move up. This one was a voice-triggered class-two storm. When Ginia set it off, targeted on her missing spellcubes, anyone standing within ten feet of a stolen spell would end up extremely wet.

Sierra looked up at her partner in crime. "Do you need some way to amplify your voice, too?"

"Sure. That way I don't have to blow game points to do it." Ginia squinted at the spellcode, and then started giggling. "It's gonna rain purple dye? Too awesome. How long will it take to wear off?"

"Dunno. But it should be long enough for you to find the spell thieves. A few hours, at least." Sierra proofread her code one more time. Bad spells cost a lot of game points, and she didn't have a lot to spend yet.

83

An icon started flashing on her screen. "I sent you the controls for one of my minion avatars," Ginia said. "That way, you can be in level seven with me."

Jeepers. Minions blew more game points than she earned in a year. "You don't need me—the spell should be pretty easy to set off."

Ginia grinned. "Are you kidding me? We're going to make it rain purple in Realm. You gotta watch from the inside— Gandalf's gonna totally lose it."

Sierra logged in to the avatar's controls. A whole hour in level seven. It was like Christmas. "Ready."

They landed their avatars on a high perch of rock. Ginia didn't like hanging out in her castles—apparently Gandalf had a bad habit of locking her in towers. While Sierra would have had serious fun in a castle, the view from the rock was definitely cool. They could see pretty much all of Realm.

Ginia unloaded a huge stockpile of spells out of her backpack. This was serious business. Once they identified Gandalf's raiders, they had to deal with them. Sierra wasn't entirely sure what that meant—Ginia didn't have much of an army for a level-seven player. She mostly relied on magic, stealth, and alliances.

Moving carefully, Ginia laid out her spellcubes and then pulled out the spellshape Sierra had coded. Her eyes lit up as she grabbed Sierra's hand. "On three?"

Oh, yeah. Sierra pulled out the amplifying spell, ready to broadcast Ginia's voice all over Realm. It was a standard air-transmission spell with a small twist that should carry sound through walls. They didn't want anyone to miss this.

She could see Ginia count down from three on her fingers. At "go," they both triggered their spells. And stood together on a pointy rock giggling like maniacs as Warrior Girl's voice rang out through Realm. "GANDALF! Spell thief and miserable excuse for a warrior. SHOW YOURSELF! Fight like a witch! You have ten seconds to fly a pink flag from your main castle keep, or I will have no recourse but to TAKE REVENGE. Ten seconds, Gandalf. YOU HAVE BEEN WARNED!"

Sierra was pretty sure ten seconds was just long enough for everyone else in Realm to hear and find a good place to watch the action. She hoped they were under cover. Things were going to get a little wet.

Exactly ten seconds after the ringing pronouncement ended, storm clouds formed all over Realm. Not what they'd expected at all—where was the stolen cache?

Ginia's eyes opened wide, and she started counting. "Holy crap—he's stashed my spells all over the place. No wonder I could never find them all." She squinted. "Where's he hiding them, exactly?"

That was something a level-three spell could solve. Sierra pulled up her spell menu and activated a pair of magical binoculars. She focused on the areas directly under the biggest clouds. Each one hung over a small building with a door, tucked out the back of houses and castles. Some kind of storage shed? She grinned as thunder began to reverberate throughout Realm. Almost time for purple rain.

The rain started—and nothing happened. Well, lots of purple water falling, but no guards, no mad Gandalf—nothing. Crap. Maybe they'd goofed the spell somehow.

Ginia scowled. "What are those dumb little buildings, anyways? Maybe it's an illusion spell and they're really concrete bunkers or something."

Sierra itched for just one decent air power stream. "Too bad we can't do real magic. Just one little tornado, and I bet we could get some of those buildings out of the way."

"Yes!" Ginia danced in place. "Build me one. In real life—I can use Net power to suck it in-game. Can you keep it under class three? The safeguards won't let it in otherwise."

Sierra leaned back in her chair and grabbed enough power for a big, bad, baby tornado. Then she split the power stream into ten parts, attaching one to each of her fingers and thumbs. Carefully, she set them to whirling. Then she realized she had a small problem.

Giggling, she glanced over the top of her screen to where Ginia sat on the other side of the table. "I don't have any fingers left for my trackpad. Can you pull them from here?" She held up her hands.

Ginia's eyes bugged as she looked at the tiny spinning tornadoes. "How many did you make?"

"Ten." Sierra grinned. "And they're gonna get a lot bigger in about thirty seconds."

"What?" Ginia squealed and dove for her keys. "Mama will kill us if we make a huge mess in her kitchen. Hang on, and I'll pull them in."

As soon as a couple of fingers were free, Sierra touched her trackpad and dove back into the action. She grabbed her binoculars again and looked out over Realm. The little buildings were no match for her tornadoes.

And O. M. G. There were mad purple people dancing where each of the buildings had stood, pants around their ankles. Ginia doubled over, gales of laughter rolling out over Realm. "Unbelievable. He hid my spells in outhouses. No warriors guarding them—just poop. Gandalf, you're such a GEEK!" This last yelled out into the wind.

Sierra had a serious case of the giggles. *This* was what happened in the exalted top levels of Realm? "So how do we get your spells back?" She totally drew the line at digging through poop.

A RECKLESS WITCH

Still watching the action below, she winced as one of her tornadoes knocked over the wing of a castle. "Oops. Maybe that one had a little too much juice."

Ginia's giggles died beside her, eyes wide as she looked at the crumbled tower. "Uh, oh. I still have four more I need to put somewhere. I can't leave them in Mama's kitchen."

Sierra tweaked her power streams, mildly disappointed. "It's okay. I turned those ones off."

"You can do that?" Ginia's eyes got even bigger. "What did you do with the backlash?" And then squealed as the Realm tornadoes doubled in size. "Never mind—I see it!"

Sierra reached out to gentle the tornado, and then remembered real-life magic didn't work in-game. She covered her eyes as the biggest one headed straight for the Enchanter's castle—and then uncovered them as Realm went completely silent.

Ginia sat down hard. "Admin override." She sucked in a deep breath, looking at the devastation below. "Man. My sisters are gonna kill me when they have to clean all this up."

An admin message pinged onto both their screens. *You splatter purple poop all over Realm, YOU get to clean it up. Love, Uncle Jamie. P.S. You might want to go pick up your spells—the tornadoes spread them out all over Realm, too.*

Sierra let out one last errant giggle. "I'll help."

Ginia groaned. "You can't. Your minion won't last much longer."

A new message popped up. *Oh, yes it will. Admin override for purposes of poop removal.*

Ginia looked up at Sierra and rolled her eyes. "Know any good cleaning spells?"

Sierra let one last giggle loose. Maybe her new life wasn't so glamorous after all.

87

~ ~ ~

Lauren frowned at Nat's belly. "She threw me out again, little punk." She looked up. "Now what?"

Nat grinned. "Don't look at me. I'm just the vessel."

Too true. Nat's mind was at the other end of the spectrum from the tantruming creature in her belly. "Yeah. Where's Jamie when I really need somewhere to lay blame?"

Nell laughed. "Blame the Sullivan genes. Always a handy scapegoat."

Moira chortled. "That blood runs in your veins, too, my dear."

"True." Nell reached for an apple. "But I take after Mom." She grinned at Nat. "I think your girl takes after Devin."

"Are Devin and Jamie really that different?" Lauren reached out with a gentle mindlink and felt the baby's mental kick. She was one annoyed witchling.

"Heck, yeah." Nell snickered. "Jamie's feet only move faster than his brain about half the time. With Devin, it's a permanent condition. Matt's the least insane of the three, but that's not saying much."

"You guys are so reassuring." Nat wiggled, trying to find a more comfortable position, and shot Sophie, asleep on the couch, an envious gaze. "I nominate each and every one of you as babysitters."

Lauren grinned. They'd be lining up for the chance, feisty witchling baby or not. "Babysitting I can handle—you just get her out here where I can see her. In the meantime, anyone have any bright ideas on teaching her how to barrier? I'm trying to layer over her mind channels like Aervyn does so I can show her what to do, but she keeps tossing me out."

"Independent little witch, is she?" Moira stroked Sophie's hair gently. "I've known one or two like that in my day."

Moira had been training witches longer than Lauren had been alive. "So if I can't tell her, and I can't show her, what does that leave?"

Nat smiled softly and rubbed her belly. "Invitation." She shifted again. "Right now, I'm trying to invite her to move her feet out from under my ribs."

Lauren raised an eyebrow. "And how's that working for you?"

Nat shook her head. "I think she's mad."

Nell snorted. "She's such a Sullivan. Start blaming Jamie now, Nat. It's all going to be his fault." She reached for her glass of root beer, and then pulled out her phone as it began to beep. "Sorry. Jamie's tagging me, and he's got Aervyn with him."

A couple of texts later, she started laughing. "Gotta go. Apparently there's purple poop all over Realm." A moment later, she winked out of the Witches' Lounge.

Lauren looked at Nat and shook her head. Just another normal day at Witch Central.

~ ~ ~

Devin sat down at Moira's kitchen table and sniffed appreciatively. "You didn't have to bake for me."

"I didn't, my dear." She set a cup of strong tea down in front of him. "Elorie's husband Aaron is always sending me over lovely tidbits—I'm just warming them up a bit."

He was eternally grateful. Much as he loved Costa Rica, they'd somehow managed to move there with all the Sullivans who couldn't cook. His parents were terrible in the kitchen, and while Nell and Jamie had both become excellent cooks in self-defense, his and Matt's skills had remained sadly primitive.

Moira finished puttering and sat down across from him. "So, my dear boy—tell me why you've come for a visit."

He grinned. "To see if you'll marry me, of course." It was a standing joke. He'd been three the first time he asked her.

She chuckled and patted his hand. "I do believe the time for me to accept grows short. It won't be long before you'll offer those words to another woman, I'm thinking."

His brain stuttered to a stop. "Have you been reading tea leaves again?"

"Not at all." She stirred her tea, eyes twinkling wickedly. "But when a man gets to a certain age, it's time for him to find the other half of his soul. Yours is finally getting ready for that matching, I think."

Not if he could help it. And he didn't believe for one moment she hadn't been digging into his future. Then again, she'd always known precisely how to make him squirm.

Which was exactly why he'd come to visit. When you needed advice, there was no one wiser or less likely to tell you pretty nonsense. "All I'm trying to get ready for at the moment is the birth of my new niece."

Moira leaned back, studying his face. "Aye. And it's a very interesting choice they've made, asking you and Lauren to lead the circle."

He knew she loved him dearly—and that she'd tell him the truth. "Did they make a mistake?"

One more long look, and then the smile that had prompted offers of matrimony over thirty years ago. "No, my boy. And the fact that you can ask that question only makes me more sure." She got up to check on whatever gift to his stomach was currently warming in the oven. "You have a wonderful partner to work with."

"She's an awfully new witch."

"That she is." Moira pulled out muffins and blew a gentle cooling spell before dropping one on a plate for him. "But she's as steady as they come, and she loves Natalia like a sister."

He nodded. Pretty much what he'd already seen with his own eyes. "Neither of us knows anything about birthing."

Her giggles sounded like those of his triplet nieces. "You weren't picked to help deliver the placenta, my love."

Good thing, since he wasn't precisely sure what that was. "I'm there to handle fire. In case our little girl comes out guns blazing."

"No." She shook her head, eyes back to serious. "You'll do that and do it well, if need be. You were chosen because that baby has Sullivan genes. And while Jamie got the fire magic, you carry the full weight of the blood that runs through your veins."

He grinned. "I'm reckless, am I?"

"That's a fine word for it." She handed him another muffin. "And a bit slower to grow up than some, but you're making us very proud along the way."

She'd always been genius at handing out a compliment and life advice in the same sentence. "So how do I keep a possibly reckless babe safe on her journey to be with us?"

"You already know the answer to that, sweet boy. Trust that huge heart of yours." Moira leaned forward and patted his cheek. "Invite her into love. It has been, and always will be, love that keeps a reckless soul safe."

~ ~ ~

Sierra lay down on her bed and fingered the ugly orange frog hanging on the chain around her neck. She'd always been able to fall asleep anywhere—on a train, in a strange room, or just curled up on Momma's shoulder. And in foster care, she'd willed herself to sleep simply to make the days go by faster.

But here, with all these cool people, sleep only came after she'd wiggled around for an hour or two.

Weird. Maybe it was all the cookies they'd eaten during the Great Poop Cleanup.

She rolled over one more time—and was positive she heard giggling. Then her door squeaked open, followed by some loud bumps and more giggling.

Must be the triplets this time. Aervyn had snuck in several nights, but he just ported.

Sierra grinned and prepared a slime spell, layering it over her duvet cover. When the invaders hopped onto her bed, the squealing was loud enough to wake the dead. She giggled. "Shh. We're supposed to be sleeping, remember?" She lit a small firelight.

"Ugh!" said Mia, in a loud whisper. "What *is* that stuff?"

"Witch goo. It keeps me warm while I sleep."

"You sleep in slime?" Shay was trying to wiggle away from the goo, without much success. "That's disgusting."

"You two are such dorks." Ginia held up a handful of slime closer to Sierra's light. "Hey, can you show me how to make this stuff? I think it would be good for some of my healing salves."

Mia snickered. "I want some for the next time Aervyn tries to borrow my iPod without asking."

Sierra giggled and disappeared the slime. "It's really fun to slide on. Momma used to take me hiking to find secret waterfalls and stuff, and then she'd make a goo slide on one of the rocks so we could slide into the water." It had always made her feel like a big otter, shimmying around on her belly.

Shay snuggled closer. "You must miss her a lot."

"Yeah." Sierra touched her fingers to the frog.

"Is it true that she just disappeared?" Ginia cuddled into her other side. "We hear stuff."

Pulling her knees up to her chest, Sierra tried to figure out how to tell a story she still didn't truly understand. Maybe the short version was best. "We were in New Orleans for Mardi Gras. That's like a big party they have down there. She left me at the hotel one night and didn't come back."

"You were all by yourself?" Mia's eyes were as big as plates.

Sierra knew lots of people thought Momma had made a bad mistake leaving her alone. She tried to explain. "I was twelve and everything, so it was no big deal."

Mia shook her head. "Our brother Nathan's twelve, and Mama would never leave him alone in a big city."

Shay elbowed her sister, and they all got very quiet.

Sierra tried not to feel the squeeze of pain. Why did everyone think it was Momma's fault? "Nothing bad happened to *me*. It happened to Momma."

"Did they look for her?"

"Yeah. But not very hard." The police had been sure Momma had just walked away and left Sierra sitting in New Orleans all alone.

Ginia reached out a hand in comfort. "Maybe we can find her. We know lots of people who could help look."

Sierra shook her head. For reasons she had never understood, she was very sure Momma was gone. "She's dead."

Ginia's eyes were no longer nine years old. "Then maybe we can find out what happened. So at least you'd know."

Sierra smiled sadly. They were sweet—but they were just kids. "Will you guys sleep with me tonight?" The nightmares didn't come when she had company in her bed.

Mia rolled her eyes. "Duh."

Chapter 8

"Two meetings in as many days." Moira hugged Govin, noting the worry creases on his forehead. "It must be serious for you to leave your data for this long." She looked at the rest of the group assembled in the Realm Witches' Lounge. His wasn't the only concerned face. It took something serious to call witches to a meeting before breakfast.

Govin squeezed her hand one more time and invited her to sit. "We have a lot of new information about Sierra, and I thought it might be good to talk as a group."

The witching community worked best when they brought all their talents together. Moira nodded in approval. "So what have we learned about our young weather witch?"

Sophie grinned. "She's made everyone who built an outhouse in Realm regret that decision."

Ah, yes—the Great Poop Caper. "The poor girl probably has no idea how long that particular bit of mischief will be remembered." Witches had long memories, especially for particularly funny pranks.

Jamie snorted. "Since people are still talking about stunts Devin, Matt, and I pulled when we were three, she's probably labeled for life."

They *had* been rather memorable young boys. She leaned over and patted Jamie's hand. "It's the one where you turned yourselves into ballerinas that will always be my favorite."

Jamie groaned and looked at Govin for moral support. "See what I mean?"

Moira chuckled. In seven decades, she'd seen plenty of rambunctious witchlings turn into responsible citizens. Sierra followed in a proud tradition. "It seems to me that with all our girl has been through in her young life, a little bit of play is a good thing."

Nell looked thoughtful. "I agree with you—but I think part of our problem is that she thinks of all magic as playing."

"Funnels aren't just toys." Govin leaned forward, very earnest. "With the kind of power she has, she needs to take her magic a lot more seriously. I'm not saying fun is out of the question, but the kind of play she does right now could easily cause catastrophic weather effects. With her power, she needs to be extra careful—and she doesn't even begin to understand why."

Moira watched as a blanket of seriousness settled over the room. And she knew what her role was on this day. Weather modeling was far beyond her—but a witch in need of training, she knew how to handle. "We need a plan, then."

Govin nodded, clearly relieved. "She needs training in using magic safely. That Realm stunt was funny, but only because it was in cyberspace."

"Training, yes." Moira shared his urgency on that, but it wasn't all that mattered. "But we must also take care of the witch, and not just her magic. Sierra's a young girl. She's not a rogue witch—she's one who doesn't know any better." She held up her hand as Govin started to speak. "It won't be rules and magical protocols that keep Sierra's magic in check. It will be love and commitment. She's one of us now, and we need to help her feel it."

She smiled at Nell. "Our Aervyn controls his magic because we ask him to. Sierra doesn't have many reasons to trust us yet. We need to give her some."

"On that already." Nell looked very pleased with herself. "I've got my girls ready to help her pick paint colors for her new apartment. We can decorate in a day or two. Normally I wouldn't suggest a gender split, but she needs sisters and aunts right now—she's really missing Amelia."

"Of course she is." Moira nodded sagely. "And there's no shame in women's work done for the right reasons." She smiled at Jamie. "Which leaves men and small boys as her training team."

He rolled his eyes. "I can paint."

Nell grinned. "Pretty sure it's going to be girly."

Jamie held up his hands in surrender. "Fine. I'll help train." He looked at Govin. "Aervyn will be useful too, I think—she likes him. I'm going to suggest Devin as well, at least for as long as he's here."

Govin frowned. "He's not exactly a role model for magical caution."

Jamie shrugged "No, he's not—but I think he's the one most likely to understand Sierra."

Silence hung for a moment. Moira waited patiently and trusted Govin's analytical mind to follow the data.

"You're saying I'm the wrong mentor." He sighed. "You're probably right. What I see as reckless, Devin will see in an entirely different light."

"Aye." Moira leaned forward, proud of her boys. "Which is why you are a good pair to work with her." Magic was always about a complicated balance of personality and power. Govin would speak to Sierra's magic, Devin to her heart. And whatever Nell might think, the girl needed honorary big brothers and uncles, too.

Nell grinned. "Can I sell tickets? Those are going to be some rather interesting training sessions."

That they were.

~ ~ ~

Nell set down a second helping of waffles covered in a mountain of bananas and whipped cream. She figured eighteen-year-old girls weren't all that different from their younger counterparts. "Here you go. After three hours of cleaning poop yesterday, you've earned it."

Sierra grinned. "It would have taken a lot longer without all those people showing up to help." She licked a bit of stray whipped cream off her finger and spoke more quietly. "That was really nice of them."

"Ha. They all wanted to see the biggest mess ever created in Realm. You two made yourselves famous." And it would probably take three days for Aervyn to stop giggling. Poop pranks were particularly funny if you were male and four.

"Purple dye is kind of hard to spell out of stuff." Sierra winced. "And I didn't mean for the tornadoes to get so big. In real life, I can adjust the power as they form, but with a pre-made spell, I couldn't do that."

Which was one of the things Nell wanted to talk about. "Yeah, one of the things we're learning about putting together spells for the WitchNet library is that you have to build in a bigger margin of error. The witches who pull the spells out often don't have the necessary magic to adjust them either."

"I wonder… maybe you could build a control mechanism into the spell." Sierra downed her milk in three gulps. "Kind of a step-switch, where you could step the funnel speed up or down a few notches. Give voice command to whoever activated the spell."

That was freaking brilliant—and not at all what Nell had expected. It was a decidedly non-reckless idea. "That's a great thought to explore with Govin. I don't think we're likely to be putting too many funnel spells into the library, though. We don't really want a non-weather witch with that kind of power in her hands."

"Even just to play? I could make a really baby funnel for kids to ride on."

Nell sighed. It was like dealing with Aervyn in his more exuberant moods. "How much damage could a baby funnel do if someone activated it in their living room, or near a toolbox full of nails?"

It was obvious neither of those possibilities had ever occurred to Sierra. "I'm so dumb—I never thought of that."

"Hey." Nell reached out, her mama instincts wanting to comfort. "We're all new to this idea of making spells for other people to use. Like you saw in Realm, it can be a lot of fun, but it can also have some unplanned consequences. We want you to work with Govin to help make weather spells that are really helpful, but also as safe as possible."

Sierra looked down at her hands. "I'm not sure Govin likes me much."

Nell debated for a moment, then chose the hard road. "He's spent his entire life trying to keep people safe from some of the planet's harsher weather patterns. He sees your talent as a risk."

She reached out for Sierra's hand as the girl's face fell. "You need to show him that you can be a help, and that you can work safely."

Sierra twiddled with a cookie. "How do I do that?"

"Tell him about your spell-control-mechanisms idea." No way Govin could resist that one. She hoped.

"I want to help." Sierra blushed. "But maybe funnel riding wasn't such a good idea on my first day."

Nell disagreed—she'd have paid big money to see Govin whirling around upside-down. "I think you can learn from each other. Govin needs to remember to relax and play a little, and you're good at that."

"Okay." Sierra's solemn nod reminded her very much of her youngest son. Very willing—and still not really understanding.

Ah, well. If three hours of cleaning up poop hadn't made an impression, a few words over cookies weren't going to alter lives either. It was a beginning, at least. Hopefully the other item on Nell's agenda would be easier.

She grabbed her bag off the counter. "Got some stuff for you." Opening an envelope, she started pulling items out. "A debit card, attached to the bank account where your paychecks will be automatically deposited. We advanced you a month's salary, so you should have plenty in there to take care of whatever you need. A transit pass—standard employee benefit." At least it was as of today.

Nell dug into the envelope one last time. "Keys and a map to your new apartment. It's about six blocks from here and a short walk from the water, so Lauren hopes you like it. You can start fixing it up next Saturday. We figured you'd want a few days to paint and things before you moved in."

Sierra nodded dumbly, looking delighted—and hopelessly lost.

Nell had some ideas about that. Right on cue, three curly heads invaded the kitchen. "And this is your painting crew. All you need to do is pick a color." She leaned over and whispered. "Don't let them talk you into pink."

"Mama!" three voices protested in unison. Ginia grinned. "Sierra can pick whatever color she wants. So long as it's not boring." She upended an entire backpack of paint chips on the table. "We hope you like one of these. We picked all our favorites."

"I've never picked my own paint." Sierra's sniffly giggles arrowed right into Nell's heart.

Mia sat down, reaching for a couple of paint chips. "Here's two I like. Bikini Pink and Pearly Purple."

Nell hid her amusement as fierce debate broke out. She had twenty bucks riding on Bikini Pink in the betting pool.

~ ~ ~

Lauren looked over at Sierra, breathing in the salt-misted morning air as they walked down the beach. She could feel the girl's mind streaming relaxed gratitude as they walked. It was the same way Nat's mind felt after yoga.

Nat smiled and copied Sierra's breathing. "It smells good. I always wonder where the air's come from, and where it will head to next."

Sierra stopped and looked out at the water, tilting her head. "It's blowing from the northwest, so..." She grinned. "I think it's only the whales that have seen this air since it left Siberia."

Lauren laughed and pulled down on the edges of her hat. "Well, that would explain the temperature."

"Want me to warm it up a little?" Sierra wiggled her fingers. "It's warmer right above this fog, so it wouldn't take much. Just a little fire magic."

Nat shook her head. "No, thanks. My belly bean here is finally sleeping, and fire magic wakes her up." She grinned. "Lauren's from Chicago—she can take it."

Lauren was feeling like she had weak California blood now, but she was hardly going to insist on waking up the baby. She reached into her pocket to double-check that her phone was on. Good realtors knew emergencies happened when you weren't prepared. If Nat went into labor on the beach, she wanted a teleporting witch available, stat.

Sierra was staring at Nat's belly, fascinated. "How does it feel?"

Nat walked a little closer to the waves, daring the water to grab her toes. "Lately, like I'm really a bowling ball with toothpicks for my arms and legs."

Sierra giggled. "Momma used to tell me she was seriously happy the whales came to swim with her when she was really pregnant, because they made her feel sort of graceful again."

Lauren looked out at the ocean and tried to imagine a morning dip. Brr. "Did she do that often? Go swimming in the ocean?"

"Sure." Sierra nodded absently, looking out toward the horizon. "We went out all the time. I haven't gone out here yet, but when I swam in Oregon I had to be careful—it scared people if they saw me out there."

She went swimming in the Pacific Ocean by herself? Lauren exchanged glances with Nat. No way that sounded like a good idea, but you didn't just tell an eighteen-year-old what not to do.

Nat touched Sierra's hand. "Maybe we can find somebody here who would like to swim with you."

The girl shrugged, unconcerned. "It's no big deal. I just swim far enough out so people can't see me, and it's fine." She frowned. "It's going to be harder here, though. More people on the beaches. In Oregon, the coast is pretty quiet in the winter."

Lauren shook her head, sure her ears hadn't heard that right. "You go swimming in the winter?"

"Uh, huh." Sierra was still staring out at the horizon. "I use fire magic to stay warm."

This was rapidly exceeding Lauren's areas of expertise as a fairly new witch. Maybe ocean swims in the middle of winter were normal for someone with water talents. She'd freak out quietly for now.

Sierra started bouncing on her toes. "They're coming. The dolphins—do you see them?"

Nat laughed as a graceful arc broke the horizon. "Did you call them?"

"Nuh, uh." Sierra shook her head. "You did. They love babies who are just about to be born."

Lauren grinned, hearing the teasing edge to Sierra's mental voice. She made a face at her best friend. "Maybe it's just because you look like a beach ball."

She danced a few steps backward as Nat threatened to dump cold water down the back of her jacket. It was probably an idle threat. For now.

~ ~ ~

Govin tapped his keyboard aimlessly and sighed. He was getting nowhere on the new WitchNet weather spell organizing. Partly because the spells were a total hodge-podge, and partly because his brain was still out at Ocean's Reach.

Sierra was an amazing witch—and she scared him silly. He had no idea what to do about it.

TJ wheeled back from his desk. "Wanna talk about it?" He grabbed a bag of chips in anticipation. TJ never talked without food present, preferably the kind that came out of crinkly bags. It was the kind of annoying habit only tolerable in an old friend.

Govin headed to the fridge for some grapes and cheese. Occasionally TJ could be convinced to expand his snack to more than one food group. "It's probably no big deal."

His buddy snorted. "You've been stewing since you got back from lessons yesterday morning. What's up? The girl not any good?"

Crap. TJ had been listening. Usually he managed to ignore stuff muttered in the general direction of the office wall. "Our new intern? She's very talented. Best weather witch I've seen in a very long time."

TJ sat up straighter, then turned back to his desk. "Strong enough to affect the planetaries?"

"Yeah." Govin grabbed a chip. "And no, we didn't play quite that big yesterday. You won't see any alerts." But they'd come close. Very, very close, and Sierra had clearly not been using anywhere close to peak power. The list of witches strong enough to mess with planetary weather was very short. It was killing him to think the list had been short a name. How had they missed her?

"She got decent control?"

"Yeah. Very decent. She can make a storm funnel sit and wag its tail."

TJ blinked. "And this is bad, because...? We could use more help around here."

"She's dangerous, Teej." And explaining why to a non-witch would be a challenge. "Her mother trained her, and she skipped over most of the stuff we do to keep big spells safe. The girl's been playing with huge power, the kind with no room for error. She's lucky she's still alive."

TJ's chip-loaded hand paused in mid-air. "Probably some other people aren't so lucky."

Govin felt his nameless unease morph into dread. That was it, exactly. Trust TJ to nail the problem in one. Sierra was still alive. But when weather witches messed with big magic, it was far too easy for someone else to die. "Exactly. And she probably hasn't always had this kind of control."

He could see TJ's massive brain cranking. "Do you know where she lived?"

When you had to ask the awful questions, it was really good to have a friend walking beside you. "Traveled all over with her mom until six years ago. I don't know all of where, but I know she was in Fiji summer of '02, Indonesia the following March, and New Orleans when her mother vanished." That much he'd picked up from her casual conversation with Aervyn.

TJ turned back to his computer. "Lemme look at our anomalies file." That was where they tracked unexplained weather disturbances, which were unfortunately legion. "Yeah. I got stuff in Fiji, and stuff off the south coast of Indonesia in spring '03." He looked up. "The Fiji one is where we had to make it rain for three weeks straight to dampen the tsunami reverbs." You had to send weather energy somewhere—and rain was better than killing waves.

Govin shoved his fingers through his hair. He was too well-trained a mathematician to jump to easy conclusions. "Think it was her?"

TJ shrugged. "Dunno. Maybe her and her mom working together? As anomalies go, they were pretty small. I could try to cross-ref, but I'm guessing the kid probably doesn't remember what kind of magic tricks she was doing eight or ten years ago."

A decade ago, no. Govin stared at the anomalies file. Oh, shit. He grabbed his cell. "Hey, Nell. Do you know where Sierra's lived for the last six years?" He waited a minute while Nell shuffled some papers around, then wrote down her answer.

Then he hung up and looked at TJ. "New Orleans six years ago. Stayed in Louisiana for a few months, lived inland for a while." Inland didn't matter—you needed an ocean to mess with planetary weather patterns. "She's been on the Oregon Coast for the last two years. Near Florence."

TJ blinked. "She's our Oregon anomaly?" He ran a quick search in his file. "Yeah. First reading's from twenty-three months ago, and a lot higher frequency in the last six." He looked up. "She's getting stronger."

"Yeah." Most weather-witch talents peaked in adulthood. And Sierra was already a major force to be reckoned with. The good news was, she probably hadn't been able to wreak worldwide weather havoc for very long. The bad news was so many kinds of bad, it hurt his brain just to think about it.

"It really is a rogue witch. Damn. I was sure we had aliens." TJ grabbed another monster-sized handful of chips. "She's gotta get things under control before she messes with something serious." He frowned back down at his data. "Assuming she hasn't done that already. How the hell does she pull warm currents all the way from Hawaii?"

Govin shook his head. All he knew at this point was that two bachelor geeks weren't going to fix the problem by themselves. Time for another meeting. Sierra was the kind of seriously dangerous they needed to deal with right now. Painting parties and making her feel loved could damn well wait.

He reached for his phone to call Nell again. And froze as klaxon bells started ringing on TJ's desktop. That meant the trouble was high alert—and local.

"We've got twenty-foot waves headed at the Channel Islands. From the north. Point of origin is here." TJ was already pushing maps to their screen bank. "Arrival time, less than an hour. They'll swamp the beaches."

Govin grabbed his phone. "I'll alert the Coast Guard to move the tourists to high ground." Fortunately, the Channel Islands, just off the southern California coast, had plenty of high ground. The people, they could probably get out of the way. The birds and wildlife—at this time of year, there wouldn't be too many nests full of babies, but still.

TJ grabbed his arm. "I'll do the alerts. You go find our witch."

"You think she's causing this?" Govin was already headed for the door.

"Dunno." TJ was hammering on the keys with one hand, his cell phone with the other. "But she sure as hell can help you fix it."

Govin stopped halfway out the door. Water witches. The beach. He wasn't thinking straight.

He slammed back in his chair and messaged Jamie, very grateful when his friend's face popped up on his screen. "What's up?"

"I need all the water witches you can scramble, on the beach as fast as you can. Do you happen to know where Sierra is?"

Jamie turned white. "Walking on the beach with Nat and Lauren. Are they in trouble?"

Govin turned to TJ for confirmation. "No, but I think they might be connected to big trouble heading elsewhere. Can you port me to wherever they are?"

Jamie nodded. "I'll suck you through Realm. It'll be easier, and I can push you out at Lauren's location—she's got her phone on. Part of the new WitchNet protocols." He looked down at his own phone. "Dev's got Aervyn with him, and superboy will port them both to the beach." He glanced back up. "We've got you a team coming. Get moving."

"I'll be on my way in the chopper in case you need to get closer." TJ grabbed his bag and tablet and ran for the door.

Govin grabbed the Realm transport spell blinking on his screen and activated.

DEBORA GEARY

Chapter 9

Sierra froze as power rippled and four witches popped into existence on the beach beside her. Four very serious dudes. Holy cow, what was this, the witch SWAT team?

Jamie grabbed his wife. "Are you okay?"

Govin grabbed Sierra. "What are you doing? What magic?"

Jeepers. "Just a little spell to play with the dolphins." She pointed out at the water. "They're swimming along with us, so I'm just saying hello. I used a groundline."

He shook her shoulders, hard. "Saying hello *how?*"

Govin. Lauren's mindvoice drilled into all their heads. *You'll get answers faster if you explain the emergency.*

"Sorry." Govin let go of Sierra's shoulders. "Sorry. I didn't mean to scare you. But we have twenty-foot waves heading toward the Channel Islands south of here, and your magic might be causing them."

Waves? "I'm not making any waves. Just swirling a little warm water for the dolphins to play in." The ocean waters were chilly this time of year, and the babies liked the warm currents.

He frowned. "How are you heating the water?"

That was the hard way. "I'm not. I just pull it from Hawaii."

He paled. "That's your idea of a little spell? Sierra, we have local currents here that you could totally mess up. Crunch a couple of swirls together the wrong way and you get big waves."

Okay, she could see that. But why all the panic? "So I'll just fix the waves." She reached for power, seeking the fluctuations that would help her locate the problem.

Govin grabbed her hands. "They're too far away to reach from here. And you can't just flatten them. The ocean is like an air mattress—if you flatten a wave one place, another one will pop up somewhere else. There are way too many people on the beaches in Southern California, even in the winter. We need to be incredibly careful about how we do this."

Sierra shook her head, frustrated. She and Momma had played a game where they'd squished waves just to make a bigger one pop up somewhere else. She knew how to be careful. "It's not a problem—I'll just head the big waves out to sea." They could go play with the whales in the middle of the ocean. Whales liked big swells.

Govin got very, very still. "That's how you make a killer tsunami, Sierra."

His voice was barely a whisper, but it cracked against her heart. She could feel her own panic rising, not even sure why. "What are you saying?"

"If we don't handle this exactly right, people will die. And you might be the only one with strong enough magic to fix it." He held up a hand as several voices clamored in protest. "She needs to know. With the power she has, she needs to know."

Devin touched his arm. "Your ride's here." They could see a helicopter approaching in the distance.

Govin shook his head. "We can't get there fast enough. Besides, the chopper can only carry four. The more witches the better, right now."

Jamie started herding them toward the landing chopper. "We'll all go. You have three air witches at your disposal. And Aervyn and Sierra don't weigh much. We'll get there fast enough. It will be easier for Sierra if she can see the waves."

Sierra tried to find air to breathe as the weight of all their expectations crashed onto her shoulders.

Devin took Sierra's hand. "And me. Two water witches are better than one." He squeezed her fingers and spoke quietly. "Any girl who can spin a funnel with one finger can handle this. Let's go." The band around her lungs eased a little.

Two minutes later, she was strapped in the back of the helicopter and headed out to sea. She looked out the window, watching the dolphin babies still playing even though the warm waters had gone away.

And then Aervyn and Jamie turned on the magical afterburners.

"Holy hell!" TJ whooped, hanging onto the rudder for dear life. "How long can you keep this up?"

Jamie held up a bag of cookies and grinned. "At least a couple of hours."

Govin's face was grim. "We won't need that long. This will all be over in an hour, whatever happens."

Sierra just held on and tried not to puke.

~ ~ ~

Devin loved speed. He was exactly the guy you wanted in an emergency—grace under pressure and all that. Under normal circumstances, a super-powered helicopter ride to the rescue was the stuff his dreams were made of. He just couldn't find any joy in this one, however. Sierra's white face had been a foot away from his for the last twenty minutes.

He elbowed Govin. "How much farther?"

Govin switched to a private channel on his headphones. "Dunno. You're the water witch—you'll probably feel it before the rest of us can see it." He eyed Sierra. "Can she do this?"

Devin had no idea. "We're about to find out."

He could see the disapproval hanging in Govin's eyes. For some reason, it made him feel inordinately big-brother protective. "She's a kid, Gov. And you scared her crapless back there."

"There could be people on those beaches."

He was well aware of that. As was every adult in the chopper. But it wasn't going to make Sierra's magic work any better to keep leaning on how bad this could be. "Magic is play for her. If you're just going to paralyze her with fear, you might as well have left her on the beach with Nat and Lauren."

He saw understanding hit Govin's eyes. "Got it. I'll try to ratchet it down a little."

Devin grinned, trying his own brand of doing just that. "Try math formulas or something."

Govin just rolled his eyes, but his stress levels eased off a little. Good. Mission accomplished.

Instead of looking out the window one more time, Devin cast out with a light finger of water power and thought he caught the edge of something. He nudged Sierra. "Can you feel it?"

She frowned, and then he felt her power surging. Man, she was a powerful witch. A moment later, she nodded. "Yeah. Three big waves, and probably a couple more forming in the backwash."

Govin leaned forward. "How close to the islands?"

Sierra closed her eyes again—and then turned whiter. "Really close. Maybe... three minutes."

She's close to panic, Dev. Jamie's voice rang in his brain.

Devin grabbed Sierra's hands and pulled her eyes to his by sheer force of will. "Forget the islands. Just the water, Sierra. Go there with me. We need to figure out how to mellow out those waves a little. You lead—I'll provide the assist."

Use Aervyn too—I can handle the chopper for now. Jamie sounded low on gas, but someone else was going to have to deal with that.

He felt his nephew's power stream sliding alongside and nudged Sierra. She took a huge breath and started to work.

Devin watched her spellcasting for a moment, weaving a complicated dance he could hardly follow. Then Aervyn's mental picture blasted into his brain. Apparently the four-year-old understood Sierra's plan just fine. Devin stood where he was told and pulled every ounce of power he could find.

He watched in straining awe as Sierra handled it all and asked Aervyn for more. Shit. Even wonderboy wasn't limitless.

He's okay for now, Jamie sent. *But she's really pushing it. Do enough grounding for all three of you.*

Devin backed off a fraction and planted both magical feet as firmly in the speeding landmass to their left as he could, feeling the desperate pull and swirl of an ocean of water power in mid-spell. And then braced as he realized what was about to happen.

Power smacked into him, a tsunami of energy pouring through him and out the groundlines. He felt Govin and Jamie jump to handle the overflow. Holy shit. Channels screaming, he took as much of the weight off Sierra as he could, well aware she held the business end of the fire hose.

Hang on tight, said Jamie grimly. *That was just the first one.*

There was no time for fear.

Twice more, they all got drilled by a wave of power bigger than anything Devin had ever handled. Twice more, they frantically cleaned up the overflow. He hung on by his fingertips.

And then everything went magically silent.

Devin opened his eyes—just in time to see Sierra's face blaze with victory. And then her head fell to the side as channel shock knocked her unconscious.

He grabbed for her—and nearly crunched heads with his brother. His very pale brother. Crap. Every witch on the chopper was in pretty bad shape. "TJ! Can you put this thing down?"

"Yeah," TJ yelled. "We'll set down in the islands. Be there in ninety seconds." He looked down at his tablet. "Lauren said she's sending reinforcements."

Thank God. They needed the cavalry right about now.

~ ~ ~

Lauren tried not to stumble as she landed on a waterlogged beach. This popping into her phone and out somewhere else was still a very strange experience. She wasn't sure a mind witch could help a lot with magical exhaustion, but Nat had been very worried about Jamie, and no way were they sending a nine-months-pregnant woman to an evacuation zone.

She covered her ears as the chopper landed. *Yeeks*, it was loud. Then she grinned gratefully as Nell and Sophie popped into existence beside her. Apparently it was okay to send pregnant *healers* to an evacuation zone. Nell's eyes were glued on the helicopter. Lauren reached out. "I can feel his mind. He's okay. They're all in one piece."

Nell's mind beamed white-hot gratitude.

"Ginia's coming in a moment with supplies." Sophie's eyes were on the people exiting the chopper, her mind all business. "And we've got a bigger team on standby if need be."

Lauren quickly texted Nat as she saw Jamie step down and reach up for Aervyn, and then followed Sophie over. She was grateful when TJ cut power before her head blew off. And then stunned by the wave of exhaustion that rolled off the helicopter's occupants. She hadn't caught a fraction of it while they were landing.

Holy God. She'd done full circles with Aervyn spellcasting that hadn't left anyone nearly this exhausted. Even wonderboy's mind felt oddly faint. She stepped to Sophie's shoulder as Nell scooped up her son. "How can I help?"

Sophie, leaning over Devin, shrugged a shoulder toward Jamie. "Mindlink with him and find out what happened. I can do the first round of channel clearing without that, but it will help make sure we catch everything." She glanced over at Nell. "Aervyn's okay—he looks worse, but his channel shock is minor compared to the others. He just needs milk and cookies."

"They protected him." Nell cast one last concerned look at the others and then walked a little away, carrying a disturbingly limp boy in her arms.

"Cookies will fix him." Ginia, just arrived, touched Lauren's arm. "Honest."

Lauren shook her head. Only witches prescribed cookies for healing. Then again, Nell's Nutella cookies weren't your average baked good. She took Jamie's hand and reached out with a gentle mindlink. His exhaustion nearly swamped her.

Cookie. Begging.

Ginia leaned over with a cookie and some sort of nasty green concoction. "Energy drink first, then you can have a cookie."

Jamie scowled. *That's no energy drink. That's one of Moira's brews.*

She shook her head, giggling. "Nope. It's one of mine."

He sipped suspiciously and made a face. *Tastes worse.*

Ginia's glare was worthy of a much older healer. Jamie manned up and tipped back his glass. *Totally revolting, niece of mine. Make sure Dev and Govin get a glass too.*

She turned away, woman-to-be on a mission, as he crunched into his first cookie.

Lauren didn't know if it was the teasing or the green goo, but the seeping exhausting in his mind was waning. "Can you tell me what happened? Sophie needs to know. I've never seen you or Aervyn hit this hard."

Jamie glanced over to where Sophie still bent over Devin, who held Sierra in his lap, just now starting to stir. "The two of them got hit the worst. Tell her it's not just overexertion—it's probably some backlash, too. Sierra sucked the energy out of the waves back through the five of us."

Lauren frowned. His voice was fairly nonchalant, but his mind was anything but. "It was risky."

He nodded, eyes very serious. "Yeah. She took the brunt of it into herself. Govin and I managed to shield Aervyn a bit, but..." He sighed. "And Dev took more than he should have, trying to spare her. He's going to have a hell of a headache, even with Sophie's talents."

Lauren could feel his anger swirling under the surface, but she wasn't sure of the target. "Is it her you're mad at?"

He blinked. "No. She's just a kid. She did the best she could, and it was big magic—I don't know anyone who could have done more. Not sure we should have done it, but..." *We used a dangerous witch. Stopped a disaster, but still.*

He winced as Aervyn's giggles drifted over the sand, and Lauren finally understood the last piece. *He's fine, Jamie.*

His eyes were bleak. *Yeah. But it's the closest he's ever come to not being fine. We didn't do enough to protect him today.* He looked over at Sierra. *Her either.*

Devin crawled over and snagged the half-cookie in Jamie's hands. "Is my brother trying to take all the blame for this?"

"Pretty much." Fascinating, Lauren thought. His tone was teasing, but his mind was pure steel. Jamie's skulk of self-recrimination was about to walk into a brick wall.

"You took care of Aervyn, bro." Devin's face was more serious now. "Just like you promised Nell you would the day he was born. Kid's in better shape than anyone else."

"I left you hanging."

"Yeah." Devin's eyes drilled into his brother. "And if you ever have that choice again, you do exactly the same thing, or I'll be the first witch lining up to give you hell."

Their exchange was hammering two things into Lauren's mind. One, Devin loved Aervyn with the same fierceness Jamie did. And two—whatever Sierra had done out there, it had scared the crap out of both Sullivan brothers.

Neither of them scared easily. Hell, as far as she'd ever seen, neither of them scared at all.

Then Aervyn's anguished cry pelted all their minds, and she knew what true fear really felt like. Every witch on the beach raced to his location—and found him tucked in a small, wet crevice, holding a very still baby bird in the palm of his hand.

"I'm sorry, sweetie." Nell, face dry, but mind full of tears, tried to cuddle him. "I'm so sorry."

He just rocked, keening into the wind, the inarticulate sadness of a small boy with a broken heart.

Lauren felt hers bleeding too—and then realized her pain was a faint shadow of the girl's next to her.

Sierra reached out a finger and ever so gently touched the bedraggled down of the dead bird. "We didn't know it was here." She looked up, cheeks streaking with tears, and her face just crumpled. "Maybe I could have saved it. Maybe if I'd just tried a little harder. I thought a little wave would be okay."

Aervyn cuddled the bird to his chest and lashed out. "You made the waves, Sierra. You killed my bird." He breathed big, gulping sobs. "You killed my bird."

"I know." Her voice was an anguished whisper.

Lauren turned as Sierra fled—but it was Devin who reached her first.

And held her as her heart cracked in two.

~ ~ ~

Nell touched her small boy's head as he slept, feeling her heart squeeze one more time.

"Come," said Sophie, her voice gentle. "The sleep spell will keep him under for a couple of hours. Come have something to eat—I think Caro brought over lasagna."

Bless the Witch Central pipeline. They'd have a steady supply of food arriving for as long as they needed it. Nell stepped into the hallway and laid a hand on Sophie's arm. "Thank you for coming. This was pretty big for Ginia to handle all on her own, especially with her baby brother involved."

Sophie smiled. "Do you have any idea how wonderful it is to be *able* to come? To not have to watch from afar and pray? So thank those girls of yours who have been busy building the Realm shuttle service." She turned to head down the stairs. "And if the day comes when I can't get here? That girl of yours will deal. She's amazing—just like her mama."

Nell managed to find a grin. A good healer always took care of the collateral damage as well, and Sophie was one of the best. "I'll be okay. Aervyn had both uncles there to keep him safe, and it's only channel shock."

"I could say something comforting, but honestly?" Sophie touched her belly. "I don't know how you do it. Really. I find myself hoping sometimes that Seedling just has a touch of plant magic or something. Nothing big."

With two major earth-witch healers for parents? Not likely. Nell chuckled. "I could say something comforting, but—"

Sophie rolled her eyes, amused, and started down the stairs. Nell followed her down and shook her head when they found her brothers and Nat sitting in the living room. "Didn't Sophie tell the two of you to go take a nap?"

Devin held up a cookie. "There's more than one way to deal with channel shock. I'll be okay. Made Govin lie down, though."

Nell snorted. Govin was the one adult male in her life who usually followed common-sense instructions.

Jamie grinned and put an arm around his wife. "And I'm not taking a nap unless she takes one with me."

Sophie chuckled. "That's not the kind of nap I meant." She looked at Devin. "Did you get Sierra settled in okay?"

He nodded. "I did the manly part and carried her to bed. Lauren's taking care of the rest."

"She's settled," said Lauren, coming in from the hallway. "And Caro said she'll bring out the lasagna when it's done."

Nell sat down in her big recliner and let her head rest on its ugly orangeness. Crisis over. She looked over at her two brothers. "You kept my boy safe today. I owe you one."

Devin scowled. "You owe Jamie. I tried to keep our weather witch from blowing herself up. I wasn't much of a cover for Aervyn."

Even Nell's feeble mind powers could pick up his guilt. "My kiddo came out of today in way better shape than any of the rest of you. He's more traumatized by that poor baby bird than by the magic you all did." She eyeballed Devin with her best big-sister stare. "And keeping stray weather witches safe is part of the deal, too."

He looked at her silently for a moment, and then shook his head. "Man, you're good at that."

Yes, she was. She looked at Jamie, trying to figure out if he needed the same treatment.

He just grinned and held up a hand in mock surrender. "We have a fractious little fire witch arriving any day now. Feel free to owe me as much as you like—I'm pretty sure we'll be claiming payment shortly."

Truth. Nell looked over at Lauren. "How's Sierra? My boy broke her heart out on that island." And every mind witch present had felt the echoes.

Lauren shrugged. "Hard to tell, honestly. Even with the sleep spell, she's pretty agitated. She feels responsible, and she's got the image of that bird in Aervyn's hands imprinted on every brain cell."

Jamie sighed. "And that's not actually the worst thing that happened out there."

"I don't think she understands *that* at all." Lauren flopped on the couch, and then looked up in surprise as Devin wrapped an arm around her shoulders and pulled her in.

He grinned. "I'm cold. Humor me. We water witches like a couch full of warm bodies."

Nell blinked. Devin had always been friendly, but there was a blanket right beside him.

She got distracted by Jamie's worried tone. "How are we going to handle things tomorrow? We have two pretty distraught witches in the same house right now."

Yup. And when her little boy was hurting, he had some formidable weapons to make everyone else miserable too, even if it was largely accidental. However, she was sitting in a room full of exhausted witches. Nell took a deep breath, ready to issue mama marching orders. "Everybody go home, get some sleep. I'll page you in the morning when I need you."

Jamie nodded and stood, helping his wife out of the couch. "That nap's starting to sound like a really good idea."

Lauren's quiet chuckle had them all turning. "Apparently someone else thought so, too."

Devin was snuggled into Lauren's shoulder, sound asleep.

Jamie snorted from the doorway. "That dude's always been able to conk out anywhere." He grinned at Lauren. "Just push him off. He'll never notice."

Nell stared at her awake brother, wondering if she was the only one paying attention. Then she caught Nat's eye. Nope. And Nat was very rarely wrong.

Chapter 10

Sierra raced through the still-dark streets of Berkeley on Jamie's borrowed moped, hair streaming in the wind. Dumb helmets anyhow—you couldn't feel the air on your face that way. Momma never would have made her wear a helmet.

She'd woken under the bed, crying from the nightmare she could never remember and haunted by a dead baby bird and the awful hurt in a little boy's eyes.

He'd been right. It was her fault.

Her magic wasn't safe. Even playing with the dolphins wasn't safe, and she'd been doing that her whole life. How many other baby birds had she killed and not even known it?

And why had Momma let her do it? Why didn't she know how to do magic properly?

She peeled around a corner, heading straight for the ocean. She needed the water. And then she needed to leave. Anywhere far away from Aervyn and the awful truth in his eyes.

Catching the tang of saltier air, she let out the throttle a little more—and then screamed as everything in front of her went blank.

Strong arms wrapped around her, pulling her in. "Sorry. Shh. Sorry, sweet girl. You're okay. We've got you."

Nell. Sierra desperately tried to suck air into her lungs, oxygen walled off by the terror layered over the aching hurt. Nell just rubbed her back and held on.

"Sorry about that." A new set of hands, a new voice. Jamie. "Porting at speed is a bit tricky. I didn't mean to scare you."

Her brain tried to turn on—and all that came was a flood of anguish.

"Shh now." Nell's voice was warm and soft and wrapped her up like Momma's once had. "You need to rest, sweet girl. I'm going to use a small spell to help you sleep. We'll figure things out in the morning."

She hadn't planned to be there in the morning. God. They wouldn't even let her run away.

No, we won't. You're ours now.

The words reverberated in her head as the fog of the sleep spell hit. *You're ours now.*

~ ~ ~

Devin pulled his bike up outside Nell's house. She'd called for backup—and in the tone of voice that would have had him coming on the dead run no matter where on the planet he was.

With both Aervyn and Sierra under her roof, it wasn't hard to imagine why she needed help. Although besides making his world-famous pancakes, he didn't have a clue how he was going to do that.

Walking in the door, he ran into the first problem. Aervyn sat just inside the entrance, hat pulled down over his ears and sad-looking blankie in his hand. Devin was pretty sure the blankie hadn't been out of its storage box in over a year. "Hey, bud." He squatted down beside his nephew. "Having a rough morning?"

"I was waiting for you. Mama said I could, and maybe you can help my heart feel better."

Oh, sure. Leave him with the easy job. "I can try. Are you still sad about the bird?"

Aervyn snuggled in and nodded. "I bet its mama is sad too."

Baby birds born out of season often got abandoned by their mamas, but this wasn't the time for a nature lesson. "Sometimes really bad things happen. It's okay to be sad."

Aervyn just cuddled for a bit, thinking. "Is Sierra a bad witch?"

She's a witch who knows all too well how an abandoned baby bird feels, thought Devin, but he didn't say that, either. "No. She's a really strong witch, like you are. But you know how Uncle Jamie teaches you all kinds of stuff about how to be careful and safe?"

Aervyn nodded, eyes still drenched in sadness.

"Well, nobody taught Sierra those things. So she did some magic yesterday, and something bad happened, but she didn't mean to."

A long, long silence. And then a big sigh. "So she's probably really sad too."

That was a heck of a piece of growing up for a four-year-old. "Yup. She's really sad too. We need to teach her how to be a safer witch, but maybe we can help her feel a little better first. You can't learn magic when you're all sad inside."

Aervyn thought a bit longer, and then took his hat off. "'Kay."

He turned and walked down the hall, small boy on a mission. Devin followed and hoped he hadn't committed a big uncle screw-up.

Sierra sat in the kitchen with Nell, a plate of untouched waffles in front of her. So much for the pancake idea. Her cheeks were streaked with tears, eyes haunted—and when she saw Aervyn, she practically stopped breathing.

Devin held up a hand as Nell moved to intercept her son. It was a gamble, but he didn't make half-assed bets.

Aervyn went and stood at Sierra's side. He tilted his head sideways, waiting until she looked at him. "Can I sit on your lap?"

Sierra just stared—so Aervyn climbed on up.

He looked right into her eyes. "I'm sad too." He held out his ratty old blankie. "If I cuddle this, it helps me feel better. Maybe we can both hold it for a while."

Sierra sat frozen for a long moment. Then she wrapped her arms around witchling and blankie and they began to rock, sharing sounds of incoherent sadness.

Nell turned away, tears flooding her eyes. "Thank you," she mouthed.

Devin wrapped an arm around her shoulders and they stood together, watching as two hearts grieved and healed a little.

~ ~ ~

Jamie reached for a wrench, ready to re-attach the bumper to his moped. He'd ported Sierra into Nell's backyard with as gentle a landing as he could manage on four hours of sleep. The moped hadn't been so lucky. Not that it was any stranger to bumps and bruises.

Although to the best of his recollection, it had never been used in an attempt to run away. He'd have to ask Mom. And then ask her to give Sierra the same "wear your helmet or get shackled to my leg for the rest of your life" speech she'd once given Devin. It had been extremely effective.

She had always seemed to know how to keep Dev just this side of insanity, even through their rather eventful teenage years.

He was beginning to think he needed to sit Mom down, get her talking, and take notes. The little girl cozying in Nat's belly was showing her own brand of Sullivan charm already. And with magic on board, they were likely to have a fairly interesting ride. Starting day one.

He felt Nat's presence before he heard her. Her mind was like a soft breeze on his cheeks—it always had him turning, seeking more. "Sorry, did I wake you up?" Banging the dent out of the bumper probably hadn't been the best of ideas while she was still sleeping.

"It's 10 a.m. Hunger woke me up." She dropped down on the grass beside him and handed over half her bagel. "Should have had some breakfast before I went back to bed."

Nell's "witch AWOL" page had woken them both up in the wee hours of the morning. He'd crawled back into bed after the rescue long enough to snuggle Nat back asleep, and then fixed himself breakfast. Tracking and porting a fleeing witch had used up a lot of energy, and he couldn't sleep with a gas tank clanging on empty.

Nat reached out and touched his cheek. "How's Sierra?"

"Still in Berkeley, and eating her waffles." He and Nell had kicked themselves three ways to Sunday for leaving her sleeping alone after such a traumatic day, but all they could do now was try to repair the damage. "Nell says Dev's working his usual magic."

"He would understand her." Nat took a bite out of her bagel. Their baby girl must be hungry.

"Yup. He's the original reckless witch." He handed back the rest of the bagel. "Or maybe that honor belonged to Sierra's mom."

Nat laughed. "I'd guess Moira could give you a long list down through history. I doubt the reckless gene got started in the last generation."

She had a point. He laid a hand on her belly, and got a good swift kick for his troubles. "Think we've got the next generation of reckless in here?"

"Maybe." She shrugged. "It feels strange to slot her into a box before we even look into her eyes."

Maybe. But Nat hadn't felt their little girl's hands reaching for power. "Are we ready if she is?"

Her smile was gentle. "No. But at least she won't be able to drive a moped for a few years yet."

Jamie remembered the look on his mom's face the day Devin had first straddled the moped. And finally understood the terror in her eyes. He gulped. "Maybe she'll prefer walking."

Nat's laughter rang in his ears long after she headed back inside for another bagel.

~ ~ ~

A hand slapped down on Govin's desk. "Five more minutes to sulk, and then you gotta snap out of it." TJ walked back toward the kitchen. "I'll even cook us some breakfast."

That got Govin moving. TJ was an abysmal cook. "I'll do it. What do you want?"

"I got some of that sausage stuff you like, and fresh eggs, and rolls from Caro."

Govin stopped dead. "You went to see Caro?" The last time those two had been in a room, actual sparks had flown—and not the happy kind.

TJ's head was buried in the fridge. "She makes good rolls."

This from a guy who ate potato chips that had been sitting in a bowl for a week. Govin reached for the eggs, absurdly touched. "Thanks. After all the magic yesterday, I'm pretty hungry."

"So what the hell happened yesterday, anyhow? I got readings that will confuse my models for a year."

Explaining complex magic to a ruthlessly logical mathematical genius was never easy. Govin tried the short version. "Sierra sucked the energy out of the rogue waves. She pulled it into herself and passed it back out through the rest of us, down our groundlines."

He could see TJ's brain doing the calculations. Then his eyes got scared. "That's insane."

Govin just nodded. "Yeah."

"Dude." TJ frowned, and then cracked a grin. "If I'd known that, I'd have gotten you more sausage."

Govin snorted, amused. TJ had always used humor to diffuse the frequently life-and-death stress of their jobs. And it almost always worked. "Let's just say I'm not lining up to do it again anytime soon."

"Better do a good job of training her, then."

"Yeah." Just one of the issues he'd been moping about. Sometimes it sucked to be right. "Any ideas on that?"

TJ sat down with a bowl of chips big enough to ruin any other man's breakfast. "You're the witch, dude. I'm the data geek. Does she like data?"

Since only about three people on the planet liked data as much as TJ, the odds weren't high. And in his limited experience with eighteen-year-old girls, bubbly, outgoing Sierra didn't strike him as having a big dose of inner geek. However, smart mathematicians played the long odds.

Govin poured the egg mixture into the frying pan, happy with the crackle and smell of frying butter. "Feel free to show her your models. Maybe she'll love them."

"What's not to love?" TJ leaned back and grinned. "Can I show her my aliens stuff?"

Govin laughed. "I think you have to tweak your aliens model some to take our rogue witch out of the picture." Sierra was the likely source of a number of the weather anomalies TJ had tagged as "of alien origin" over the years.

"She's not rogue, Gov." TJ's face was suddenly dead serious. "She's dangerously ignorant, but think about what she did yesterday."

He shrugged, irritated. "Blasted the hell out of every witch in the chopper?"

"No, not that part." TJ tapped the table. "She used your groundlines. To reroute the energy."

"Yeah." Govin could tell he was missing something.

TJ rolled his eyes. "Didn't she just learn about groundlines like two days ago?"

Govin froze, spatula in mid-air.

TJ nodded, obviously six steps ahead as usual. "She did huge magic, under serious pressure, and not only did she remember grounding, she used it to solve a very big problem."

"She didn't need to do so much." Govin wasn't sure why he was fighting this. "The beaches were clear—she put five witches at risk for a few birds."

TJ's eyes were back to serious. "When's last time she worked with four other witches?"

Crap. Never. Govin shook his head, realizing just how difficult a task Sierra had faced. And how little credit he'd given her for what she *had* done.

"Don't think so hard." A tossed banana thudded off his chest. "Train her. Maybe she's not the hardcase you think she is. And don't burn my breakfast. I stood in line at the farmers' market at six freaking a.m. for those eggs."

~ ~ ~

Nell looked around the Witches' Lounge and took a deep breath. Even her pretty feeble mind powers could sense the buzz of unhappiness, uncertainty, and fear in the room.

It had been a very rough twenty-four hours. And while they'd managed to pull everybody back from the brink, there were very few days she could remember when Witch Central had been in this much turmoil. She was pretty sure it was going to get worse before it got better.

Assessing the room, Nell saw Moira watching her steadily and sighed. She knew that look. Handoff. There was no way this meeting was going to stay calm, but they could start off that way.

She held up a hand for silence. "Okay, all. We have ourselves a bit of a situation. I know we each touched different pieces of the drama yesterday, so maybe we can hear from everyone before we start trying to fix anything."

Jamie rolled his eyes as she borrowed a tool straight out of Mom's family meeting handbook—let everyone have a say before you laid down the law. Nell wished someone could actually walk in and straighten this one out. Some parts of being a kid were kind of handy.

Trying to start with one of the less volatile minds in the room, Nell tipped her chin at Sophie. "You want to kick us off?"

Typical of an earth witch, Sophie took a moment to contemplate before she answered. "I saw a whole lot of witches who pushed the edges of their personal safety. Aervyn's mostly emotional distress. The rest of you ran yourselves pretty dry."

"Not much choice," said Devin quietly. "It was either that or cook a witch. You don't put down a spell like that."

Sophie raised her hands. "I'm not arguing with that. But it's a rare day we have that many drained witches."

Jamie nodded slowly. "We're good at scrambling whatever resources we have in an emergency. We scrambled Sierra, knowing she's got big power and some serious training holes." He sighed. "At some level, what happened after that is on us."

"What, are you channeling TJ now?" Govin shook his head. "He said the same thing this morning. We're used to working together with a team. She's not. We're very lucky she didn't cook someone's channels."

Nell felt the dread in her heart rising again. One of those "someones" had been her baby boy. "Realm makes scrambling a team a lot easier. We need to add some thinking steps."

Jamie looked guilty. "Ones like not putting four-year-olds on the crisis-response team?"

Much as she wished the answer to that could be yes, she knew she couldn't keep Aervyn in a box forever. "Not necessarily." She smiled wryly at her brother. "But you might consider skipping the supersonic helicopter magic next time."

Every man in the room looked totally mystified. Nell sighed. "Southern California has plenty of Internet access, and more than one witch. You could have beamed through Realm to get closer."

If things hadn't been quite so serious, the look on Jamie's face would have been high comedy, at least for the two seconds it lasted. Then he looked horrified. "Shit. I didn't even think of that."

Nell relented. "Me neither. It hit me about six o'clock last night." About eight hours too late.

Govin's hands looked like they were trying to find something to break. "Those are details. Important ones, but let's get to them later. We have a loose cannon. She's dangerous. There could have been people on those beaches yesterday."

"Her dangerous, combined with our stupid." Jamie looked at Nell, abject guilt on his face. "There was more than one bad decision yesterday, and Sierra didn't make all of them."

Just for a moment, Nell wished she'd never come up with the damn fetching spell.

"You're smart witches." Moira's voice was balm to the stress-filled room. "We'll figure things out. Govin's right. Today our job is to figure out how to help our loose cannon use her magic more safely. One step at a time. She'll need training, and quickly."

"I don't think it's going to be fast." Govin was pacing. "We can teach her basic safety precautions, and after yesterday, she might even understand the need for them. But her magical judgment stinks." He scanned the group. "That's really what we teach to our witchlings with all the practice and magic tricks and games. We teach them to use magic wisely. Amelia taught Sierra the games, but none of the judgment."

"Amelia didn't have the judgment." Moira looked as distraught as Nell had ever seen her. "We tried for years. If Sierra's head is as hard as her mother's..."

Jamie shifted restlessly in his chair, nodding. "She added groundlines when we asked her to, but she couldn't see why. And she blasted us all nearly to the ground yesterday, but she has no idea. Even if she's less resistant than Amelia was, we'll be trying to undo the way she's used magic for years."

Nell debated, and then added her biggest concern to the top of the pile. "It's a lot more than that. Magic is her strongest connection to Amelia. The way she currently does magic is her mother's legacy, and it's one Sierra treasures."

"We have to fight memories of a dead woman?" Govin rested his forehead against the wall for a moment. Nell felt his frustration and fear. If they couldn't adjust the way Sierra used magic, and quickly, he'd be on the front lines of trying to keep the damage contained.

Then she swallowed against her own dose of fear. If it got really messy, there was only one witch capable of shutting her down. And he was currently asleep in his bed with his old blankie.

~ ~ ~

Lauren had seen it happen in big real estate negotiations. Fear would leak in one corner and infect the whole room, like a nasty oil slick. She'd just never seen it happen in Witch Central. Some of the most capable people she'd ever known were trying to psyche themselves into losing a war.

And an eighteen-year-old girl was going to be the casualty.

Somebody needed to be on cleanup. Two somebodies. There was only one other witch in the room who wasn't swimming in fear. And after watching him croon to a girl in the throes of heartbreak, she was pretty sure Sierra couldn't ask for a better defender.

A really smart negotiator knew when to act—and when to work behind the scenes. Swiftly, she reached out to Devin's mind, knocking lightly. *You're the only one who's not scared.*

He didn't even blink at the mind contact. *Yeah. You wanna lead off, or should I?*

Jeebers. How the heck had he figured out how she was feeling? *What, is my poker face losing its touch?*

Yup. His mindvoice carried a touch of humor, and more than a touch of respect. *You look like Electra ready to bust some heads.*

Nine months of hanging out with wonderboy, and Lauren was totally up on her superhero references. *Not every woman would think that was a compliment.*

You're not every woman. Devin looked around the room. *Can you pipe me a mind feed? This'll go a lot easier if I don't have to guess how everyone's feeling.*

That wasn't precisely ethical. However, it was right. Lauren set up the feed and settled back. She was pretty sure this was going to be impressive.

Devin stood up—and the moment he did, he owned the room. He looked around, meeting every set of eyes. "She's an eighteen-year-old girl. An orphan. Since when does that make Witch Central cower in fear?"

It had been right to have him go first. Only someone raised in their midst could have said something that harsh and gotten everyone listening.

A RECKLESS WITCH

Lauren felt him check in with the mind feed—and then double down. "We fear her power." He held up a hand as Govin started to protest. "I get it, dude. I really do. We've had two hurricanes hit Costa Rica in the last year. I've cleaned up the bodies."

Govin winced. "We tempered the first one a little. The second, we couldn't touch."

"I know." Devin's eyes held on to those of his old friend. "And I know the pain you feel for every life you can't save. But I also held the hand of the little girl who looked for her mama after the first storm—and found her, right on the edge of the flood zone." He paused. "Alive, Gov. The lives you save mean something too."

Govin scraped his hands through his hair. "So how do we deal with a witch who might put more faces up on my mental dead board?"

Devin's mind was part friend, part avenging angel. He looked over at Moira. "We follow the advice of one of the wisest witches I know. We love her. It has been, and always will be, love that keeps a reckless soul safe."

It was then that Lauren realized how thoroughly she'd underestimated Devin Sullivan. In three sentences, he'd sucked half the fear out of the room.

Moira nodded in quiet acknowledgment. "We talked about that in our last meeting. If anything, this makes welcome blankets and painting parties all the more important."

Only witches would carry paint chips into battle.

"We all need some time to recover, anyhow." Sophie was wearing her healer glare again. "None of you, Sierra included, needs to be doing any magic for the next day or two."

Lauren could feel Govin's impatience. And his dread. She piped both through to Devin. *He's not convinced.*

135

He stepped up to Govin's shoulder. *I know. And I don't blame him. He's got the most to lose if we're wrong. But sometimes, you have to relax in the eye of the storm, or you don't make it out the other side.*

That wasn't exactly comforting.

Chapter 11

"How's our Sierra doing?"

Nell looked over at where Moira sat, needles clicking, and tried not to curse her own knitting swatch. She was one of the few fire witches who really disliked knitting. Weird, but true—and heresy here at Caro's house. "Settling down, I think. She's been pretty quiet. Headed out to the beach this morning for a walk."

Sophie, knitting next to Moira, frowned. "Is it a good idea for her to be out there alone?"

Nell shrugged. She'd tangled with exactly the same question watching Sierra walk out the door. "She's not a child."

"Still needs some mothering, though." Moira smiled. "She'll be fine. A walk on the beach will soothe her soul. We water witches need our time to commune with the sea. I often do exactly the same when my mind's in turmoil."

That was one of the things worrying Nell. "More numb than in turmoil at this point, I think."

Sophie leaned forward, in healer mode. "Is she clearing the trauma, or bottling it?"

"I'm not sure." Nell gestured toward Lauren. "I asked her to come visit later today. My mind-witch powers aren't up to the task. You might give her some pointers on what to look for—she hasn't been around a lot of traumatized witches yet."

Sophie grinned. "I'll do that in a bit. I think she's rather busy at the moment."

Nell looked over at Lauren's frustrated face, sympathetic. Some people found knitting a twelve-inch swatch the work of a few minutes. Lesser knitters would take a few hours. Poor Lauren, who had never knit before, was probably going to be at it for days.

Ah, well. Moira had decreed that Sierra needed a welcoming blanket, so a welcoming blanket she would get. Nell glanced over at her son, sitting beside Caro, who was helping him with repairs on his swatch and sneaking in a row or two as she did it. There were some advantages to being four. Or almost five. "Are you guys coming for Aervyn's birthday?"

"Of course." Moira smiled. "Where else would we be?"

Nell grinned. "I don't know. I thought you might have some other plans for Winter Solstice."

"And that we do. But we'll get them done and still make your wee boy's party, and mayhap a birth as well."

Nat sat over by Jamie, quietly knitting away on the swatch resting on her belly. "You think she'll crash Aervyn's birthday, do you?" That would figure. Babies had impeccable timing. Not that he would mind.

Moira's voice got that eerie, otherworldly tinge it sometimes got. "Aye. That baby girl's got the blood of ten-times-ten generations of witches running in her veins, and power already running through her fingers. Destiny will call to her this Solstice."

Nell shivered. It was hard not to believe in destiny and portents when Moira used that tone. "I'll make extra birthday cake."

Sophie grinned and spoke in a stage whisper. "It's so creepy when she does that, isn't it?"

They giggled quietly together. Or rather, she and Sophie giggled. Moira positively cackled.

A RECKLESS WITCH

~ ~ ~

Lauren frowned over at Devin, her emergency knitting instructor. Apparently she was lacking in a key witch life skill—everyone else in Caro's living room seemed to know what they were doing. "I have to make it how big?" The swatch hanging on her needles wasn't growing very fast.

He grinned and glanced at Aervyn, tucked in by Caro's side. "Dunno, but probably at least as big as his. And preferably with a few less holes."

It was more than a little embarrassing to be out-knit by a four-year-old. "Does every witch learn how to knit?"

"The ones around here do." Devin reached over and adjusted her yarn. "All fire witches learn as a way to channel their magic. And since Jamie's a fire witch, Caro decided Matt and I needed lessons too."

She eyed Caro's flashing needles. Any woman who taught triplet boys how to knit deserved serious respect. "And when was the last time you picked up a ball of yarn?"

He laughed. "Probably the last time they wanted squares for a welcoming blanket, but it's like bike riding. You don't forget."

Devin's hands were quick and competent, and damn, if a man knitting wasn't oddly sexy. Lauren checked her mental barriers. There were some thoughts you definitely didn't want leaking. "It's amazing how relaxed everyone is."

"Eye of the storm." Devin caught the ball of yarn that had rolled off Aervyn's lap and tossed it back over to the couch where he sat. "Sierra's not the first witch to make life interesting. If you don't relax when you can, the stress builds, and that doesn't do anyone any good."

The planet might be better off if a whole lot more people took that advice. "So we knit and wait for the rest of the storm to hit?"

Devin grinned. "And we eat. Don't forget that part."

Even a newbie witch knew that much. Witches and food were never far apart. And since she was probably going to be sitting here for the next three days finishing her swatch for Sierra, she might as well take care of another hole in her witch knowledge. "So, tell me about birthing circles. What exactly have we been volunteered for?"

"Well, I can tell you what they're usually like." He shrugged. "Or I can give you my best guess about what we're in for."

Why did she never get the easy witch stuff to do? "How many birthing circles have you led?"

His eyes flashed humor. "None."

That's what she'd been afraid of. "What kind of crazy people put two newbies in charge of a circle at a birth everyone seems to think is going to get a bit nuts?"

Devin's eyes got suddenly serious. "You're the mind witch. You know exactly why."

Sigh. Yeah, she did. "Because they trust us."

He nodded, his mind radiating the kind of sure strength you'd want beside you in an emergency. Or the birth of a fire witchling. Watching him in action with Sierra had been a pointed reminder that for all his goofing around, this Sullivan brother had a deep core of strength, just like Jamie. Nothing was going to go wrong on his watch.

Knowing they'd both go to the wall for the people they loved was comforting. She'd learned a lot about teamwork in the last few months, but this was for Nat. "How do we get ready?"

And just like that, his mind switched back to happy-go-lucky Devin. "Not much to get ready for. We just roll with whatever comes."

Not a chance. In real estate, negotiations could get tricky, and Lauren knew how to fly by the seat of her pants. But preparation still made the difference in a lot of deals. She also knew better than to waste her breath trying to convince Devin of that. "Run me through a couple of what-ifs and how you'd roll with it."

He just raised an eyebrow.

She held up her pathetic knitting swatch. "Humor me. I'm still new to this witching stuff. In the world I come from, a doctor comes out to the hospital waiting room and tells you everything's fine and the baby's a girl."

"We already know she's a girl." He reached over for her knitting. "You're making holes again."

Sometimes you had to pull out the big guns. *Talk, or I'll tell Nell who swiped her last batch of Nutella cookies.*

He actually turned a little white. "Shit. I had that buried. You're a damned good mind witch."

Such flattery. "And only a mind witch. How will that impact the birthing circle? Nell said Aervyn won't be in the inner circle, and he's usually my connection to everyone else." It was thoughts like that keeping her up at night.

"You really *are* new to this." He looked up, his brain suddenly serious again. "It's not like our normal full circles, although it can morph into that if needed. Part of the reason we were picked is because we have the primary talents they expect to need. Water magic in case our little girl comes out blazing. Mind magic to help the healers keep her calm and feeling safe. Birth is a pretty big transition, and some babies handle it better than others."

Lauren was pretty sure *her* face was going white now. "That's kind of a big responsibility for someone who's never actually seen a birth before."

"You can handle it." He spoke casually, still fixing the holes in her knitting swatch, but she could feel his sincerity.

"Why are you so sure?" It was nice to be trusted, but they'd never worked magic together.

He handed back her neatly repaired square. "I've seen you in action. But more than that, you hold the power streams for Aervyn in full circle. If my sister and my brother trust you enough to do that, I'd trust you with my life." And he meant it. Just that simple. Then his grin flashed. "Besides, no way I'm letting you abandon me to watch my sister-in-law give birth alone."

He clearly meant that, too.

Nat was going to have a baby. That still rocked her to the core when she really thought about it.

Devin touched her shoulder. Back to the intent eyes again. "They'll be awesome. Can you think of any two people you'd rather trust with a baby than Jamie and Nat?"

She grinned. He was right—they would be awesome. And maybe their backup wasn't as shaky as she'd thought. However, she was going to sit Sophie down and grill her, first chance she got.

Right after she got her knitting swatch done and Devin's eyes out of her head.

~ ~ ~

"Are you cold? Do you need to put your feet up?" Ginia tucked a blanket around Sophie's expanding waist and pulled out a bottle of water to put on the floor beside her. "It's non-toxic paint, but I still think it's a good idea to leave the patio door open."

Sophie grinned. Ginia sounded like a miniature Moira. "I'm fine, sweetie. And you can't get out of painting by taking care of me all afternoon." Nell had shuttled her through Realm to come supervise the painting of Sierra's apartment—and to pick up some clues about what kind of furnishings she might like.

Ginia grinned. "Sierra's still trying to decide on all her colors." She motioned to the group over at the counter. "Come over here—maybe Sophie can help us decide."

In moments, there were about a hundred paint chips spread out over the floor. At least half of them were pink. Tahiti Sunrise. Bubblegum. Pinkify Me. It was a selection that had nine-year-old girl written all over it. Sophie grinned at Sierra. "It's your apartment—do you have a favorite color?"

She giggled. "Well, I like pink. But I'm not sure I want to live in the middle of an entirely pink room."

Indeed. Time to impart some gentle decorating advice. "I usually like to pick a pretty relaxing color for my main room. Then you can use funky colors in small spaces, or on furniture, or art."

Sierra laughed, sweeping her hands around the empty room. "I don't exactly have a lot of furniture."

Not yet. Sophie spread out her arms. "Tell me what it would look like if it was done up any way you wanted."

Sierra just blinked. Clearly no one had asked her a question like that in a very long time.

Ginia held out a paintbrush and tapped her on the shoulder. "I am your Fairy Godmother Giniarella. What kind of room can I bring you, oh lucky peasant girl?"

Now Sierra giggled, obviously more comfortable with goofy games than serious questions. She closed her eyes and spun around a few times. Mia grabbed her just before she bumped into a wall, and four giggly girls collapsed on the floor.

Sophie hoped Sierra offered up some clues soon. The real fairy-godmothers-in-waiting needed the inside scoop, and she really needed to pee. This whole being-pregnant thing was starting to get uncomfortable.

Sierra looked around at her walls, considering. "Maybe something watery. I'd kind of like to feel like I'm floating in the ocean."

That sounded like a good fit for a water witch, but oceans came in a lot of different moods. Sophie dug a little. "In Nova Scotia right now, that would mean all gray and blustery."

"Uh, uh." Sierra rolled over. "Warm blue water, like Hawaii in the summer, or Tahiti."

The girl had been to Tahiti? Lucky her. But they could work with a Hawaiian-ocean theme. "What else can you see as you float?"

"Happy fish. I used to like the yellow stripey ones best—they were the most curious. And the huge old green sea turtles, and big red flowers on my favorite beach towel." Sierra was lost in memory now, eyes closed and a smile on her face that tugged at Sophie's heart.

Then her face fell, and Ginia and Sophie both reached out, the heartache that had just hit obvious to any healer. Ginia touched Sierra's cheek gently, offering comfort even as her nine-year-old heart struggled to understand. "Did you go there with your mom? To Hawaii?"

"Yeah." Sierra sat up and cuddled her knees. "We went back there a lot. I was born in Hawaii, in the ocean."

Ginia's eyes opened wide. "That's so cool."

Sierra grinned. "Momma said she felt like a whale, so it made sense."

Sophie giggled quietly and rubbed her belly. She was beginning to understand how that felt, and she was nowhere near as big as Nat yet.

Shay got up and started collecting blue paint chips. "Are any of these the right kind of watery color?"

Sophie watched as the four girls put their heads together and began debating the merits of Blue Moon, Tropical Turquoise, Forget Me Not, and her personal favorite, Love In a Mist. Quietly she pulled out her cell phone and began to text instructions to the waiting brigade of shoppers.

And then she needed to contemplate Sierra a little longer. The girl was putting on a good front. But Sophie was pretty sure she wasn't feeling nearly as bubbly as her exterior might suggest.

~ ~ ~

Nat tried not to grunt as she extracted herself from the car. It was sad and pathetic to drive less than four blocks to go shopping, but Jamie insisted on having the car nearby these days. Which was pretty funny when he could have teleported her the four blocks home.

Mostly she just wanted an anti-gravity device that would make her feel a little lighter. She hadn't been upside-down in three months, and every organ in her body had settled in somewhere under her ribs.

And that was enough very-pregnant-lady whining. She smiled over at Jamie, who was reading the incoming text on his phone. "Do we have our mission?"

"Yeah." He frowned. "Hawaiian ocean in spring. Aren't we supposed to be getting shopping instructions?"

He was so cute. "Those are instructions, sweetie."

"Not. Instructions are things like 'eight-foot couch' or 'table and four chairs.'"

Well, she hadn't married him for his shopping skills. "We know Sierra needs all that stuff, but this is about more than making sure she has a place to sit and sleep. It's about making her a home." Nat tried to imagine Hawaii in spring in her mind. It sounded lovely.

"Eight-foot couches are homey." Jamie pointed hopefully at the furniture store.

She started waddling in that direction. Everyone waddled at nine months pregnant. It was humbling. "Well, we need to find a homey couch that will remind Sierra of Hawaii in spring."

"One couch with palm fronds, coming up."

Nat tried not to giggle. It wasn't a safe activity with a belly this big. "I don't think we have to be quite that literal."

He leaned down to kiss her forehead and opened the store door. "Fine. I'll judge the comfort factor. You figure out if it will pass the decorating committee's standards."

Ten minutes later, two things were obvious. One, furniture salespeople got *really* nervous when very pregnant women sat down on squishy couches. And two, most comfortable couches were insanely ugly.

Nat sat down carefully on a footstool and sighed.

Jamie looked over from his prone couch-testing position. "Maybe we're going about this backwards. What would the perfect couch look like?"

She closed her eyes and tried to imagine. "Curvy lines. Watery, so squishy and soft. Sophie says the walls are going to be a soft blue color, so maybe a darker blue for the couch, with a really soft fabric." She touched the footstool. "Most of these are way too scratchy. We want it to feel like water, not carpet. Some pretty pillows and throws—I think Caro and Moira are taking care of that."

"We're in the wrong place, then." Jamie grinned. "I know the perfect couch."

Hallelujah. Levering up off the footstool, she took his hand. "Where are we going?"

"Home." He laughed as she stopped in confusion. "You know that ugly monstrosity in our basement?"

It was olive green and coffee-stained—and one of Jamie's most prized possessions. "You're going to give her The Monster?"

He shrugged and headed for the door. "Sure. It's perfect. Big as an ocean and comfy and curvy. It just needs a new cover. I'll call Nell—we must know someone who can sew."

The generosity of the witching community still made Nat catch her breath with regularity. Her husband would give up his couch, get it a new cover, and think nothing of it.

She was a lucky woman. And maybe not the only one. Things were stirring for another Sullivan brother. "So what do you think about Devin and Lauren?"

"What about them?"

"You think what's flying between them will go anywhere?"

Jamie stopped dead in his tracks and stared at her. "What are you talking about?"

She grinned. It was serious fun figuring things out faster than a mind witch. "I think it started at our wedding, actually, but it's getting really obvious now. Did you see them at knitting this morning?"

"Dev? And Lauren?" Jamie was practically squeaking.

Yeah. Not the likeliest of pairs, on the surface. "The beginnings are there, but they might just ignore it. Lauren's always been really happy on her own. She needs a guy less than anyone I know."

Jamie stared another long moment—and then his face slowly lit with mischief. "Well, that might be the one thing Dev would find irresistible."

Possibly. Nat kissed his cheek. "Resist the urge to meddle."

"Oh, we've already done that." He grinned. "We put them together in our birthing circle."

She was missing something. "And how is that meddling?"

"They're going to be scared witless, depending on each other, and overwhelmed by our gorgeous girl." He snickered softly. "Mom will be thrilled."

Nat shook her head, amused. "It's not exactly a done deal yet."

His eyes shone with the kind of glee she usually saw in his four-year-old nephew. "No, but Mom will be here in a couple of days. And no one meddles better than Retha Sullivan."

They stepped out of the store into the much busier street—and two feet kicked into Nat's ribs hard enough to make her double over. Jamie grabbed her arm, concern all over his face. "Contractions?" Then he shook his head. "No, I can feel her mind—her head hurts. Too many people."

He laid a hand on her belly and closed his eyes for a minute. She could feel the baby instantly quiet. "Whatever you did, she's much happier now."

He nodded. "I threw up barriers, just like I did for Lauren once upon a time. I think all the strange minds confused her."

Nat tried to breathe and roll with the newness. "Ginia's been coming over to clear our channels every day. Is there more we need to do?"

He shrugged. "Ideally we teach our sweet girl to barrier, but as Lauren's discovering, that's tricky just yet. I tried lessons with Aervyn before he was born, too. Some stuff worked a little, some didn't. Lauren's a way better mind witch though, so maybe she'll have better luck."

Magic lessons for an unborn witch. She definitely wasn't in Kansas anymore.

Chapter 12

Lauren walked into Nell's living room and laughed. "Didn't any of you go home?" It was pretty much the same crew who had been there after the Channel Islands emergency.

Jamie grinned. "Shopping exhaustion. And we were hungry. A little bird said Caro was bringing over food again."

Nell rolled her eyes. "Dev and Jamie came over to do a magic lesson with Aervyn, but he's napping." Her face softened. "He asked Sierra to come tuck him in, and when I went upstairs, they were both curled up together."

The two of them had bonded deeply in the last twenty-four hours. Aervyn's capacity to forgive was humbling.

"Done." Sophie put down her needles, with what was presumably a swatch for Sierra's blanket. "Napping's good for people with channel shock." She looked pointedly at Jamie. "You're still tired—you could use some extra rest too."

He *was* tired. She could feel it. Lauren stood up. Witches who refused to take naps could at least eat. Nell's kitchen always had cookies.

She made it about halfway out of her chair before her head exploded, pounding with the incoming flood of desperation and sadness and incoming death. Oh, holy God. Not in the eye of the storm anymore. She fought for control—and then she heard Aervyn beginning to panic, overwhelmed by the trauma hitting his sleeping mind.

First things first. *Jamie! Get Aervyn out of there. Then get him barriered.*

She could feel Jamie's fear, even as they both bolted for the stairs. *Don't know if I can. Once I port him, I won't have much left.*

On it. Caro's mental voice from just outside the house stopped them both in their tracks. *Consider it done. You move him, Jamie—I have his head.*

Jamie nodded. *Moved.* He was sheet white again.

Lauren squeezed her eyes shut in relief. Caro was a strong mind witch—Aervyn would be safe. She took one more moment to send an order to Nell. *Barrier Jamie, or get him out of the house.* He was almost empty.

Sophie touched her arm, and then reached for Jamie, who was clutching the newel post, swaying. "I've got him. Go."

Thank goodness witches flocked to food.

Lauren charged up the stairs and heard footsteps at her heels. She whirled on Devin. "Stay out—I can't protect your mind and deal with her too." Closer now, she was picking up Sierra's dream—hurtling waves as big as a mountain, bearing down on a tiny island. "She's reliving what happened."

"I'm mind-deaf, Lauren." He grabbed her shoulders. "Whatever's happening, it's not hurting me."

She had no idea how anyone could be deaf to the tsunami of feeling coming from the bedroom where Sierra slept, but there was no time to argue. Yanking open the door to the room, she froze, barriering spell crashing to a halt.

The poor girl was off the bed, trying to squeeze into the tiny space between the mattress and the floor, mewing like a tortured kitten. Her mind was one keening wail of pain.

"Can I touch her?" Devin's voice was an ocean of calm. "Is it okay to pick her up?"

Lauren clung to his steadiness, fighting for control against Sierra's devastation. "I don't know. Move slowly—I'll let you know if it gets worse."

Carefully he moved in beside Sierra, laying a hand on her shoulder. "Shh, sweet girl. Shh, now."

Lauren motioned for him to keep going—and then realized he'd do a lot better job if he wasn't flying totally blind. She connected into his mind and sent a tiny fraction of what Sierra was feeling down the pipe.

He nodded in thanks and slowly picked Sierra up, settling her in his lap like a small child. The pain in her mind dialed down a notch, and the awful mewing stopped.

Lauren closed her eyes, trying to figure out what to do next.

Can you hear me? His voice surprised her, but probably shouldn't have. He'd been joined at the hip to a mind witch his whole life.

Yeah. I'm going to try to dampen her emotions a little.

No. His mind was very decisive. *Not yet.*

She's in agony, Devin. Lauren turned up the volume a bit so he could see for himself.

He winced. *Stop that, damn it. I'm not a stupid witch—I can see how bad it is just looking at your face. You're whiter than Jamie.*

She dialed the volume back down, suddenly ashamed.

And don't freaking apologize, either. There's no way this is all about a dead bird. You're empath and telepath both, right? Focus on her dream—we need to know what's hurting her like this.

Lauren froze as his words sank in. He was right. She'd seen waves, but no birds at all. If Sierra was reliving the past few days, the bird would have been all over her dream. She swung around mentally and tried to pull dreaming images out of the flood.

Hey! Devin had a hell of a kick for a guy who wasn't a mind witch. *Hook me in. Don't you dare go into a dream alone.*

Freaking bossy Sullivans. He was right, however. Lauren threw him a line, and then dove into Sierra's mind torrent, seeking—and glad for the guy who had her back.

When she found the dream source, she backed off a step. Monitoring dreams was a tricky and dangerous business. Monitoring a nightmare...

I've got you. Devin's mindvoice was rock solid.

Checking her mental anchors once more, Lauren grabbed hold of the roaring dream. And hissed as she suddenly found herself flying over the surface of the ocean at insane speeds. Holy God.

Sierra's desperate fear had nothing to do with the flying, however. Lauren looked up—and saw a mountain of water racing front of her. Just beyond it, a tiny island in the middle of the ocean. And on the island, a woman, blonde hair streaming—her back to the killing wave.

She felt Devin's harsh intake of breath. *That's Amelia. Oh, shit—Lauren, that's Sierra's mother.*

It was all too clear what was about to happen. And no way in hell did Sierra need to go through it again. Not today.

Lauren reached for power, wrapping her own mind around Sierra's. She grabbed the flow of the nightmare and folded it over, ripping out a large chunk of what came next.

It took practically everything she had. Devin was right—this was a dream sequence with a long history, and it deeply resisted the change she imposed on it. She fought the overwhelming urge to make it permanent.

Tying off the ends, she hit Sierra with the best sleep spell she could muster—and then reached for the floor as she felt the backlash hit.

~ ~ ~

Sophie cursed as Devin carried Lauren into the living room. "What now?"

Lauren lifted her head off his shoulder. "I just need a cookie. Or seven. I'll be fine."

"Sit." Sophie glared at Devin and pointed at the couch. She'd had more than enough witch heroes in the last few days. Reaching out for Lauren's hands, she started a basic healing scan. And had to laugh. "What, you thought I hadn't had enough practice with channel shock? What happened up there? Jamie thought it was just a bad nightmare."

"Beyond bad." Devin spoke with a mouth full of cookie. "Sierra watches her mother die. Thanks to Lauren, she watched it one less time."

Sophie frowned. "She sees it? She was there?"

"I don't think so." Lauren leaned back against the couch. "When she's awake, she believes her mother's dead, but she doesn't know for sure. I don't think she was there."

Sophie wasn't so sure. "Recurring dream?"

"Oh, yeah." Lauren took the cookie Devin handed her. "Strong little bugger—I tried to loop out the worst part and just barely got it done."

Nat and Nell walked in, bearing bowls full of soup. It smelled like heaven—Sophie was pretty sure even her toes drooled. "Where's Jamie?"

"I hit him with a sleep spell." Nell grinned. "He never does see those coming."

Good. One less patient to worry about. Sophie reached up as Nat handed over a bowl. "It's a crazy day when the woman who's about to give birth is taking care of the rest of us."

Nat smiled. "It's better than being the watched pot, trust me."

She had a point. And the soup tasted even better than it smelled. French onion, heavy on the onions and topped with strands of melty cheese. Pausing to savor the first few spoonfuls, Sophie breathed deeply—and then turned her mind back to their main problem. "So, Sierra knows how her mom died. She dreams it."

Nell sucked in air. "What? I thought she was reliving the helicopter flight. We got vague images of chasing big waves before I managed to get a decent wall up."

Devin shook his head and looked at Lauren. "Can you project the face of the woman on the island?"

She managed half a grin. "Can I have more soup after?"

Sophie frowned. Mind-projection was pretty basic—clearly Lauren had pushed awfully close to the edge upstairs. In an emergency, a witch did what she had to do—but this had only been a dream.

Lauren shook her head, meeting Sophie's eyes. *Not just a dream. Watch.*

It was only ten seconds of replay. And if Sophie had possessed mind power, she'd have ripped the nightmare out of the fabric of time and tossed it into the depths of hell.

She looked at Lauren and tried to clear the horror from her mind. "I'm a healer sworn, and I don't know if I'd have had the guts you did. It was right to leave the dream in her head—we don't know what it's attached to, or how much of it she remembers."

"Thanks." Lauren's voice was raspy. "I needed to hear that."

Sophie had known it was more than channel shock rocking her latest patient. Sometimes the very hardest choices involved having the magic—and still doing nothing.

Devin looked at his sister. "That was Amelia, right?"

Nell nodded slowly, eyes glistening. "But how could Sierra have seen it? Maybe it's just a nightmare, pieced together from other experiences?"

Lauren shook her head. "No. Or at least, I don't think so. Most dreams feel a bit unreal. This one reads like a memory. The imprint's really deep."

Nell frowned. "But how's that possible? Amelia was out alone in the middle of the ocean."

A few months in Fisher's Cove, where a long-dead five-year-old boy still cast a big shadow, and Sophie knew the answer. "She might have traveled."

Devin turned white, but shook his head. "She's been on her own for six years, Soph. No way an astral traveler lives that long without proper anchors. She'd have just drifted away."

"Some people only travel in times of enormous stress or fear." And watching your mother die had to top the fear charts.

"Sometimes it's hereditary. We should ask Moira if Amelia ever traveled." Nell cuddled a knitted pillow to her chest. "But it could also just be a dream. Sierra's had a lot to deal with in the last six years. This might be one way her mind has tried to help her cope."

"No way." Devin's voice was almost as raspy as Lauren's. "It tears her apart. There's no way that's a healing dream."

It could be. Sophie knew well that sometimes healing hurt. "Her subconscious might prefer it to not knowing." A mother killed by a big wave might be better than believing she'd walked away and left you alone.

Lauren shook her head, as if trying to clear cobwebs. "Wait. Our two choices here are a dream that feels very real, but isn't, or a twelve-year-old girl who got pulled out of her body because her mother was in danger?"

Sophie nodded. At a different time, she might have been amused—astral travel was always good for freaking out newbie witches. "Pretty much. At some level, I'm not sure it matters. It's still a horrible thing for Sierra to have stuck in her mind."

"The dream's bad." Devin's eyes were darkly intent. "But it told us something really important."

He had the attention of every witch in the room—and Lauren, at his shoulder, was nodding in quiet approval.

Devin looked at his brother. "Can you fetch Moira and Govin? I have something to say." He put an arm around Lauren's shoulder. "*We* have something to say."

~ ~ ~

Lauren sat quietly, waiting for everyone to get settled. Govin was already sitting in the corner, chatting with Jamie. Nell handed Moira a cup of tea and turned around, perching on the arm of a chair. "Okay, you two. We're all here. Talk."

You wanna be the good cop, or the bad cop?

Devin's question startled Lauren. She hadn't realized her mind connections were that open. And then realized they weren't—to anyone except for him. Leftovers from handling Sierra's nightmare. *You start. I'm a better deal closer.*

He put his hands on his knees and surveyed the room. "We've really screwed up, and Sierra's paying the price. She's Amelia's daughter, and therefore, we've assumed she's like Amelia. She's not. Not even a little." He waited a beat. "Sierra Brighton's not reckless, and we have to stop treating her like she is."

Lauren could feel the stark confusion coming from everyone. Except Nat. That figured.

"She's dangerous, Dev. We've seen it." Govin was the most agitated witch in the room. "She's got enough power in those fingers to let loose a disaster."

"Do you really think she's ever going to do that again?" Devin's quiet question hammered into every mind in the room. "Look around your fear, Gov. Heck, it's our fear that's the whole problem here."

He turned to his sister. "You're scared she's going to put Aervyn at risk again. Or that she represents what he might become if we can't keep him hooked into community."

Bull's-eye. Lauren felt Nell's mind quake.

Next, his brother. "You're scared for Aervyn—and more scared that the girl in your wife's belly might be the next Amelia Brighton."

Three for three. That fear resonated even for Nat.

Devin turned to Moira, and didn't say a word.

She met his gaze for a long time, and then looked down at her tea. "I'd be scared that our Sierra has her mother's blood in her veins. The sins of the mother, living on in the child. It's not right, and I'm sorry for it."

"It's okay to be scared." Devin reached for Moira's hand, speaking quietly. "It's not okay to dive-bomb Sierra because of our fear. Our last meeting, we laid out a plan of attack. It's time to stop attacking."

Nell's face was white. "She's still dangerous, Dev."

Lauren leaned forward. Her turn. "No. She's not."

Every head swiveled to look at her, most of them still wildly skeptical.

Govin spoke first, frustration lacing every word. "How big a wave does she need to make to convince you?"

Lauren dug for words—and then decided in this case, a picture was worth thousands of them. Reaching into her memory banks, she found the image of Sierra, staring at the dead bird in Aervyn's hands—and projected it to everyone in the room, complete with the abject, horrified guilt that had been in the girl's mind. Then she hit them with Sierra's dreaming anguish as a magically caused, killing wave chased down her mother.

Man. You fight dirty. Devin winced—and nodded in approval. *They'll see it now.*

You're the only one who's never been at all scared of her, Lauren sent softly. *You've always known.*

Yeah. Which means I screwed up the most. His mental voice was bleak. *I didn't fight hard enough for her.*

Cut yourself a break, Sullivan. It's been less than a week since she arrived. And you're fighting for her now. Let's get the job done.

Together, they faced the room. And waited.

Moira breathed out and sipped her tea, hands shaking. "She's really not Amelia, is she?"

"I never knew her mother." Lauren smiled as Sophie's hands gently settled over Moira's, offering more than one kind of love. "But you've all been worried that, like Amelia, Sierra is going to be hard to teach. Hard to convince."

"You think a dead bird will make that much difference?" Jamie rubbed a hand absently on his wife's shoulder. "We tried to show her groundlines a few days ago, and she didn't seem all that convinced. Even tried to show us what she could do, before Aervyn shut her down."

Lauren blinked. That was news to her.

"Think, bro." Devin leaned forward. "All we had was words. It's like when Mom used to tell us we were going to fall out of the oak tree in the front yard if we kept climbing that high."

Jamie found half a grin. "She wasn't all that persuasive until Matt fell out."

"Exactly," Devin said. "And Matt's not the reckless Sullivan."

Nell snorted. "It only took one fall to convince *you*, Jamie. Dev was a harder sell."

"Which is the whole problem here," said Lauren. Her turn again, and Nell had given her a perfect opening. "You've all been assuming Sierra has a head as hard as Amelia's." She elbowed the guy beside her. "Or Devin's here."

The stress levels in the room settled substantially as everyone laughed at his wounded look. Good. Sometimes humor could drive home a point far better than fear ever would. Lauren paused, waiting for quiet—and hit them with the echoes of Sierra's emotions one more time. "It seems to me that anyone that distraught over one baby bird isn't going to be hard to teach."

~ ~ ~

Oh, how proud these two made her. Moira wrapped her hands around her still-warm mug of tea and watched Devin and Lauren step up and call them all on the carpet.

They were a fierce duo. And they *were* a duo—Moira had seen enough mindconnected tag teams in her lifetime to recognize one in action.

She tried not to grin. It wouldn't help the very important and serious point they were trying to make. Ah, such an excellent team they would be for the upcoming birth. And perhaps beyond. Her fingers ached for her scrying bowl.

Sophie touched her hand lightly. "Behave."

Ah, she wasn't the only one that saw possibilities here. "I am behaving. I haven't selected them a wedding gift yet."

Lauren looked over, eyebrow raised, as tea nearly squirted out Sophie's nose. "Is there something you'd like to share with the class?"

"Nope." Sophie was turning shades of purple. "Sorry. Baby's kicking my ribs."

Which wasn't precisely a lie. The baby had indeed started kicking in reaction to Sophie's mirth.

Moira rode to the rescue before anyone dug deeper into Sophie's thoughts. "So, we have a young girl who might not be so hard to train after all. What happens next, then?"

Jamie shrugged. "We still need to get some work done with her, and soon."

Govin nodded. "Even if she's going to be receptive, the safety layers on weather magics are tricky." He folded his arms. "And I still think she needs to be made aware of the risks in what happened two days ago. Gently. But she needs to know."

"Try coming in the back door with that." Devin, relaxed now, looked nothing like the warrior who'd stormed the room five minutes earlier. "Teach her the right way to work with the excess energies and with a team. She's a smart witch. Let *her* figure out why what we did in that helicopter was risky."

"Aye." Moira winked at him. "Even the most stubborn witches do better working things out for themselves."

Devin just rolled his eyes.

Nell laughed. "I'm pretty sure that was one of Mom's favorite lines."

"She had plenty of practice, dear." If Devin was going to offer himself up as an object lesson, Moira was happy to help. She had one small bit to add to the point he and Lauren had driven home. "Many parents raise a child in their image. Your mama was smart enough, and strong enough, to parent each of you the way you most needed."

She paused a moment, waiting to see which of the smart witches in the room would understand her first.

It didn't surprise her at all when it was Devin. "Sierra was raised reckless. She wasn't born reckless. And we've been confusing the two."

Moira knew when to give credit where credit was due. "Isn't that what you've been trying to tell us all along?"

"Yeah." He nodded slowly. "Yeah. I think it is."

Chapter 13

Lauren looked up from her desk as her office door chimed, not at all surprised to see her best friend. "Hey. You hungry?" She'd been pondering a donut run.

Nat held up a box. "One step ahead of you." She grinned. "Sophie said Sierra's nightmare was pretty rough on you, and you could probably use some extra sugar."

The witch line of duty had been hard on a lot of people recently. "I'm okay. I have a lot more respect for Sierra, though. She's a sweet kid, but I don't think I was really giving her enough credit for how she's held her life together without much help." Lauren met her friend's eyes. "Reminds me of someone else I know."

"There are good people who will love her now."

There were. And none of that explained the determined look in Nat's eyes. Alarm bells went off in Lauren's mind as her visitor sat down in the comfy chair on the other side of the desk. "What's up?"

"You and a certain Sullivan brother." Nat patted the box of donuts. "If you talk willingly, you can have two apple fritters."

It was an excellent bribe. Unnecessary, but appreciated all the same. Lauren sighed. "What do you want to know?"

"He's a good guy. What's scaring you?"

Lauren laughed. "Got any easier questions I can start with?"

"Nope." Nat patted her belly. "I could pop any minute. Or have to pee. I've learned to get right to the point."

Lauren rolled her eyes. "It's hardly a new skill." Nat had always zeroed in fast on the most important things. "I'm not sure he scares me, exactly. I'm just being careful."

"Careful is fine." Nat grinned. "But fast and spontaneous can sometimes be fun too."

That idea shouldn't be firing sparks in her belly. "Just because you had a whirlwind relationship with a witch doesn't mean the rest of us should." Lauren licked apple-fritter heaven off her fingers. "I'm pretty happy with my life the way it is. I don't know that I need a guy in it."

"Need, no. You never have. But it's okay to want one."

Lauren squirmed. Anyone who thought Nat was all soft and nice had never been on the receiving end of one of her inquisitions. "I want, okay? But he's a tornado, Nat. Devin Sullivan doesn't come into your life without turning it upside down. In another lifetime, he'd have been one of those Wild West gunslingers."

"You ride tornados better than you think," said Nat softly. "And Devin isn't the Sullivan brother who created the biggest one in your life."

Well, that was true. Jamie declaring her a witch had been pretty radically disruptive. "Don't I deserve a nice, boring life for a while?"

"I ask myself that a lot these days." Nat laid a hand on her belly. "And then I think about all I'd be missing if I'd chosen simple and safe."

Trust Nat to hold her feet to the fire of honesty. "There's a lot at stake here, including all the people we both love. I need to figure out what I want."

"The people you love will be fine." Nat smiled, eyes twinkling. "It's not a real estate negotiation. You don't have to figure it all out before you explore things a little."

That sounded disturbingly like the little voice in her head. Lauren reached for her second apple fritter. "I don't think Dev's the kind of guy who explores. He dives in head-first and trusts himself to pick up the pieces later."

"Yes." Nat grinned. "Yes, he is."

~ ~ ~

Moira settled into her hot pool with a sigh. The bliss of the warm water on her old joints hadn't dimmed in the six months since the circles had created her wondrous pool.

She heard a matching sigh as Sophie settled in beside her. Pregnant mamas had plenty of aches and pains of their own—and Sophie's day had been a busy one.

She opened her eyes, reaching for the nearby cup of tea. "Something's on your mind, my dear."

"Mmmm." Sophie stretched for her own teacup. "I've been thinking about Sierra."

Moira waited. A nosey old witch knew when to keep quiet.

"She's a convincing actress." Sophie shrugged. "No, that's not quite right. She's not faking it, but she's got depths that are hard to see. It took me an hour to see past the giggly young woman this morning."

"Ah, and what did you see in the second hour, then?"

"I'm not sure, really." Sophie reached over and pulled down a fragrant bloom to sniff, smiling. "It's so lovely that flowers bloom year round this close to the pool."

It was indeed lovely—and Moira knew an attempt at distraction when she saw it. "What are you pondering, dear girl?"

Sophie sighed. "Tell me about Amelia."

That was a wide and painful topic. "Is there something in particular you want to know?"

Sophie nodded slowly. "Tell me why you think she spent so much time away, traveling."

Ah. Tricky waters for a witch who had only very recently come home herself. "There are all kinds of reasons why people separate from their community. You did it to spare Elorie the pain of your presence, which was an act of great love. Marcus did it—well, for complicated reasons."

"To escape."

Moira smiled gently. "That's how it seems, doesn't it? But I often wonder if he stayed away for so long so we couldn't help him heal."

Sophie's eyes were sad. "Because he blames himself for Evan's death."

"Aye." And there was more work to do there yet, but Marcus wasn't the topic of the moment. "And Amelia left to avoid growing up, I think—both as a woman and as a witch."

"She must have grown up some, having a baby."

Moira certainly hoped so. Motherhood brought maturity and wisdom for some, but Amelia had shunned both most of her life. "I wish I knew. On the one hand, Sierra is a lovely girl. On the other..."

"Amelia left her daughter alone in a hotel room in New Orleans and went off and did something foolhardy." The critical tone in Sophie's voice was exceedingly rare.

"It's easy to think that." After seventy years, being honest shouldn't still make you squirm. "But we don't *know* it. Sometimes magic goes terribly wrong, and it's no one's fault. And sometimes parents walk away from their responsibilities." Moira sighed. "But I can't find an explanation that doesn't hurt my heart and make me wonder one more time whether I could have done better by Amelia."

"You're a wonderful trainer. I can't imagine you left anything undone."

"On the training, no." And this was the point she'd been thinking on ever since Devin and Lauren faced them all down in the Witches' Lounge. "But perhaps I focused too much on the witch, and not enough on the girl. I'm not sure she found true acceptance here for who she was, for the adventurer's heart beating inside her."

"If that's true, the fault lies with all of us." Sophie laid her head back against a convenient rock. "But I doubt it. There have been plenty of witchlings through the years with a reckless streak, and I've always had a sneaking suspicion you love them best."

Moira chortled. Love was never that simple, but it was true she had a soft spot for the troublemakers. "How can you not love a pregnant belly singing a wee pirate song?" Sean's latest caper had nearly given Elorie heart failure.

"And that's my point," Sophie said softly, laying her hand on Moira's. "You love, and when the witchling has a restless heart, you love perhaps even a little more."

"It wasn't enough for our Amelia." And that still felt like failure.

Sophie plucked a tired and dying bloom off a nearby stalk and trickled magic into its petals. "Or maybe, like Uncle Marcus, she was just a slow learner, and life didn't give her enough time to come back to us."

Moira felt that thought sink into her soul and find root. Sometimes, the right words really could heal.

Maybe Amelia would have come back.

And with her daughter's arrival, in a very real way, she had.

~ ~ ~

Sierra stopped in the hallway outside Nell's kitchen. It had taken almost the whole day to paint her apartment. And the whole time, she'd watched the triplets.

Ginia had magic. Shay and Mia didn't. They still did lots of the same stuff as their witch sister, and they had really cool jobs helping out with Realm.

And they weren't dangerous.

Magic had always been her favorite toy—and in the last six years of foster care, it had kept her from going crazy. Momma had promised it would always be there for her, something to make her feel special.

But Momma had lied. Magic wasn't a toy, it wasn't simple, and it wasn't something little girls should do just to have fun. It was complicated, and dangerous, and if you screwed up, people died. Or baby birds.

So she'd made a decision. And now she needed to go ask for a job. Because when little girls grew up, they had to pay the bills.

Sierra stepped into the kitchen and clutched at the strap of her bag. "Can I talk to you for a minute?"

Nell turned from the computer parts she had scattered all over the counter. "Sure. Want to give me a hand with this while we talk?"

It looked like the computer had puked its innards. "What are you doing?"

Nell held up a small silver part and laughed. "Trying to figure out where this goes. Aervyn took this machine apart and tried to put it back together, but he left a couple of parts out."

Wow. "Does it run?"

"Nope." Nell seemed awfully cheerful. "But it didn't before he started, either, so no great loss."

"Isn't he kind of little to be doing this stuff?" Sierra realized that probably sounded critical and hurried to explain. "I don't mean it's bad or anything, but it doesn't sound like something most four-year-olds do." Not that she knew a lot of four-year-olds.

"My brothers were always taking stuff apart. Jamie swears it's a boy thing." Nell shrugged and held up the part again. "Maybe he can figure out where it goes."

"Sorry, I guess I'm not much help." And that was probably bad right before you asked for a job.

Nell looked up, suddenly alert—then turned to the fridge, voice very casual. "Want some ice cream?"

Always. "Sure." Sierra took a deep breath. "I have something to ask you."

Nell set two pints down on the table. "Sure. Shoot."

"I need a job."

Nell blinked. "You have a job."

Cripes, she wasn't doing this very well. "I need a different job. I'd really like to keep working for Realm, and I'm a pretty good coder and everything, but I can't help with the WitchNet library anymore."

Nell nodded as if she heard confusing stuff like that every day. "Okay. Why not?"

It felt like half the air was suddenly missing from the room. "Because I have to do magic for that. I'm not going to use power anymore."

Nell took another spoonful of ice cream. "That sounds pretty serious."

"I'm dangerous—everybody says so. And they're obviously right." Sierra looked down at her hands. "So if I'm not a witch, then I can't be dangerous anymore."

"It's not that easy, sweetie. You can't just turn off the power switch."

Yes, she could. "I've done it before. After Momma died, I didn't do any magic for almost a year because it made me so sad."

Nell frowned, eyes full of sorrow. "You're a strong witch. That must have been incredibly hard."

That whole year had been impossibly hard. But if she could survive that, she could do this. It wasn't really something she wanted to talk about anymore. She just wanted to get it done. "So, can I have a job? A non-witch one?"

"Okay." Nell nodded slowly and reached out to squeeze Sierra's hand. "Done."

Sierra breathed out. That had been so much easier than she'd expected. "Thanks."

Nell licked off her spoon. "I'll call a meeting."

Huh? "Why?"

"So you can tell everybody else." Nell shrugged. "It'll be faster than telling them one at a time, don't you think?"

Sierra stared, trying to figure out why her stomach had suddenly tied itself in a Chinese knot.

~ ~ ~

Nell sat down on the end of one of the Witches' Lounge couches, waiting on her second impromptu meeting of the day. After a quick debate, she'd left her kiddos at home. None of them, witches or not, would understand choosing to walk away from your talents. And Sierra didn't need any more little Walkers bruising her heart accidentally.

The grownups would probably handle that perfectly well.

There was one fairly immutable law in the witching world. With great power came great responsibility. And Sierra had great power. There was an abundance of support in learning to use that power, and every attempt made to let a witch grow into her talents slowly—but in the end, the hard truth was that a big piece of Sierra's path had been sketched out the first moment she touched power.

They would not force her. It wasn't the way of witches.

But they could throw their weight hard on one side of the scale. Nell trusted that those in attendance would understand their roles and rise to the occasion, since she hadn't actually had time to tell anyone why she'd paged them all.

She looked over at Sierra, hands in her lap, sitting on the other end of the couch, and felt her heart beat with empathy. But she couldn't let this one slide. Sierra's decision might have sounded like teenager drama—unless you could feel the calm finality in her mind.

Devin and Jamie popped into the room. "Hey, sis."

What's up? Jamie slouched down into a chair, totally nonchalant. His mind was anything but.

Give the rest of the crew a couple of minutes. Let's just say Devin and Lauren were right on the money.

He raised an eyebrow, but said nothing.

Moments later, Sophie, Moira, Lauren, and Govin had all arrived and grabbed seats. Nell listened to the murmur of casual conversation, noticing with a quiet twinge of amusement that Devin couldn't keep his eyes off Lauren. Something was going on there, and when she had a spare moment, she intended to find out exactly what.

Right now, she needed Lauren for something else. *Hey—can you patch us all into Sierra's outer mind? Gently? I don't want to invade her privacy, but I don't want to bruise her any more than necessary, either.* Devin's earlier speech was still riding heavy on her mind.

I thought we were trying to ratchet down the intensity for a while?

Nell rolled her eyes. *No one gave Sierra that memo.*

Lauren shook her head, amused, and a few seconds later, Nell felt the light thunk of an incoming mindlink. Reaching for a plate of cookies, she opened the meeting. "Hey, all. Sierra had something she wanted to share, and I thought it would be faster to get us all together."

Ball in Sierra's court. Nell sat back and watched her squirm. It took every ounce of parenting instinct she had not to offer comfort.

Mindlink gave them all two seconds of warning that Sierra was going to come out of the gate fast and defiant. "I'm not a witch anymore. I'm not going to do magic. I asked Nell for a different job at Realm."

Nell gave her serious props for looking a lot calmer than she felt. And one thing needed to be laid to rest right away. "The job is yours. No matter what."

Jamie, eyeing his sister, was rapidly catching up. "You're a good coder." He grinned. "The more people like you I have around, the less work I have to do."

Sierra cracked a smile, and they could all feel her tension ease a little. Nell suspected the relief would be short-lived, but at least the girl should be nervous for the right reasons. Worrying about a way to pay her rent wasn't one of them.

Moira leaned forward. "To do magic or not is your choice, sweet girl. But you will always be a witch. The ability to touch power will always flow in your veins, and perhaps in your children as well."

Nell hid her grin as Sierra's mind radiated blank confusion at the mention of children. Clearly not on her agenda yet. "It might be there, but I don't have to use it."

She's really serious about this. Jamie's mindvoice was a lot more awake than his cookie-eating, lounge-lizard routine suggested.

Yup.

Lauren passed over the cookies. "Why?"

Now Sierra's mind sparked. Anger—she was feeling cornered. "I'm dangerous." She looked around the room. "You all tried to show me that, but I didn't listen. This time a bird died. Next time it could be a person."

Her eyes were bleak—and every heart in the room ached for her.

Nell sat and waited. Moira and Lauren were just the opening skirmish. She kept her eyes on Dev and Govin. Her bets were on the two of them as the final one-two tag team—Govin to remind Sierra of the responsibility that came with her power, Devin to remind her of the possibilities for joy.

It didn't surprise her that Devin moved first. He got up and sat on the coffee table in front of Sierra. "You're right. You are dangerous."

Pain sliced through the girl's heart. What the hell was Dev up to? He was supposed to be reminding her of the joy of magic.

No one gave him the script either, sent Jamie dryly.

Devin leaned forward and took Sierra's hands. "But you're also an incredibly capable, powerful witch. One who can make a difference in this world. I watch my brother save lives every day with his healing magic. You have that kind of power in you. What if the next wave isn't one you made? And what if it's not just a baby bird in the path of the storm? Will you sit and do nothing?"

Holy shit. Nell blinked, hard. It was extremely rare to see Devin this intense. Wasn't he the one who'd told them all they needed to be gentler with the poor girl?

Sierra just stared, the calm finality in her mind shattered in an instant. "I have to. I'm not safe." She closed her eyes, tears trickling out. "Maybe Momma didn't have time to teach me all the lessons."

Devin wiped her cheeks with his thumbs and waited until she opened her eyes. His voice was hardly above a whisper, but it drilled into every person there. "We can teach you. You don't have to stay dangerous, sweetheart. And you don't have to give up magic, either."

Nobody breathed. He'd made the offer—and he'd made it with the kind of intensity no one else would have dared. Every heart in the room pleaded for her to take it.

Her anguished uncertainty was heartbreaking.

Then Govin stepped in, and Nell got her second serious shock of the hour. He sat down beside Sierra on the couch. "And you can teach us." He grinned. "I know about a hundred witches who would like to take a ride in a funnel."

Sierra's mouth dropped open. "A funnel?"

"Sure." He reached casually for a cookie, handing her half. "Magic isn't serious all the time. Sometimes it needs to be fun, too."

"Fun?"

Nell blinked along with Sierra. Govin was one of the best people she knew—but fun wasn't usually a big part of his vocabulary.

He turned to face Sierra, eyes bright. "That feeling? When you ride on a funnel and joy shoots through your heart? I've been thinking about that a lot today."

She nodded, dazed.

"Every witch needs that feeling." His grin lit up half of Realm. "Some of us more than others." He held out a hand. "We can learn from each other."

It was a breathtaking offer, one that wrenched at Nell's heart. Devin had offered hope. Govin offered a piece of his soul.

Sierra sat, motionless, staring at his outstretched hand. And then somewhere in her heart, a flame rekindled. The light in her eyes made the gleam in Govin's look like a dim candle. "I'd like that."

Nell let out her breath. *Now* the crisis was over. At least for the time being.

And she was pretty proud of her brother and her old roommate. Not bad work for a troublemaker and a mathematician. Witch Central might have needed a good swift kick to get moving in the right direction, but Sierra was in good hands now.

~ ~ ~

Jamie slid into the neighborhood bar and grinned. Total guy hangout. Just what he needed after a day of teenager drama and buying totally girly fabric to deface The Monster. His poor couch might never forgive him for its new, decidedly turquoise cover.

However, he trusted The Monster to do its job and remind one lost witch that she had a home now—a place of comfort and love, good food, sloth, and plenty of company whenever you wanted it.

Right now, he was in search of some of that himself. Waving at the bartender, he headed back to the pool tables, trusting that someone else had already taken care of the food-and-beer part of the evening. When he spied TJ's huge head, he was sure of it. The man never took more than five minutes to surround himself with food—or cute girls sure they could cure his bad-boy biker ways.

The girls always seemed to vanish when they found out he was a mathematician.

Dev waved a pool cue, and Govin materialized out of some dark corner. Excellent. Game on. Jamie snagged a chicken wing and a beer, and plopped onto a stool. "We playing partners, or two at a time?"

"Partners." Devin snickered. "I haven't been away that long." He waved his pool cue at TJ. "Nobody in their right mind wants to play this dude one-on-one."

TJ crunched a nacho. "You guys cheating?"

"Hell, yeah," said Jamie. "Anybody ever beat you without using magic?"

"Nope." TJ stood up. "I'll take the world traveler—his magic sucks for pool. You two can try that superheated-air thing again." He smirked. "It's not gonna work this time, either."

Jamie rolled his eyes at Govin. "You're a math geek too—how come we still always lose?"

Govin chuckled and racked the balls. "That, my friend, is a question for the ages."

Which was geek-speak for "who the hell knows."

Jamie set up to break. If you let TJ have that honor, he cleared the table before anybody else got to play. He lined up his cue and focused on the purple ball, weaving a quick air-current spell. Pool balls were notoriously difficult to steer, but he'd been practicing. Or at least *he* called it practice—Nell called it corrupting a four-year-old.

"You gonna be able to do this after that baby girl of yours shows up?" Devin chomped casually on a spicy wing.

Jamie growled. Devin's distraction tactics were notorious. And effective. Dammit. He backed away from the table and glared at his brother. "That depends on whether she gets my version of the Sullivan genes, or yours."

Dev grinned. "Could get Matt's instead."

Jamie snorted. No way his baby girl was going to be the careful, cautious variety of Sullivan. That much he could already tell.

TJ frowned. "Aren't you guys identical triplets?"

Jamie leaned back over the pool table. "That's what they tell us. But you've met Matt. Do you really think we've all got the same genes?"

TJ watched as the purple ball ran for the side pocket—and missed just left. "Nope. Matt's way better at geometry than the two of you." He shrugged. "Maybe he got grabbed by aliens. Smart aliens."

"Must have been." Govin grinned, long used to TJ's wacky theories of alien abduction, and handed Dev a pool cue. "You're up."

Jamie waited. His brother was the weak link in TJ's march to pool supremacy. He monitored Dev's mind, looking for that moment when his brother's brain fired the "go" signal to his hands, and pounced. *So, what's up with you and Lauren?*

The ball Dev had been aiming at nearly landed in TJ's nachos. "Out of my head, bro." His scowl brought back some very good memories.

Jamie grinned. "Fine. What's up with you and Lauren?"

Govin's eyebrows winged up. "Nat's friend?"

Nat's best friend in all the world, which meant he had a message to deliver. He looked at Dev. "Don't mess with her, or my wife will make your life living hell." That was a loose translation of Nat's message. Hers had too many words.

"Women." TJ munched another nacho. "Way more trouble than they're worth."

Jamie wasn't dumb enough to try to defend the institution of marriage to three confirmed bachelors. Or maybe two. Because

Devin's mind was suddenly seriously queasy. Damn. Nat was right again.

Govin looked thoughtful. "You'll make lovely babies together."

Devin's hot'n'spicy wing nearly came out his nose.

TJ patted him on the back, hard enough to send the nachos flying. "Don't let them spook you, man. They're just trying to get you off your game."

Jamie grinned. Mission accomplished. Now, time to see if they could rock the big man. "Sierra's coming to your office tomorrow. Can you chill with her for an hour or so? Govin and I will swing by and grab Aervyn and the first batch of whatever Nell's cooking, so we won't make it there in time to meet her."

TJ turned a little pale. "You want me to talk to a teenage girl? For an hour?"

Devin's belly laugh rang through the entire bar. "Focus, dude. They're just trying to get you off your game."

TJ stared mournfully at the last wing. "It might have worked."

Chapter 14

Sierra turned off the road at the address Govin had given her, grateful for the re-loan of Jamie's moped. The house was in the middle of nowhere, or at least not on any major bus routes. Ten minutes out of town, and then a driveway winding between two rocky hills. On the upside, it was heading right toward the ocean, and that was a pretty nice job benefit.

Her view suddenly widened, and she stopped abruptly, yanking off her helmet. The salty air wasn't gentle here—it swirled up the cliffs and blasted into her face. She reached out her hands in welcome, letting go a trickle of magic to play with the winter wind, glad she still had magic to play with.

It wasn't the warm teasing of Hawaii or the mist-shrouded gales of Oregon. But it was *her* wind, and she was finally alone with it. She teased it a bit, trying to get a feel. Not the thundering power of Ocean's Reach, either—just a strong blow with some tricky edges. She grabbed one of those edges and threaded the needle, weaving it back through the middle—and laughed as wind buffeted her from both sides.

"Yo. Sierra." She spun around as a deep voice yelled from the doorway of a farmhouse. "Quit messing with my wind and come on in."

She rolled the scooter up to the house, parked, and tucked away her helmet, never taking her eyes off the hulking guy waiting for her. She'd never gotten a really good look at him in the chopper—she'd spent the whole time staring at Devin's forehead and trying desperately not to puke. Nell had told her Govin's partner was really smart at math and really messy. She'd forgotten to mention he was huge and looked like a biker.

He waved her inside. "C'mon in. I'm still having breakfast. You want Doritos or a bagel?"

Okay, even she drew the line at Doritos for breakfast. "It's okay. I ate already." Nell made seriously awesome waffles, and there was always enough for three helpings if you wanted. Her belly hadn't had that awful gnawing feeling once since she'd arrived.

Mountain man just grunted and led her back to a room with papers and dirty dishes everywhere—and a bad-ass wall of huge computer monitors. She beelined for the monitors. "What are these for?" One of the screens had like fifteen flashing warnings.

"Monitoring weather. That one's tracking really local air currents, in case we need to put the chopper in the air. You set off every alarm I have—what were you doing out there?" He held out a hand. "I'm TJ, by the way. Not much time for introductions on that wild chopper ride."

"I'm Sierra." She blushed. "But I guess you know that already."

"Yeah. Govin called. He's running a little late. Said to tell you he's bringing Devin out in about half an hour and you're going to do pond magic."

She blinked. "What's that?"

TJ shrugged and snagged a Dorito. "No idea—I'm not a witch." He nodded his head toward the monitors. "Wanna see how my toys work?"

She was already staring at the monitor with all the warnings, trying to figure out what it meant.

TJ sat down and clicked a few keys, and all the flashing lights disappeared. "This shows air currents in a one-mile radius in 3D. Line thickness shows speed, and color shows temperature."

"So all the lines are blue because it's winter?" She followed the thickest blue swirl for a minute. "And the air's faster up high—that's weird. Does it always do that here?"

He looked at her in surprise. "You've worked with weather models before?"

"Nuh, uh." High school wasn't nearly this cool. "And the air's getting warmer where it blows over the ocean. How come it's all tangly over here, though?"

He grinned. "This isn't live. It's playing back the last five minutes. That's you out there, doing whatever you were doing."

She watched in total fascination as the tangled lines spun and then threaded the needle. "That is *so* cool."

The rest of the big bank of monitors suddenly shifted and showed the same kind of air lines—but laid over a global map. "This is the same basic thing, but bigger." TJ hit a few more keys. "And we can layer in cloud cover, temperature, precipitation…"

Her brain was ready to explode. "Can you go back to just the air stuff?"

"Sure." He clicked a few times, then crunched on another chip. "See anything interesting?"

She was looking, following the air currents in places she knew best. "What's going on here, beside Maui?" It was over the whale winter nesting grounds—not a good place for trouble to be brewing. Swimming with the baby whales was one of her favorite memories ever.

"Small storm depression. See where the little, fast, warm-air current is smacking into the bigger, slower, cold one?" TJ crunched. "Sometimes it works itself out, sometimes you get storms. I've sent a big-waves alert to the surfers on that shore. They're pretty good about keeping people off the beaches when it's not safe."

Sierra stared at the map a minute longer. "There's warmer water south of Maui. If we pulled some of that up, it would warm up the cold air and stop the storm, I think." So the surfers and the baby whales would all be safe.

"Might." TJ nodded, contemplating. "If we had that kind of reach, it's the kind of thing we would try."

Not a problem. This she could do. TJ thought it would be okay, and they all trusted him, so she could too. "I need to be outside to do it." Sierra got up, heading for the door.

"Wait." He grabbed her arm. "Are you serious? You can move the water from here?"

"Sure." And she needed to do it soon, before the storm picked up speed.

"No, wait." Mountain man wasn't letting her go. "Tell me exactly what you'd do. We need to model it, see if it would cause problems anywhere else."

Sierra blinked. "I'm just going to move a little water. I thought you said it would be okay."

"From there, sure—but if you do it from here, you'll be messing with a lot of currents between here and there."

Well, yeah. She couldn't just teleport to Hawaii. "I'll be really careful." She'd make darned sure no waves headed for any more baby birds, for starters.

TJ shook his head. "Show me which currents you'd tug on from here. Can you see them on the map, or show me outside?"

She closed her eyes a minute, visualizing, and tried to overlay that on the map. "Here, this one. It's not the straightest, but it's the easiest to pull from here."

He began madly banging on his keyboard, and half a minute later, the lines on the screens began to move. "I've asked the model to project what would happen if you tugged hard enough from here to fix the problem off Maui."

Okay, he was the coolest geek ever. Sierra watched the lines on the screen as they morphed and changed, and grinned as the storm brewing offshore in Hawaii dissipated. "It'll work, see?"

TJ didn't take his eyes off the screen. "Keep watching. If I've learned one thing about weather, it's that nothing is simple. No way you move the energies like that for thousands of miles, and nothing else happens."

Magic was so freaking complicated all of a sudden. Sierra's heart squeezed, thinking of her baby whales. She kept watching the screens, though. Seeing all those lines move was kind of mesmerizing. Suddenly TJ leaned forward and froze the screen. "There. Off New Zealand. See that disturbance? Keep your eyes on that."

It was a tiny red dot. And as Sierra watched, it mutated into a big, ugly, green-and-red mess. "What's that?"

"Class-four tropical storm. Almost hurricane status."

Get out. "All that from fixing a little storm in Hawaii?" No way.

"Ninety-two percent likelihood. That's pretty high. Might be a little bigger, might be a little smaller, but we'd probably make a lot of people in New Zealand pretty wet. Maybe some big waves, too."

She'd never been to New Zealand. Momma said it was mostly sheep. "This is just a model, right? Maybe something messed up."

"Maybe." TJ shrugged. "But probably not. I'm pretty good at this stuff."

She tried to wrap her head around messing up the worldwide weather just to keep the baby whales happier. It didn't seem right to do that—but it didn't seem right to just forget about them, either.

"Maybe there's a different way to do this."

"Maybe. From here, probably not, at least with your magic. Govin can use fire, and that's sometimes easier when we need to reach long distances." He leaned back from his computer. "But in this case, it's probably going to be just as effective to leave Mother Nature alone and put out alerts to the surfers."

"If it were a bigger storm, we'd want to do something, right?" She frowned, not quite ready to let the storm toss her baby whales around. "I could fix it more quietly if I were closer." And take a swim with the whales, too.

"Yup." TJ threw the Doritos bag at the garbage can and missed. "That's why we're trying to get things all sorted out for WitchNet. Jamie says they should be able to shuttle people through Realm—dump you out in Maui, or wherever. Or send the right spell to someone who's already there."

Okay, maybe Jamie was the coolest geek ever. "Is that what I'm going to get to do?" That would be pretty much the world's best job, zapping in and out of Realm, being a weather superhero.

"Maybe." He retrieved the Doritos bag and tried tossing it again. "Gotta solve the logistics and safety problems first."

She frowned. "What's that mean?"

TJ hit a few keys. "Here's what could happen if five witches each did something along the lines of what you just did, without realizing what anyone else was doing."

She watched as five spots on the map started flashing. Lines spread out from each, strange little ripples that traveled, and touched other lines, and sometimes met. She frowned as yellow alerts started popping up all over the world. "What are those?"

"Weather anomalies. Bad stuff the model wasn't expecting." He started pointing. "Storms here and here. Some flooding in low-lying areas, here. Big waves here and here. Those ones are forty-footers."

A new alert popped up in the bottom center screen. "What's the orange one?"

"Twenty-foot waves hitting coastal India."

That was big, but she'd seen waves that big in Hawaii more than once. "So why is it bright orange, and the other waves were only yellow?"

TJ zoomed in on the map. "Lots of villages in low-lying areas in that region, and normally very little wave action. A couple of twenty-foot waves would cause a lot of damage down there."

Sierra squinted as the alert started flashing. *Estimated death toll: 11,312.* Oh, God. "The waves would kill people? And you try to guess how many?" She stared at him in horror. What an awful job.

He nodded slowly. "It helps us figure out where we can help most. Save the most lives."

"What if you can't help enough? What if you can't fix it?"

He didn't look like a Dorito-eating biker anymore. "Then we have really bad dreams."

~ ~ ~

Govin sat on the small dock by his weather pond and looked over at his two companions. They both made him nervous, and for some of the same reasons.

They already knew Sierra had enough power to wreak havoc—and very little understanding of the potential consequences of her actions. Devin wasn't nearly such a loose cannon, thanks to a lifetime of training, but he was reckless by birth.

They were magical risk-takers. And he was anything but.

"Thinking about the last time I was here?" Devin grinned. "I promise to be better behaved."

Govin groaned. No, he'd actually managed to forget about the hailstorm they'd made, the one that had dented the brand-new paint job on TJ's chopper. "I put up a much tighter training circle today. Feel free to help reinforce it."

Devin waved his hand negligently in a circle. "Done." He looked over at Sierra, who seemed really subdued this morning. "You might do the same—neither of us have much air power, so you're the best witch to be containing your magic."

She looked totally blank. "Sorry—what's a training circle? Is it like a groundline?"

Govin felt the knot in his gut tightening. "It's a way of containing magic while you're trying new skills. A trainer normally sets one for beginner witches, or anyone trying a new spell." He grasped at wisps of hope. "Maybe your mom used to set one for you. It's definitely something you should know how to do for yourself."

Sierra squinted and reached out with a trickle of power, clearly following the lines already blending into the training circle spell. Moments later, Govin felt the weight of her power added to the existing reinforcements.

He breathed a sigh of relief. "That was quick—you must have seen something similar before."

She shook her head. "No, not that I remember."

Devin's eyebrows shot up. "You worked out a spell you don't know that quickly?"

"Sure." She nodded, all unconcerned teenager. "That's how Momma always taught me. She'd do something, and then I'd trace it. It's how Aervyn learns spells, too—I felt him trace my funnel at Ocean's Reach."

Govin blinked. Not very many witches casually put themselves in the same sentence with Aervyn.

Devin nodded slowly. "That would make sense—explain how he picks up spells so quickly."

Sierra frowned. "How else would you learn a new spell?"

Hard work, practice, and lots of mistakes. Govin chuckled ruefully. He should be glad his new student was a quick learner. "Let's put your tracing talent to good use then, shall we?" Freaking out that she'd done magic for eighteen years without training circles or groundlines could wait until later. For now, he had a witch to train. The faster they started, the safer she'd be by dinnertime.

He pointed to the pond, calling power as he did so. "This pond is like a mini-world. We make small-scale magics here and watch how their effects travel outward." Working carefully, he created a very small funnel, using a wisp of fire power to heat a curling stream of air.

Sierra sucked in her breath. "That is so cool—how'd you do that? Fire magic, right?"

"Govin's the master of baby magics." Devin grinned to take the sting out of his words.

"If you can't control a spell when it's small, you have no business making a big one." Govin fired off the usual retort, and then winced as he realized Sierra didn't know the thirty years of history behind their bantering. "I use micro-versions of weather magic to practice."

She nodded solemnly. "Do it again, please."

Govin complied, moving a little more slowly this time.

"Ah." Her eyes brightened. "I get it. You're using fire magic to heat the air instead of water. That's a lot faster, but I don't think I have enough fire power to do that for a full-sized funnel."

He shrugged. "And I don't have water power at all. We use what we have."

She cocked her head. "So you're a weather witch with fire as your strongest talent?"

"Yup. He's a weirdo." Devin tossed a pebble into the pond. "He was born with a brain for weather, so he decided to be the only fire-powered weather witch in the universe."

Govin snorted. "Says the guy who spends his life trying to do fire magic with water power." He grinned, very glad to have his old friend back in town. Even if he was really annoying.

Sierra just sat watching the two of them, yearning written all over her face. It suddenly struck Govin how insanely lonely the last six years must have been for her. He was an only child—but with the Sullivan brothers as friends, no guy would ever be lonely unless he wanted to be.

Sympathy stirring, he looked at Devin, hoping his friend's very occasional mindreading was online. And then realized he was way behind. Devin wasn't here to support Sierra's training. He was here because she needed a friend. Trust a Sullivan to figure that out first—they'd always been the family adopting stray frogs, puppy dogs, and witches.

Devin winked. "Analysis complete, dude?"

Govin nodded ruefully. Sometimes a big brain didn't work nearly as fast as good instincts. "Ready to make some weather, guys?"

Sierra straightened and swirled her fingers, suddenly all sporting two-inch hurricane funnels.

Govin gaped and closed his eyes to see her energy flows. Holy hell. She'd split air power ten ways—and then used water to swirl the left-hand funnels, and fire for the right-hand ones. Twenty-five years of practice, and he was darned sure he couldn't do five at once. Okay. Maybe putting herself in the same sentence as superboy hadn't been totally crazy.

He rapidly revised his plans for the morning's lesson, pulled out a stopwatch, and selected one of his more advanced drills.

"Can you lay those out on the pond in a way that none of them will amplify for at least sixty seconds?" Amplification happened when two funnel effects ran into each other.

Sierra squinted out at the pond. "Can I do stuff to the pond water too?"

Seriously? It had taken him a month to figure out that was the only way to solve this little problem. "Yeah. But only at the beginning. Whatever you set in motion needs to run free once the clock starts ticking."

He watched as she carefully laid out her funnels on the pond's surface, water currents eddying and ripple effects heading out to the rest of the pond. The first three, she impressed him with her understanding of spatial relationships. The next three, she astonished him with her easy skill weaving water currents.

She didn't step wrong until funnel number eight. As soon as she let that one go, it was clear to Govin that disruption was coming. Funnel eight sat spinning quietly—but one of its side ripples began to create havoc over on the left edge of the pond.

And Sierra noticed nothing. Her eyes were fixed on funnel nine's pretty dance—she'd just set that one down. She didn't notice until the combined entity of funnels two and five bounced off the edge of the pond and ricocheted back through the center. At that point, a blind man wouldn't have missed the chaos.

Her face fell.

Devin waved his hand to calm the energy flows, and then elbowed Sierra gently. "Congrats. I don't think I've ever managed to create two-foot waves in a duck pond."

She frowned, clearly not ready to let go of failure. "I was really close. What went wrong?"

Govin debated how to approach his answer. She'd laid down seven funnels before disaster hit. That was two more than he'd ever managed. Which made her later blindness all the scarier.

And hopefully more correctable. She's not reckless. Not reckless. He tried to remember Devin's words as he faced a witch who still scared him silly. "You've got the mind of a mathematician. Your initial layout was brilliant."

She scowled at the pond. "I still had one more to add. I'm not sure where that one was going."

He was pretty sure TJ and all his models couldn't have solved that one either. "That's part of the work we do—needing to judge when we can't safely do any more."

Her eyes opened wide. "You lay out funnels on the ocean?"

He'd forgotten how literal teenagers could be. "No. But we look at existing weather patterns and try to intervene in ways that solve problems without creating more. Sometimes the ocean's pretty clear, and it's like laying down your first couple of funnels. Sometimes the weather's pretty gnarly, and getting even one small intervention in place is impossible."

She nodded slowly. "So sometimes eight funnels fit. But not nine."

"No." Damn, she really hadn't been watching. "It was your funnel eight that caused the problem. Sent a left-turn swirl toward funnel five that was a little too strong."

"Eight?" She scowled, clearly not getting it.

"Yup." This much he was sure of. "Five ran into two and caused the big funnel to form."

He didn't really expect her to understand. She'd spent her whole life doing magic without a care for the consequences.

She looked out at the pond, mirror calm now. "And if I screw up like that with a big spell, people die."

Govin looked at Devin in concern. Damn, he'd been trying really hard not to whack her over the head with that. And then he knew what must have happened. TJ's models had been all over the wall monitors when they'd arrived.

Sierra held up her hands, ten more funnels spinning. "I want to try it again. The same thing first, so I can see what went wrong." She stared out at the water, eyes fierce. "Then I'm going to fix it."

Chapter 15

Sophie plunked down on The Monster between Nat and Moira. "This looks like the closest thing to an island of sanity in this place."

Moira chuckled and handed over a cup of tea. "We old people and pregnant ladies occasionally need a break. Besides, the decorating is coming along very well."

Nat looked over at Mia, atop a ladder with a hammer in her hand. She was hanging artwork, with Lauren behind her holding frames and offering input. "I think Jamie was a little offended when Mia threw him out so she could use his tools."

Sophie grinned. Somehow decorating Sierra's apartment had turned into an all-girl affair. "He does have cool tools." She'd had to veto the table saw and bit router—they were decorating a one-bedroom apartment, not building it from scratch.

Sipping her tea, she looked around. They'd done a nice job. The walls had a lovely watery feel and gave the entire main living space a mellow vibe. Which was good, because the kitchen was Roaring Raspberry, the bedroom was Laughing Lavender, and the bathroom was Tahiti Tangerine. Totally wild, as were various bits of furniture pilfered from all over Witch Central. "Do you think Sierra's brain will hurt when she walks into that bathroom in the morning?"

Nell walked over, bearing grapes and cheese. "Dunno, but my girls are currently lobbying to be let loose on our house with paintbrushes, so I suspect I'm about to find out."

"Sorry." Sophie winced in sympathy, trying not to look too amused. "They've done a great job here."

Nell shrugged. "It's paint. If it's really awful, I'll teach Aervyn a color transmutation spell."

Nat blinked. "You can do that?"

"It's not a difficult spell." Moira smiled. "But only one of our three lead decorators here is actually a witch, so this way, they all got to make a real contribution to Sierra's new home."

Nat grinned. "Well then, can I either borrow the girls, or a witch who can keep a secret?" She lowered her voice to a loud whisper. "Jamie thinks he painted the nursery orange, but it's salmon pink, I swear."

Nell snickered. "I'll come over tomorrow. There should be a law against salmon pink."

Any more opinions on Jamie's painting skills were interrupted by Lauren. "What do you think? Do they look good from over there?"

Sophie turned a little to see the display of pictures Lauren and Mia had just finished hanging. Jennie had dug up some negatives from an old trip to Hawaii, and the wall sang with color. "Wow. I so know where I want to go next time I get on a plane. Those are awesome pictures." Not surprising, given a glorious location and the talents of a world-famous photographer.

"I think we're about finished too." Caro stood up from an easy chair in the corner and stretched. She and Ginia had been piecing together the welcoming blanket—a huge, multicolored throw for Sierra's bed, made up of almost a hundred hand-knit squares contributed by the witching community. The colors clashed, knitting skills seriously varied, and some witches clearly had only a vague idea of how big twelve inches was. It should have been an eyesore. It was gorgeous.

Moira smiled. "It's absolutely lovely. She'll go to sleep at night cuddled under magic and love."

Sophie's eyes misted, and she patted her belly. Normally welcoming blankets were made for babies—she'd sent her square for Nat's little girl, and there was surely one underway for her Seedling, as well. But they hadn't known about Sierra when she was born. It was good to know that no child was ever too old for a proper welcome.

Caro folded the blanket neatly. "Nothing holds a candle to that throw you made, Moira. I've never seen anything knit that so resembled water."

"It was my Sophie who dyed the yarn for that one."

Sophie grinned. Aunt Moira had been an exacting taskmaster—they'd tried four batches before she'd been satisfied with the result.

"Really, now." Caro's eyes gleamed. "And how might I go about getting some of that for my yarn store?"

Sophie laughed. "I'll need an apprentice." She was no dummy—every water witch on the continent was going to want some of that yarn. It was totally luscious.

Nell laughed as hands shot in the air. "How about three?"

Sophie had no idea when the triplets slept. They seemed to be involved in everything these days.

"Does it require magic?" Nat touched the throw meditatively.

Sophie's eyebrows shot up. Nat wasn't a knitter. Yarn shouldn't call to her like that—unless she was nesting. And when someone was nine months pregnant, nesting only meant one thing. She reached out for Nat's hand—and met Moira's knowing eyes.

Carefully, she dropped into healing scan, lightly following the energy strands linking mom to babe. The baby was fine, cocooned in the safety of a warm, dark womb and a room full of happiness.

Everything okay? She heard Lauren's mental question, lightly shaded with concern.

Then she remembered Lauren had shields in place for the baby. Perhaps those were affecting her readings. "Can you drop the baby's barriers for a minute? I want to have a quick listen."

"I can, but in this crowd, it might give her a headache." Lauren grimaced. "I still can't figure out how to teach her to barrier for herself. Every time we try, she just gets mad."

Moira chuckled. "Our little fire witch is throwing tantrums already, is she?"

Nell snorted. "No surprise—she's got a full set of Sullivan genes." She winked at Nat. "Good thing you really love my brother. If there's justice in the world, any child of his is going to be a handful."

Sophie leaned in as everyone laughed, still feeling a need to scan the baby.

Nat grinned. "Didn't you just check ten minutes ago?"

Normally Sophie tried to avoid making those in her care feel like watched pots, but something was niggling at her. She nodded at Lauren—she wanted those barriers down.

And when they came down, she knew why. This babe was preparing for arrival. She squeezed Nat's hand gently. "It won't be more than a few days now. She's ready."

~ ~ ~

Devin set down the tray loaded with fast food. "Two burgers enough for you, or do you want more?"

Sierra grinned. "I'll let you know."

Fair enough. Witches were always hungry, and she'd blown a lot of magical calories on Govin's pond. "You were pretty impressive out there today."

She grabbed a fry and scowled. "I didn't ever figure out how to get ten funnels down."

"Govin says it can't be done."

She shrugged. "Math is cool and all, but it can't figure out everything."

Neither could magic. "Govin and TJ are pretty genius with that stuff." He held up his hands. "Not saying they can't be wrong, but not every problem has a solution." And cripes, that made him sound really old.

"What if it was real, and people were in trouble?" Her eyes were dark and serious. "Just because the computer can't find a way doesn't mean there isn't one. We'd try to help."

Man. How had they turned their witch from reckless to carrying the weight of the world in less than a week? "Sure. But *try* is the important part. Weather can be big and mean, and magic can't always fix it." Devin had a fair amount of experience throwing magic at the impossible. He could see that same need in Sierra, and it worried him. "Govin and TJ save a lot of lives with the work they do."

"But not all of them."

"No." And it took a special person to handle that kind of work on a daily basis.

She suddenly looked young and very sad. "It's all gotten so complicated."

"Weather's always been complicated." He tried to tread carefully. "You've got a lot of talent, but even a basic weather spell is pretty tricky."

She looked down, toying with her fries, but he could hear the tears in her voice. "I always thought spells were so much fun. Momma and I used to do so much magic together. It was like getting to play all day long."

"Not feeling like a game anymore, huh?" For some witches, it could be. But not one with Sierra's power. At least, not all the time. And it sucked to be one of the people pushing that truth on the poor kid.

She shook her head slowly. "No. Rules, and training circles, and problems that if we can't solve them, people might die."

All true—but not the whole truth. If magic were nothing but a weight to carry, a lot more witches would have been kicking around the world seeking freedom with Amelia. There was something seriously wrong when Witch Central didn't seem like *any* fun. Devin decided someone needed to be in charge of fixing that. "Wanna ride a broomstick?"

Her giggles seemed to escape by accident. "What?"

"Eat." He levitated her burger. "Aervyn's been trying to figure out how to fly on a broomstick like Harry Potter. We're going back to Ocean's Reach in a couple of days for another lesson." He grinned. "You have to wear a cape and a pointy hat. Aervyn's rules."

She shook her head, more giggles spilling out. "I don't have a cape."

"That can be fixed." He took a bite of his burger. "I think Mia has a pink princess one you could borrow."

She held out a French fry like a sword. "Over my dead body."

He considered for a moment. "Finish your food. Then we'll go shopping."

More giggles. "For a cape?"

"Yup." It would solve two problems. One, Berkeley thrift stores were like a trip to an alien world—Sierra couldn't help but have fun. And two, it would keep them busy for another hour. If he delivered Sierra to her new apartment before 7 p.m., the decorating squad would be very displeased.

A RECKLESS WITCH

~ ~ ~

"You don't have to walk me up." Sierra grinned at Devin. "I know the way."

"I do so. Honorary-big-brother handbook, section 23.2."

She still wasn't entirely clear how she'd acquired a big brother. But she'd never forget where. They'd been in the third thrift store of the evening, trying to complete the set of Ugliest Dishes in the World. He insisted she'd need them to feed him properly. Apparently little sisters cooked for their big brothers. Also in the handbook.

Devin set several bags down in front of her door with an exaggerated sigh. "Girls always buy too much stuff."

"Ha. You're the one who picked the bowls with the cute painted pink pigs." She was slowly getting the hang of this little sister gig.

"Those are not cute pigs. They're totally ugly. I so won the contest."

"Did not. The ones with the guy in the kilt were way uglier."

His eyes lit with victory. "Yeah, but you didn't actually buy those."

Well, that was true.

He elbowed her. "You're not supposed to let me get the last word in. Little-sister handbook, section 17.8."

She needed to have a serious chat with Nell about this sister stuff. Sierra dug in her bag for her new set of keys, a bit wistful the night was over. It was nice to have her own place. It was just kind of... empty. Literally—she had three cups and one folding chair. Shrugging off the tugs of sadness, she picked up one of the bags. At least she had dishes now. And a Superman cape.

Devin pushed the door open, and she nudged her way inside. A strange noise caught her attention—and then sound exploded from the walls. "SURPRISE!!!"

Sierra tried to get her racing heart under control, astonished she was still clutching the bag of dishes.

"Oops. We forgot to turn on the lights." Ginia's voice came out of the dark, followed by some thunking and cursing and a lot of giggling. Then light flooded the room.

Wow. Just. Wow.

There were people everywhere. And stuff. Couches, and pictures, and pretty lights. It looked like a room out of a magazine. Ginia bounced over, her sisters half a step behind. "Do you like it?" She looked up in concern at Sierra's face. "If you don't, we can change it—honest."

Sierra felt the happiness in the room dim—and belatedly realized she was the cause. She tried to find her words. "For me? You did this for me?" She cuddled her dishes in inarticulate joy. Only Momma had ever loved her like this.

"Come sit down, dear," said a voice from the couch. "We've overwhelmed you. Come—there's a bit of space right here by me."

Devin took her bags and gently nudged her dysfunctional feet in the direction of the voice. She sank down into the couch between Nell and the older woman she remembered from her last visit to the Witches' Lounge. Moira.

"Welcome to your new home, darling girl." Moira smiled, deep welcome in her eyes. "I haven't had a chance to tell you yet, but you look just like your mama. You have her twinkling eyes and those same hands that are always moving. Your mama could tell a story just with her hands."

And with those words, memory drilled into Sierra. Momma's hands painting pictures in the night shadows, telling one more tale before they drifted into sleep. Tears spilled over even as she felt herself cuddled into a warm shoulder.

"Let them out, sweetheart." It came as a gentle command. "The Irish have always believed tears are a blessing."

She cried. And when she finished, wiped her eyes, and looked up, discovered half the room had cried along with her. Somehow, that felt just fine.

She took a moment, appreciating the home they'd made for her. Her hands traveled over the soft fabric of the biggest couch in the universe. Ginia grinned. "It's called The Monster. It used to be Uncle Jamie's."

Sierra sniffled. "It's totally gorgeous."

"Ugh." Jamie groaned, eyes twinkling. "Don't insult The Monster. He's already feeling all dolled up and girly."

Ginia stuck out her tongue. "Maybe The Monster's really a girl." Then she doubled over laughing as both her uncles started tickling her ribs.

They were so goofy. And it was a totally awesome couch. Sierra reached out again, running her hands along The Monster's curves—and her fingers touched magic. The knitted throw was beautiful, but that's not what had called to her. She wrapped her hands in the soft folds, letting her power hum with delight. "What *is* this?"

Moira smiled, eyes filled with pleasure. "Just a small gift from my hands to your house. I put my great-granny's best blessing spell in there. She was a water witch of some repute."

Magic flowed out of the blanket and into Sierra's soul. It was like... floating in warm ocean waters. Sierra cuddled the throw to her cheek, completely unable to put it down.

Mia tugged on her hand. "There's a bigger one on your bed—come look!"

Sierra let herself be swept along by the friendly crowd into the lavender haze of her bedroom. The blanket that covered her bed was the last thing she expected. Dizzy squares were stitched together in a drunken mess of uneven color. Mia put her hand on a bright red square. "This one is mine."

Ginia was next, on a square that was pink and glittery. "And this one's mine."

Devin grinned and touched a blue not-quite-square. "Mine. It's been a while since I did any knitting."

A woman Sierra didn't know elbowed him. "That's pretty obvious, my boy." She touched a square that spoke of warm fires and looked at Sierra. "I'm Caro, and this one's mine."

One by one, the crowd of people in the room each laid a hand on her blanket. Aervyn squeezed through and plopped down in the middle. "Not everybody could come tonight, so they sent squares to cuddle you until they can show up." He stuck his finger into a large hole in a fire-engine-red square. "This one's mine. Sorry 'bout the hole, but Caro says that way you won't forget which one I made." He held out his arms for a hug, all innocent boy.

Sierra hopped onto the bed and pulled him into her lap, looking up at the sea of faces. Total strangers had made her a blanket. The most beautifully ugly blanket in the world. She had no words.

Nell leaned over and touched her hair. "It's a welcome blanket. We usually make one for new babies in the witching community, but we didn't know about you until now, so we're a little late. Welcome to our world, Sierra Brighton."

Six years of ice in Sierra's soul simply melted, and she let her heart float on the swells of love in the room.

She had a home. With an ocean for walls, patchwork love on her bed, and pink pigs in the kitchen. It was every kind of awesome.

Aervyn wiggled in her lap. "Sophie and Elorie and Nat are having babies soon, so you can make squares for them if you want. I can show you how, or Caro can. She's the bestest teacher."

Very slowly, she nodded. It felt like a promise.

~ ~ ~

Lauren followed the flood of people exiting Sierra's apartment and found herself standing on the sidewalk beside Devin, shivering slightly in the crisp, wintery air.

He grinned. "Walk you home?"

Home was less than three blocks away, and she was a big girl. Then she realized he had something on his mind. "Sure."

He slipped his fingers companionably in hers, nice and warm, and they walked quietly for a while. "Do you think Sierra's going to fall asleep in The Monster?"

"Yup. I'm pretty sure that was Nell's intent." They'd all left with Sierra and three giggly girls burrowed in the couch's depths, armed with movies and a humungous bowl of popcorn. "She'll probably sleep better with the company."

"You think those girls sleep?" Devin snorted. "Besides, no one has nightmares while The Monster's in the house. And we beefed up Mom's spell, just to make sure."

The couch had depths she wasn't aware of. Lauren raised an eyebrow. "What spell?"

"Haven't heard the story?" He grinned. "Jamie went through a stretch when his precog abilities were emerging where he had a lot of nightmares. Used to wake up screaming. One particularly memorable time, he thought a girl had been kissing him." He paused a moment. "Huh. I wonder if that was Nat?"

Boys. "Sounds like the stuff of nightmares."

"When you're nine? Pretty much." Devin sobered. "Some were really bad, so Mom told him The Monster ate nightmares, and he'd be safe if he slept there. It worked great. I found out ten years later that she'd spent three days bespelling the darned couch to keep his nightmares away." He paused a minute, reaching into his pocket for his phone and pulling up a picture.

"This is the three of us. Eighteen and cocky, headed off to college."

In a pickup truck, with The Monster hanging off the back end. "How far did you drive with it like that?"

He shook his head. "Dunno. Couple thousand miles, I think. Jamie loves that couch. It's moved all over the country with him."

"And he gave it to Sierra." There were still times when the quiet displays of love in Witch Central totally flattened her.

"Sure." Devin shrugged. "She needed it."

There it was—that same casual generosity. On the surface, Jamie and Devin were very different—well, once you got past their identical looks, anyhow. She'd never had any problem telling them apart. Their minds felt very different. But the same values beat in both their hearts, and for some reason, that kept surprising her.

As did the curling in her belly she felt any time Devin was around lately. Suddenly acutely conscious of their interlocked fingers, she tightened up her mental barriers. For a non-mind witch, he was very perceptive. And until she figured out what she wanted from him, she'd prefer to keep the fact that he tickled her belly and snuck into her dreams to herself.

They were almost at her house. She looked over at him, remembering the focused feel of his mind as they'd left Sierra's apartment. "Was there something you wanted to talk about?"

"Hmm? Nope." He wrapped an arm around her shoulders, dropping a casual kiss on her cheek. "I just like being with you. Have a good night."

She walked into her small yard, pulling keys out of her bag, and turned to wave. He stood, leaning against the lamppost, effortlessly sexy. The curls in her belly multiplied. Damn. Definitely time to figure out what she wanted.

Chapter 16

Lauren glared at Jamie. "See? She just kicks you out!"

He feigned innocence. "What? It's hardly my fault."

Nat rubbed her belly. "I think everyone's in agreement that all her difficult genes come from you, love."

Jamie rolled his eyes. "Then they don't know you very well."

Lauren leaned back, amused. "I think it's illegal to insult your wife when she's this pregnant." They'd been conducting another short magic lesson before breakfast, trying to teach Nat and Jamie's unborn baby how to mind barrier. They were getting exactly nowhere. "She's pretty determined to figure stuff out for herself already."

Jamie groaned. "She's just like Devin. We're cursed."

"Thanks a lot," said Devin, walking into the room. "Just for that, I'm eating all the food Nell sent over." He leaned over and casually rubbed Nat's belly. "Except for yours, sweet girl. You need to come out soon and play with me."

"If you can make that happen," said Nat, grimacing as she shifted positions, "you'll be my favorite brother-in-law forever."

He grinned. "Much as I'd like to have that to hold over Matt's head, I got nothing for you. Sorry. Well, except for French toast with some pink stuff on it."

Nat's eyes gleamed. "That'll do."

Lauren revised her opinion of Devin yet again. In two minutes, he'd managed to reduce the frustration level in the room ten degrees and Nat's tension along with it. Baby magic lessons weren't easy on the mama, either.

Do we try again? she mindsent to Jamie.

Either that, or you're going to have to barrier her for however long Nat's in labor. He sounded glum.

Nat stared pointedly as Devin laid a plate on top of her belly. "Feel free to have that conversation out loud, you two."

Devin looked over. "What's up?"

"Our baby's got your stubborn, I-want-to-learn-it-by-myself gene," said Jamie. "We're trying to show her how to mind barrier. She's not cooperating."

"She's hardly the first stubborn witchling in the history of the Sullivans." Devin scooped a forkful of Nat's breakfast.

Which earned him giggles from Nat—and more points from Lauren. Her best friend had grown up with none of the normal fun of siblings and close family. It seemed like Devin was taking personal responsibility for filling in the gap. He got a lot done for a guy who looked like he wasn't up to much of anything.

Devin plunked into an armchair and looked over at Lauren. "How are you showing her?"

"Mental hand over hand." It was the only way she knew, at least the only way that didn't require words. "I can't exactly tell her to watch." Or at least, not without being a lot more invasive than she wanted to be.

Devin looked pensive for a moment. "I wonder if that tracing thing Sierra does would work."

Jamie's fork stopped halfway to Nat's plate. "Damn. Why didn't I think of that?"

Devin grinned. "You got the looks, I got the brains."

Lauren was smart enough to duck as the pillow left Jamie's hand, since she apparently wasn't yet smart enough to keep herself out of the line of fire in the first place. "Are either of you going to explain what tracing is?"

"Nope. Sierra can show you." Jamie looked out the front window. "That's her now—she just ran back to her house for more clothes. It's gonna be cold out at Govin's this morning." He laughed and got up as the doorbell rang. "Somebody needs to tell her witches don't have any manners."

Truth. Lauren still wasn't used to people bursting in her front door at all hours of the day. She'd come home more than once to a gathering in her living room, quite comfortable to raid her fridge and chat while they waited for her to arrive.

Jamie came back into the room, Sierra on his heels. She looked contagiously happy. "Good morning, everyone!"

Witch Central strikes again, thought Lauren. Sierra's new apartment had been put together with generosity, love, and unique decorating flair—and clearly it had totally hit the mark.

"How's The Monster treating you?" Jamie handed her a plate of food. "Lost anyone under the cushions yet?"

She giggled. "I think Mia and Ginia slept on it all night, but we can't find Shay. Maybe The Monster's a cannibal."

Devin snorted. "If it wanted a witch to eat, there's been plenty of opportunity."

"Maybe it was waiting for a small and tasty girl." Sierra stabbed a piece of French toast. "You guys *are* kind of old and stringy."

The guys had her upside-down, shrieking with laughter, in two seconds flat. Without moving from their chairs.

Lauren just shook her head, amused and impressed—by both the magic and the obvious message of brotherly love behind it. The Sullivans had taken in another stray. *Don't break her,* she sent to Jamie. *We need her to help teach that little girl of yours, remember?*

A couple more shakes, and they dropped Sierra in a giggling puddle on the floor and resettled her neatly rescued plate of breakfast in her lap. Devin sat down beside her. "While you eat and mock your elders, can you tell Lauren how you trace magic spells?"

"Sure." Sierra cocked her head, her mind suddenly jittery. "Why? Do I do it wrong?"

Devin's mental curses rang in Lauren's ears, but outwardly, he just rolled his eyes. "No. Because us old, stringy witches don't know how to do it."

Her eyes got big. "Seriously?"

"Yup. You said Aervyn does it, which explains how he picks up magic so fast."

"Hmm." Mouth full, Sierra thought for a moment. "Maybe he learned when he was a baby, just like I did."

Lauren caught the sudden interest in the room. Jamie leaned forward, eyes intent. "You were born with magic?"

"Uh, huh. Just water magic at first. That's why Momma went into the ocean while I was born."

Jamie nodded slowly. "If she didn't have a circle to help her, that was smart."

Sierra grinned. "Momma was really smart. And she said I wanted to play with magic right away after I was born, so she gave me a tiny bit of her spell and let me follow it around."

"And that's how you learn magic, right? You start at one end of a spell thread and feel your way through."

Sierra nodded, mouth full again. "Yup. It's totally easy."

Lauren tried to wrap her head around a newborn following spell threads. Weren't they just supposed to eat, sleep, and poop?

You think that when my girl already kicks you out of her head? sent Jamie dryly. *Can you monitor Sierra while she traces a simple spell of mine? See how she does it?*

No rest for weary witches. Yeah.

Lauren mindwatched as Jamie created a simple fire globe—fire lines were easiest to visualize. And watched as Sierra gently untangled the end of a small spell thread, kind of like finding the beginning of a ball of yarn.

Then she jumped in shock as another mind reached for the dangling thread. *You've got company*, she sent carefully to Jamie.

His mind was full of wonder. *I know.*

Lauren watched, fascinated, as a small presence traced the lines of the spell—and then her eyes flew open at Nat's sudden intake of breath.

Suspended over her belly was the twin to Jamie's fire globe. Their little girl had done her first magic.

From the baby's mind—pure joy. And from her teenage teacher—astonished pride.

~ ~ ~

Moira set three cups of hot chocolate on her table. It was a wondrous gift in her old age that people from thousands of miles away could just pop in for a visit. And there were few guests she loved better than her girls.

Even if they were being mysterious.

Giggles from the front of the house suggested they'd arrived. "In here, my lovelies."

Three girls, bigger every time she saw them, bounded into the kitchen and joined her around the table. Ginia picked up her cup, sniffing. "What did you put in here?"

Moira's eyes twinkled. "That's for you to guess, my dear. An earth witch doesn't give up all her secrets." Truth be told, Ginia could probably worm it out of her, but they'd both have more fun if she offered at least token resistance.

Mia's headshake suggested there was more serious business at hand. "We came because we need your help, Aunt Moira."

That much she had gathered from their message. "And how can I help my three girls?"

Ginia's eyes had that look that made Moira fiercely wish she'd be around to see the witch this one would become. "We want to find out what happened to Sierra's mama."

Oh, my. Moira paused a moment, shaken. This, she hadn't expected—but maybe she should have. "Has Sierra asked for your help?"

"No." Shay was usually the quietest of the three—and the most thoughtful. "But her heart asks."

Aye, it did. "I'm sure it's extremely difficult for her, not knowing." But answers weren't always comforting, either. She reached out gently for small hands. "You know the answer is likely to be very sad."

"We know." Ginia looked down at their joined hands, then tipped her head back up, eyes fierce. "But if something terrible happened to Mama, we would find out. At least then we could be sad about the right things, instead of scared of all the things that might have happened."

"She has bad dreams," Mia said.

Moira was well aware of that. "I know, sweet girl. And she still might, even if we find the answers you seek." Because none of those answers would bring Amelia back. That much, her heart knew.

Shay traced one of the petals embroidered on the tablecloth. "Will you help us?"

"Aye." It would hurt all of their hearts, but she would. "Where do you think we should start?" She was certain the girls had a plan.

"With the old and the new." Ginia sipped her hot chocolate carefully. "We're going to ask Jake to help us with the new part."

Jake was the new head of Sentinel, an organization that attempted to find and help witches in distress, particularly young ones. It had a bit of a spotty history, but Jake was as good as they came. And Sentinel's magic alert system—and long record-keeping of witch incidents—was second to none. It was smart thinking. And it suggested the girls knew more than they were letting on. "You think there was magic involved when Amelia disappeared?"

Ginia's chin jutted out. "Don't you?"

Yes, she did. Moira tilted her head in acknowledgment. "Jake's a good man. If there are records at Sentinel, he'll be able to find them. You'll need some times and dates, though, and it would hurt Sierra to ask. Your mama might have that information from the foster-care files."

"We already know all that stuff." Shay spoke for her sisters. "It was on the third night of Mardi Gras when she was twelve." She grinned. "We pay attention."

They certainly did. So far, they were taking the adults to school.

Ginia sniffed her hot chocolate again, still trying to figure out the mystery ingredient. "Jake's the new part. We need your help with the old part."

Didn't that just figure. "Well, I'm certainly old, child. What do you want me to do?" Scrying probably wouldn't help here, but she was willing to try.

Mia giggled. "You're not the old part. We need you to convince Lauren to use her crystal ball."

"Oh, my." Moira paused, savoring their quick minds. "What a very good idea. Not an easy task, mind you..."

Ginia grinned. "We know. Lauren's still a scaredy-witch on the hocus-pocus stuff."

She was indeed. They'd had a few quick lessons on how to use Great-gran's crystal ball, but unless Moira was mistaken, Lauren hadn't asked it a serious question since the day before her stroke.

Mia reached over to pat her hand. "You can do it, Aunt Moira. Lauren's a sucker for people with sad hearts."

Moira chucked, thinking the very savvy, professional Lauren might be surprised at that particular description, apt though it was. "I'll do my best."

Three smiles of approval on three identical faces. They'd gotten what they'd come for.

Moira closed her eyes, suddenly hit by the full import of the moment. She had always been matriarch of the witching community. Her granddaughter Elorie had stepped into a large part of those shoes—organizing training and service and generally gluing the community together. But she'd never had a true heir for her meddling talents.

Until now.

~ ~ ~

Jamie grimaced as Sierra's intricate air streams tangled and blew up, collapsing her spell. And then winced as, eyes fierce, she pulled on power to begin the whole thing over again.

Devin stepped back, shaking his head. "She's going to kill herself working this hard."

Or kill her trainers. They'd been out at Govin's place for four hours, and Sierra had been doing magic almost non-stop. Jamie was tired just from watching. And judging from the amount of food Govin and Dev had consumed in the last hour, they were flagging as well.

Hungry bellies, they could fix. Solving Sierra wasn't going to be as easy. "Kind of the opposite of reckless now, huh?"

"Can you blame her? We all ganged up on her, trying to convince her she was a danger to humankind. Then ganged up on her again, telling her she has to use her magic." Devin's voice carried judgment Jamie wasn't used to hearing.

He frowned. "Well, both those things are pretty much true."

Devin snorted. "If she keeps going at this pace, she's going to be the safest, most overworked witch in the west by Winter Solstice."

Which was in two days. Point taken. "You think we're pushing too hard?"

"Not anymore. She's doing all the pushing now." Devin paused, sadness in his eyes. "We all assumed she'd be hard to convince."

Jamie picked up the thought his brother didn't voice. They'd all assumed she was like her mother. And they'd steamrolled her because of it.

He let out a sigh. Time to try to unflatten a witch.

Jamie focused once more as Sierra's latest attempt hit crux—and this time, nothing tangled. He watched, with impressed respect, as she threaded the narrowest of air currents through 169 lit candles and blew out the one exactly at the center of the square—without so much as a flicker in any of the other flames.

With almost thirty years of practice, he could only handle a 9x9 square of candles. And he was one of the most talented air witches on the west coast. Sierra had just mastered a 13x13 square.

She looked over at Govin. "Add another row."

Crap, thought Jamie, reading exactly the same reaction on Govin's face. He stepped forward, cookie in hand. "I hereby name you Queen of the Candles. Take a break, wonderwitch."

She took the cookie but shook her head. "It still took four tries. I can do better."

"I can't." Govin's voice was quietly commanding. "There's no such thing as perfection in magic, Sierra. Not one of us here can do what you just did. It's enough."

"The more I practice, the safer I'll be." It was obvious she had no intention of stopping until she fell over from exhaustion.

Jamie looked at his brother. *Your turn, dude.* If anyone understood extremes, it was Dev.

He breathed a sigh of relief as Devin slid over to Sierra. And blinked in shock at his brother's mental tone.

"You're wrong." Devin's voice was hard, unyielding. "You keep practicing like this, you'll be as dangerous as you were."

Jamie shook his head as Govin started to move. He had no idea where his brother was headed—but no way was he beating up Sierra for sport.

Sierra's eyes blazed. "I'm using groundlines, training circles, doubled spell barriers, protective layers, failsafes, and I have better control than any witch here." She hurled each word at Devin. "What more do you want from me?"

"Forgiveness." Devin's one quiet word carried deep apology. He reached for Sierra's hands. "When you came here, we looked at you and saw the lacking in your magic. We've yet to truly acknowledge your biggest gift."

Nobody moved.

"You know how to partner with your magic, little sister. To ride with it and to trust."

Sierra nodded slowly, still lost. "Momma taught me that."

"Yes, she did." Devin grimaced. "And because she left out a few of the usual safety features, we missed the strength of what she *did* teach you. Don't make us live to regret that."

"I don't understand."

"If you listen too carefully to us and abandon what your mom taught you, you'll still be dangerous, but in a different way." He pointed at the candles. "You know your limits. Deep inside, you know. Can you do another row?"

It was a long moment before Sierra shook her head. "No. I barely made it at thirteen."

"Right. Groundlines and failsafes are there for the emergencies." Dev waited until he had everyone's complete attention. "They're important, but the most important way to stay safe is to know what you *can* do—and be a good judge of what you *can't* do." He touched her cheek. "Just like your mom taught you. And just like you taught that little girl in Nat's belly this morning."

Jamie felt the band around Sierra's chest loosening and wondered how his brother kept getting ten steps ahead of the rest of them.

And he wasn't done. Devin leaned in one more time, tipping up Sierra's chin. "You're as safe as you need to be. Now we just build on what you already know. When you're working with a team, you need to know everyone else's limits too." He grinned. "Except me. I'm invincible."

Sierra's smile was slow, but it came. "That's not what I've heard."

Jamie knew it was his turn. Time to trust their new witch—his brother was insisting on it. "Devin's tough. I'm kinda fragile, though." He grinned. "And you have to be really careful with Govin. Fire witches are kinda moody and unpredictable."

Sierra laughed as the square of candles whooshed into a tail of flames that stopped an inch short of his belly. Jamie rolled his eyes at Govin. "Show-off." And a message as well—no better proof of trust than not flinching when a guy tried to scorch your favorite T-shirt.

Sierra sobered. "It sounds complicated, working together like that."

Devin grinned. "That's because I suck with words. You just need a little practice. New magic lesson. Tomorrow. Eat a big breakfast and bring a broomstick."

Jamie picked up enough of his brother's thoughts to know where tomorrow was headed. He trusted Dev with his life—but he was still bringing a helmet.

Chapter 17

"Come on in!" Nell had two hands full of computer parts, and she hoped whoever was at the door wanted to help her reassemble Aervyn's latest experiment. Superboy was awesome at the destruction part. So far he wasn't showing any signs of genius at reconstruction.

It was hard to believe her Winter Solstice baby was going to be five soon. Two more days.

She sensed her sister-in-law's presence before Nat came around the corner. And realized this wasn't a casual visit. Nat's mind felt… jostled. Uncomfortable.

Nell set down her tools. "Good morning. Jamie drop you off?"

"He did." Nat smiled. "Apparently if I'm left alone for an hour or two, he's afraid he'll come home to me holding our baby girl."

Not unless she was in a heck of a hurry. "Sorry, that's kind of my fault. When I was pregnant with the girls, Nathan was driving me crazy, and I made Daniel take him out so I could have a nap. The girls weren't due for weeks yet, so they went to the zoo."

Nat grinned. "And you went into labor?"

"Yup. At four o'clock in the afternoon on the Friday of a holiday weekend. Traffic was bumper-to-bumper to get out of the city. It took him three hours to get home."

"The girls were born in three hours?" Nat looked shocked.

She wished. They'd been fifteen hours of hard labor. "Heck, no. But Jamie got to sit with me while we waited for Daniel to get back. He was a tad stressed." Truth be told, she hadn't been all that calm, either. "Moira arrived about an hour later, but I think Jamie had visions of having to deliver triplets by himself on my kitchen floor."

Nat frowned. "How did Moira get there so fast?"

"She'd left Nova Scotia that morning. Said she just knew it was time." Nell tapped her laptop with love. "You're lucky. This pretty toy will let us fetch you a healer in just a few minutes." Shuttling people through Realm was cool for many reasons, but getting a witch midwife to the right place on time was one of the coolest.

Nat was quiet for a moment. "Did you know it was time?"

In nine years, no one had ever asked her that. "You know, I suspect I did. That's probably why I wanted a little time to myself." Nell grinned. "I must've known I wouldn't get a second's rest after the triplets arrived."

Then it occurred to her that Nat might have a pretty specific reason for asking. "How are you feeling?"

"Unsettled." Nat stretched into a pose that Nell couldn't have pulled off unpregnant. "I've been having weird dreams."

Pregnancy dreams could be seriously wonky. "Any sexy hunks?" Nell remembered a very steamy dream during her last pregnancy, featuring Nathan Fillion. In triplicate. *Firefly* reruns had never been quite the same since.

"Nope." Nat blushed. "Those happened back at the beginning."

Nell waited patiently. If friendly silence didn't work soon, there was always chocolate ice cream.

"I've been dreaming about my little girl growing up. And turning into Amelia."

Nell blinked. "Sierra's mom?" That was a direction she hadn't expected.

"Yeah." Nat folded herself into a pregnant pretzel. "I'm sure it's just my subconscious putting her face on my fears."

Now they'd landed on the reason for the visit. Nell lowered onto the floor beside Nat. No way she was trying the pretzel. "And what's scaring you?"

There was no answer for a bit as a careful yogini gathered her thoughts. "I've been wondering what must have driven Amelia—what kept her so far away from community, from everything she knew, from people who would love her."

It was something a lot of hearts had been pondering. Nat's answer was likely to be more insightful than most, even though she'd never met Amelia. "And what do you think?"

"Joy in seeing the world, maybe. And fear that coming back would mean limits—chains on her freedom. Some hearts can't bear to be constrained."

Nell frowned. Something more was going on here—that last sentence was practically imprinted on Nat's brain. "You think she needed freedom that badly?"

Nat nodded slowly. "Why else would you leave a child alone—a child you loved immensely?"

For the first time since they'd fetched Sierra, Nell felt herself step into Amelia's shoes. And find, at last, a tiny thread of empathy. "You can't be a mother and be absolutely free."

They sat quietly together for a bit. Then Nell looked up, asking the question that bothered her most. "Do you think she was coming back?"

"Yes." Nat's answer was quick and sure. "She wouldn't have left Sierra in a hotel room if she was leaving for good."

Nell nodded slowly, tugging on that slender thread of empathy for Amelia she'd finally been able to find. "She would have sent her back to us."

"I think so." Nat shrugged. "I didn't know her, so I can only guess. But I know what it is to want to taste freedom from the realities of your life, even if it's just for a few hours. Maybe that's what Amelia tried to do while her daughter slept."

Those were strange words from one of the most responsible people Nell knew. And where she could no longer feel any sympathy at all for Amelia. "She left a child alone in New Orleans, Nat. Why are you fighting so hard to find empathy for her?"

"I have to." Nat's face was intent. "That quest for freedom rides in the heart of my baby girl, too. And I don't want her to grow up to be a woman who has to leave her child sleeping alone in a hotel room to get her own needs met."

Anyone else and Nell would have brushed it off as the irrational fears of pregnancy. Anyone else. "She's a fire witchling. They tend to be pretty restless. Maybe that's what you're feeling."

Nat shook her head slowly. "It's more than that." She took a deep breath. "She's not going to come out quietly. It's going to be her first taste of freedom."

It wasn't in Nell to offer stupid platitudes. "Probably. Most babies with power make a pretty loud entrance."

"We have to help her." Nat's eyes looked off far into the distance. "You tease Devin about his reckless gene."

Nell was lost. "Devin isn't Amelia."

"No, he isn't." Nat's hands folded under her belly. "But he could have been. He has a heart that seeks freedom. Amelia didn't know how to find that without being reckless. Devin does. With him, the reckless part is just for fun."

It was the best description of her brother Nell had ever heard.

"I need to help my little girl seek like Devin. To fly high, but with a rooted heart."

Her sister-in-law was one cool chick. Nell reached out. "Nat, I can't think of any two people on earth more likely to get that right than you and Jamie." She grinned. "And if your baby girl comes out flying high, we'll send Uncle Dev to catch her. Trust me. He's earned it."

Nat smiled, her mind sliding back toward its usual serene cool.

It was Nell's head that was restless now, retracing some of their strange conversational turns. "How did you manage to figure my brother out so fast?"

"He loves my best friend."

Nell tried to breathe. "You're sure?" Dev was the brother who had always flown the highest—and the one she'd caught the most.

Nat nodded, eyes sympathetic. "For now, it's just him. Lauren's heart isn't quite as quick."

That wasn't helping Nell's airflow any. "Is she going to catch up?"

Nat's face slowly bloomed in amusement. "That depends how good a negotiator your brother is."

Dev and Lauren.

Nell leaned back, trying to picture it. And decided it wasn't all that hard. If any woman could partner with her hurricane of a brother, she'd lay her bets on Lauren.

~ ~ ~

Sierra winced as Aervyn missed crashing into a huge boulder by about a broomstick bristle. "How does he do that?"

Devin grinned. "Absolute trust in his magic."

Jamie snorted. "Absolute trust in his ability to port himself out of trouble."

Aervyn wasn't the only one who could teleport. Sierra looked at Jamie. "Can you grab him before he crashes?"

"Smart question." Devin's eyes held approval. "Aervyn's been working magic with Jamie for a long time, so they know each other's limits."

Jamie shook his head. "He's going too fast. If he were slower or closer, I could probably snag him." He winked at her. "Remember that if you want me to rescue you before you hit a rock. Close and slow."

Close and slow. Check. Sierra looked at the broom in her hands, trying to mute the war inside her head. Sierra Brighton, storm witch, could hardly wait to get her feet off the ground. Sierra Brighton, newly cautious and safe witch, was trying not to puke.

Devin laid a hand on her shoulder as Aervyn skidded to a halt two inches away. "We put up a big training circle, and we're all grounded. It's a safe place to play—have some fun."

Govin, standing beside her, tried to hop into the air—and nosedived into the ground six inches away. Ouch.

Aervyn giggled. "You gotta go faster than that, or you won't stay up in the air."

"Now you tell me." Govin looked up from the ground and winked. "Any other tips before I try again?"

Aervyn studied Govin's outfit for a minute—helmet, padded vest, knee and elbow pads, shin protectors. "I think you need a cape."

Sierra couldn't stop the giggles that bubbled over. "You can borrow mine."

"I have an extra." Devin pulled a pink sparkly cape out of his backpack. "I raided the girls' costume stash."

Govin didn't bat an eye. "If a cape will help me fly, I'll wear a cape." He stood up, donned the cape, checked his helmet, and nodded at Sierra. "Race you to the rock."

It was hard to believe this was the same guy who spent half his life making baby weather on a pond. And then did math for fun. "Which rock?"

He laughed. "Any rock I can get to."

"I can help." Aervyn ran behind them. "I can give you a push off."

Devin swooped him up. "No way, little dude. No assists. Every witch must fly for him or herself. House rules."

Jamie hopped on his broom and lurched off into the air. "You guys are making me look really good," he called back over his shoulder.

Sierra watched him fly for a minute, tracing his spell lines. Aervyn used primarily earth magic to propel himself, which she didn't have. Devin used water. Water power she had, but Devin's speed control was practically non-existent. Jamie, however, used air and fire, and that gave her the missing pieces she needed. Carefully, she levitated into the air, and then floated forward, mixing air currents under the front third of her broom to pull herself forward.

Jamie zoomed back around. "Nice. Now try going faster than my great-grandmother."

The storm witch was rapidly winning the shouting match in her head. She could feel speed just a twitch of magic away. Doubling her groundlines, she shifted into second gear and felt the wind against her cheeks. It called to her. Heck, it was practically turning her inside out.

Let go. It's okay to play sometimes. Jamie grinned at her as he shot by.

Tears stung her eyes—and then blew off her cheeks as she let her magic loose. Leaning forward on her broomstick, she shot through the winter sky, shrieking in joy.

And realized she was not alone. Aervyn was on her wing, eyes dancing. "Try this!" He swung up into a big loop, zooming upside down.

It was an irresistible offer. Pulling up on the front of her broomstick, she shot skyward, following him up into the clouds—and whooped as they came racing down toward the earth. Working quickly, she wove an air net to catch them, just in case.

Aervyn grinned and nipped in to touch her shoulder. "Tag. You're it!"

He zoomed off, dipping and weaving like a drunken hummingbird. Sierra did her level best to follow him while not running into rocks or other witches. In two minutes, she'd mastered double loops. In five, they could do a corkscrew holding hands.

And Sierra's heart ached with the joy of magic shared. She clutched the orange frog hanging around her neck. Momma would have adored broomstick flying.

It took cookies to finally lure them out of the air. Nutella cookies. Lots of them.

Sierra skidded to a halt at Devin's feet, her heart still somewhere up in the sky. He handed her a fistful of cookies. "Eat. Then we'll try the second lesson."

She crammed a cookie in her mouth. "Wass' that?"

He grinned. "I'll tell you once we're back in the air. Aervyn, can you hook us up with a group mindlink?"

Wonderboy, mouth full of cookies, just nodded and grinned.

Sierra felt an incoming nudge on her head and realized she could still hear Devin talking—even though his mouth wasn't moving. *If you've got a mind witch handy, this is pretty useful for group magic on the fly. If it gets too distracting, just let Aervyn know, and he can turn it off for you.*

Voices in her head. That was so cool. Sierra grinned. *What's lesson number two?*

Devin laughed. *Hit the air–keep it to second gear. Then you'll find out.*

Sierra launched and headed forward at a sedate pace. Aervyn pulled up on one side of her, Jamie on the other. Sierra blinked—wonderboy was flying on air power now, instead of his usual earth power. Cool trick. Devin slid in front of them, flying backward. *Lesson number two. Fly in formation. Sierra, you're the lead. Think about what your team can handle.*

She looked over at Jamie, thinking hard. *Can you port yourself out of the way of a rock?*

Gee, thanks a lot. He rolled his eyes, but answered. *At this speed, yeah.*

Well then, they sure as heck weren't going any faster than this. Carefully she led her team of three through a couple of simple formations, and then flew them over to where Devin was still meandering backward on his broom.

He just shook his head. *Do-over. This time, find your team's edge. Get close, but don't go over it.*

No way. She landed them all on the ground. She wasn't having a serious conversation with a witch flying backward. "That's not safe."

He raised an eyebrow. "You did corkscrews with Aervyn."

"Sure, but he flies at least as well as I do. So if I could do something, so could he." She looked at Jamie, trying not to be rude. "I think maybe he can't do all that stuff."

Jamie snorted, looking amused. "You think?"

"You're exactly right." Devin waited until she looked at him. "You're a strong witch, Sierra. So you're often going to be working with people who can't match you. Find Jamie's edge, but don't break him."

She frowned. Lesson two wasn't sounding like much fun. "Why?"

His eyes were very serious. "Because the next time there's a big wave heading at an island, you want to know what it feels like to have a teammate reach their edge."

Her broom clattered to the ground as her legs turned to jelly. "I didn't do that. I wasn't careful." She'd done the magic she'd needed to do—and assumed they could all keep up.

She felt Devin's fingers under her chin. "You didn't know. Had you ever worked with a team before?"

No. Only Momma.

"You did the best you could with what you knew." He stooped to pick up her broom and held it out. "Time to learn a little more."

The realization she'd put her team at risk was still poking huge, bleeding holes in her heart. "Maybe somebody else can lead."

"They could."

And she would still be dangerous the next time she worked with a team. Sierra closed her eyes for a moment, wound a bandage around her heart to stop the bleeding, and looked over at Jamie. "I think you'd better borrow Govin's cape. Maybe the kneepads, too."

As they launched into the sky, she tried to figure out how to keep three separate witches safe. Watching Jamie wobble as she moved to third gear, she knew she'd better come up with a plan fast. Pink capes only kept you safe in fairy tales.

Ignoring Aervyn, she swung into a simple loop—and cursed as Jamie stalled out at the top. Panic beating in her heart, she shoved his broom from behind, pushing him around the loop. He grinned and waved, looking totally unconcerned, and her heart slowed down a little.

She shifted the team's speed up another gear. Going slow wasn't always safest. She pulled up into another loop, glued to Jamie's side—and grinned as he stepped on the gas at the top. Good. He learned fast.

A bit more practice, and they managed a couple of jerky double loops. But no way were Jamie and his broom going to make it through a corkscrew in one piece. Or whatever that thing was called where she and Aervyn buzzed each other in the sky.

Her team had reached its limit.

No. Her team had reached *Jamie's* limit.

Sierra clutched her broom, thinking hard. And then grinned. Sending out air power right and left, she extended an invitation. If they were flying on one power stream, Jamie would no longer be the weak link.

Trust the magic. Devin's words from the weather pond bubbled to the surface as she hooked her team onto a shared air flow.

Trust the magic. Sierra double-checked all the links—and then stepped on the gas.

Aervyn's glee as they streaked through the sky in formation was no match for his uncle's. She heard Jamie's exultant war whoop as they fired into a corkscrew and threw the air net a little wider—just in case he let go.

Then she leaned into the wind and prodded Aervyn's power stream. *More.*

DEBORA GEARY

Chapter 18

Nat looked over at Sophie. "How did two totally pregnant women get roped into helping with this kind of subterfuge?"

Sophie held up a bag full of baby clothes. "Officially, we were just out shopping for more newborn stuff." She sniffed. "Do I still smell like linguine?" They'd picked up two take-out helpings of Roman's insanely good signature dish at the request of some very determined triplets—and had been obliged to sit down and consume two more plates while they were at it. No one in their right mind sent hungry pregnant women to pick up takeout.

Nat leaned over and sniffed. "Maybe. But Jamie swears I can smell cookies coming out of Moira's oven five thousand miles away."

Sophie giggled. "Pregnancy will do that. Elorie can't stand the smell of onions, or basil, or fifteen other things. Poor Aaron has suffered trying to cook everything without half the ingredients he normally uses."

Nat looked down at her belly. "I'm pretty sure our guys get the easy end of this deal."

"You have no idea." Sophie contemplated whether or not to change the subject. Most women about to experience labor for the first time didn't want to hear any more stories. Nat was as centered as anyone on the planet, but pushing a baby out into the world was life-changing. And sitting on the cusp of life-changing wasn't all that comfortable.

Nat paused, leaning against a wall, and Sophie's eyes sharpened. "Braxton Hicks again?" The small, mostly painless contractions helped prepare a woman's body for what was to come. They could also be really annoying, keep you awake at night, and totally punish an already tortured bladder. She reached out a hand in healing comfort.

Nat caught her wrist and started walking again. "It's okay. Let them happen." She smiled wryly. "Feel free to come fix the ones at 3 a.m., though."

Sophie was pretty sure Nat wasn't going to be pregnant for many more middle-of-the-night stretches. And a good night's sleep now would make the birthing far easier. "Have Jamie use a small sleep spell on you and the baby tonight."

She grinned as Nat stopped in the middle of the sidewalk. "It's safe to do that? Now you tell me."

"It's not a good idea to do it too often—we try not to mess much with a baby's natural rhythms—but it will be fine for one night." And now it was really time to stop talking about babies. Nat's mind needed to spend some time elsewhere. "So, what do you think the girls are up to?" Sophie had her theories.

"What do you think?" Nat grinned. "They're meddling."

Yeah, that was pretty much her theory. "And how do you feel about that?"

The look Nat gave her was pure mischief. "Know any good eavesdropping spells?"

"We've totally corrupted you, haven't we?" Sophie hooked elbows with her friend, laughing. "Sadly, none that work through walls."

~ ~ ~

It was time to make a witch squirm. Moira sat in her favorite chair in the Witches' Lounge and waited for Lauren to arrive.

Nell grinned. "Be gentle. Remember, she didn't grow up with all the hocus-pocus."

Moira snorted. "Show a little more reverence for your roots, my dear. Lauren may not know any better, but you do."

That little speech had no effect at all on Nell's amusement. "Is this what my girls have been all whispery and giggly about lately?"

An old witch never told. "Aren't all nine-year-old girls giggly?"

Nell's sharp look was interrupted by Lauren's arrival—holding her crystal ball, as instructed. And a glass pitcher of something vaguely yellow. "What's that, my lovely? Some sort of potion?"

Lauren looked mildly horrified. "It's eggnog. It's been popular in my office lately, so I brought some to share."

Yummy. "Did you know that eggnog started as an old witch remedy? It's easily digested for those weak or ailing, and the spices can cover a wide array of noxious tastes."

Lauren cuddled the pitcher to her chest. "No spiking my eggnog."

Moira tried a stern look. "Do your magic like a grown-up witch, and I won't have to." Both members of her audience cracked up laughing. Ah, well. It had been worth a try.

"I brought the crystal ball." Lauren set it down gently on the couch and started pouring eggnog. "Is it really the best way to do this?"

"We won't know until we try now, will we?" The old magics could be powerful, but they were a tad unpredictable, especially in the hands of a still-somewhat-skeptical witch.

Nell shrugged. "Jake came up blank. He has records of some unusual energy spikes about that time, but Amelia probably wasn't the only witch at Mardi Gras."

Moira took a sip of her eggnog. It was truly delicious. "Is it your young Lizard that made this?" She'd developed a strong fondness for Lauren's assistant.

"It is." Lauren grinned. "We had one guy buying a house yesterday who asked for lifetime rights to drop by for eggnog as part of his deal."

Nell laughed. "Did he get it?"

"Of course." Lauren sat down on the couch and grinned. "We aim to please."

Such a creative, enterprising woman. No wonder Great-gran's crystal ball had chosen her. Moira smiled. "Have you figured out the question you're going to ask yet?"

Lauren scowled at the innocuous glass ball on the couch beside her. "No. It never answers the first thing I ask it anyhow."

"It's Irish, child. We like to lead into a conversation slowly." The crystal ball was old and not used to the forthright ways of modern witches.

"Well, I'm not Irish. If it chose me, it'll have to get used to not beating around the bush." Lauren picked up the ball and peered into its depths. "Tell me what happened to Amelia Brighton."

It surprised Moira mightily when the ball hazed a bit. She'd have expected it to entirely ignore such a question. Lauren had more power than she knew.

"See?" Lauren shrugged. "It's got a mind of its own."

Nell looked over at a picture on the wall, clearly stifling giggles. Moira wasn't having an easy time containing her own. "You might try a different question, dear. In general, crystal balls like to express their opinions. It rather bores them to just be asked for a quick fact or two." Or at least, so Great-gran had said.

Lauren rolled her eyes. "Why do I get the witch tool that's temperamental?"

"They're all temperamental, child." Moira chortled in delight. "Why do you think witches end up with white hair?"

Now Nell's laughter rolled through the room. "Oh, a witchling or two is enough to do that. No tools needed." She grinned at Lauren and motioned at the ball in her lap. "Pretend it's Aervyn, and you'll do just fine."

An odd look crossed Lauren's face. "That's actually helpful, I think." She studied the ball a moment longer, and then spoke quietly. "Show me the most important thing I need to know about Sierra's mother."

The surface of the ball misted instantly, swirling with a strange light. Lauren looked up, eyebrows raised, and motioned to them. "Come on over. It wants to speak to all of us."

Moira's heart caught. For over seventy years she'd asked questions of her family heirloom, and not once had it ever so much as acknowledged she existed. She reached for Nell's helping hand up out of her chair, not taking her eyes off the crystal ball.

Sitting down beside Lauren, she reached a trembling hand to the stirring globe. And squeezed her eyes shut as a river of images started flowing in her head. Too fast at first to make out, and then the flow slowed, and Moira began to pick out faces she knew.

There was Great-gran, sitting in the ancient family rocking chair, holding two babes to her breast.

Elorie, nestled in the arms of her mama.

Her departed sister, with Marcus and Evan cuddled up at her feet.

An exhausted Amelia, floating on her back in the ocean, holding a naked, howling babe to her chest. The love flowing from mother to child was big enough to fill the sea that surrounded them.

Then came Nat, her bundle hard to see. Sophie. Sierra. The faces started flowing faster again. And then the river ceased.

Moira sat, her hand resting in awed thanks on the now-quiet crystal ball. Seventy years she had waited. And what an answer it had given. She opened her eyes, holding the magic tight to her heart. "Sierra was loved. That's what it wanted us to know." The most important thing. Amelia had loved her child with all the passion of the best mothers—past, present, future.

"Yeah." Nell nodded slowly, sniffling. "Sorry. I'm sure that's the important part." She smiled. "But I saw my girls. They're going to be mamas one day."

Hmm. That was very interesting. Moira patted the crystal ball in approval. She hadn't seen any of the triplets. It must have shown them all something different. "I saw my great-gran. And our Sierra."

Lauren just stared at the ball in her lap. "I only saw Amelia." She looked up sharply. "Did either of you see Nat?"

Moira smiled as she and Nell both nodded. It might be a bit of a wild ride to get there, but Nat would cuddle her babe. "They'll be just fine."

"Okay." Lauren's relief was palpable. Then she frowned. "But this doesn't really answer what we wanted to know." She frowned down at the ball. "Should I try again?"

Ah, these young ones who thought questions and answers were linear. "We got the answer we needed, sweet girl." She patted Lauren's hand. "We know that the love they shared while Amelia lived is far more important than how she died."

Lauren nodded slowly. "Sierra already knows that."

"Aye. She does." Moira sat up straighter. "It was the rest of us who needed a reminder. Whatever happened to Amelia, it was not a lack of love that caused it."

A musical ring scattered their attention. Lauren grabbed for her bag. "Sorry. Lizard's still trying to finalize that deal, and I told her I'd stay available." She glanced at the messages on her phone. "Gotta go."

Waving goodbye, she carefully picked up the crystal ball. And ball in one hand, iPhone in the other, whisked out of Realm.

Great-gran would have been highly amused.

Nell scooped up the pitcher of eggnog, refilling Moira's glass. "I'll take the rest of this back with me. It'll be a good excuse to drop in on my three girls and see if I can find out what the heck they're up to."

Moira tried to look innocent, which was difficult. She was in this one up to her neck.

Nell laughed. "They came to the champion meddler for lessons, did they? I thought so." She shook her head. "I just hope you thought things through a little more than they did."

"A good witch always thinks."

Nell was still laughing as she vanished.

Moira smiled, well satisfied. Somewhere in that river had been Lauren with a babe in arms. She was sure of it.

~ ~ ~

Devin frowned again at the message from Sierra on his phone. *I need you to come to my place. 6 p.m. Bye!*

Not exactly informative. But when a sister, of the real or honorary kind, paged him, he usually went. Part of the big-brother handbook. Didn't mean he couldn't give her a little grief, though.

Pulling open the door to her building, he grinned. Who was he kidding—he'd cut her a mile of slack tonight. The ride he'd taken on her corkscrew train, his broomstick wedged in line between Jamie and Aervyn, ranked as one of the coolest experiences of his life. And he'd have been a cinch for photographer of the year if he'd had a camera when the pink-caped Govin had been pulled through his first loop, clinging to his broom and laughing like a banshee.

They'd had fun today—and one teenage witch had been utterly generous with her magic. So if she wanted to be a little demanding tonight, he'd deal. That's what brothers did.

He knocked on the door to Sierra's apartment, and then turned at footsteps in the hallway.

"Hey!" Lauren waved, halfway down the hall. "How was broom flying?"

He grinned. "To quote Sierra, 'awesome cool.' You gotta try it."

She laughed. "I'm in line right after Moira. I figure if she comes back in one piece, I might too."

He was pretty sure he could convince Moira to sit on a broom with him. Or with Aervyn. She had a serious soft spot for the little dude. He'd put Lauren on *his* broom. "Deal."

She blinked. "Moira's going to fly on a broomstick?"

"Sure." He winked. "I can be very persuasive."

Lauren stared a long minute and then snorted. "No wonder Nell does such a great job with Aervyn. She's had three brothers' worth of practice with that 'I'm cute, so give me a mile' look." She turned to the door and knocked. "How come you're here, anyhow?"

He was pretty sure he'd just been complimented and insulted in one short sentence. She was good. "Sierra messaged me."

"Really?" She frowned. "Me too. Cryptic message about being here at 6 p.m."

His Spidey senses started tingling just as his phone beeped again. Incoming message. *Open the door, silly. Mia.*

Lauren, phone in her hand, started laughing. "Open it carefully. They probably have it booby-trapped or something."

He grinned. "You've been hanging around witches too long."

"Tell me about it." She studied the door. "Can you do some kind of scan for spell traces or something?"

There was apparently still a thing or two he could teach a newbie witch. "It'd be faster if you just scan for the perpetrators and mindread their devious plans." He had visions of four girls hiding behind The Monster, giggling.

"Good point." She paused a moment, and then frowned. "The apartment's empty. There's no one in there."

Huh. The Monster didn't really eat girl children, even ones who deserved it. "What are they up to?"

Lauren grinned. "We could just walk away."

"I don't think I'm genetically capable of that." He shook his head at his phone. "And those little punks know it."

She waved at the door. "After you."

He laughed and pushed the door open. "Mom taught me better than that. Water magic's not much good for shielding, but I can cover you better in front of me."

She rolled her eyes, but stepped forward, leading the way down the dark hall. He followed—and then ran smack into her as they reached the living room and she stopped dead.

His fast hands kept them both upright. At least until he took a good look at Sierra's living room.

Cozy table.

White tablecloth.

Two flickering candles. A single red rose.

And the smells of Romano's signature linguine steaming from two plates.

Uh, oh.

His phone beeped again. *Don't make us lock you in. Shay.*

Punk girl children. He knew exactly what they were trying to do. And no way in this lifetime was it going to work.

Then he looked over at Lauren, still staring at the table in shock—and realized it just might. Damn.

~ ~ ~

Lauren stared at the flickering candles, strains of Puccini echoing in her ears.

This should be funny. Nine-year-old matchmakers should be a joke. Except it didn't feel that way. There had been another moment, less than a year ago, when she'd stood in an apartment with Jamie and known her life had changed forever.

Her gut said she'd just hit another one of those moments. And there was another Sullivan standing beside her.

She looked over at Devin. He wasn't laughing either. "What do we do now?"

He met her gaze—and she felt her bones melt. "We eat. Those punk girls left my favorite food."

Lauren closed her eyes in one last-ditch effort to find the control mechanism on her heart. "No. They left mine."

His laugh was low and long—and reached deep into her belly. Uh, oh. She felt her brain trying to resist. This was Devin Sullivan, world traveler and adrenaline junkie. No way this worked—even if he did love linguine.

She could feel the panic beating in her ribs. Small deals could be made on the fly. Big ones—well, big ones needed time. And thought. And sanity.

None of which were going to happen in a room with Puccini, linguine, and the gravitational pull of a man she still needed to think about really, really hard. Lauren reached for coherent words. "I think I need to go."

He caught her hands, words soft and inescapable. "You don't want this?"

"I don't know." Honesty fought with the fluttering panic. "Maybe."

He grinned, and the intensity in the room plummeted. "Then eat some linguine with me. We'll have dinner, curl up on The Monster later. Watch a movie. Plot revenge on those nieces of mine."

Lauren just stared. She knew expert negotiating tactics when she saw them. Devin Sullivan was a very dangerous man. No way was she going to hold onto "maybe" through linguine and a date with the Monster.

Her phone beeped. *There's tiramisu in the fridge for dessert. We love him. You could too. Ginia.*

Oh, God. She was in really serious trouble.

Chapter 19

Moira unraveled some wool from her ball and continued knitting. She'd taken to popping into the Witches' Lounge for an hour or two every day. It was warm and cozy, and someone usually dropped by.

With no warning, her chair and the rest of Witches' Lounge suddenly shimmered and disappeared—and she found herself dumped rather unceremoniously on a beach. With purple water and orange palm trees. Oh, my.

Sierra landed beside her, spewing apology. "I'm so sorry! I didn't know anyone was in the Lounge. Hang on, I'll get you back there."

Another moment and her chair reappeared under her bottom, back in the Witches' Lounge, much to Moira's relief. Sierra stood right beside her, still looking horrified. "Hello, my dear. What was that wee trip about?"

"I'm trying to write a program to turn this into a beach." Sierra's words tripped over each other. "The triplets wanted to know what Hawaii looked like, so I was going to show them." She scowled. "It's more complicated than I thought."

Ah, and weren't so many things. Moira smiled and pointed to the seat beside her. "Well, the colors did look a bit odd, but the sand seemed very real."

Sierra sat down, sighing. "Sand's easy. Water's really hard. I don't know why. I thought..." her voice trailed off, yearning written all over her face.

It tugged on Moira's heart. "What is it, sweet girl?"

"I wanted to go swimming." The girl's voice was quiet and sad. "The water here's nice enough, but it's cold. I miss the warm water."

Missed the connection to her mama, too—that was plain as day.

Fortunately, this was a problem easily fixed. Moira collected her knitting and stood up. "Meet me back here in ten minutes." She smiled. "Wear a swimsuit and bring a towel."

Sierra stared, speechless, as Moira activated the spell to transport out of Realm back home. She needed a swimsuit too—and perhaps another traveler or two.

~ ~ ~

Nat giggled as her husband squirmed yet again. "Hold still, or I'll end up sticking you with one of these pins."

He was tempted to wiggle one more time just to hear her laugh. "There's got to be someone more Aervyn's size who can model this while you finish it." Several someones.

"None that know how to keep a secret."

She had a point there. Well, maybe he could amuse himself while he waited. A quick flick of power, and he activated the spell. The cloak shimmered and disappeared, along with most of the guy wearing it. As Sierra would say, "awesome cool."

Nat laughed at the part of her husband she could see. "We know the invisibility spells works, silly. Now bring it back so I can get it hemmed—otherwise, superboy will trip and break his nose as he skulks around."

Jamie shimmered back into visibility. "You know Nell's going to kill us for this, right?" He was pretty sure giving the most powerful witchling in the world a Harry Potter invisibility cloak wasn't going to make her life any easier. However, sometimes ideas were so perfect you just had to roll with them and brave the sisterly wrath.

Nat pulled the last pin out from between her lips. "I suspect she'll just get even."

Crap. That could be even worse. Nell could be frighteningly creative. "Hopefully she'll wait until our little girl is walking, at least." That might buy them some time to redeem themselves.

"By then, we might not be too worried about Nell." Nat undid the cloak, moving it to the table. "Okay, I just need to hem this, and then we're done. I've heard stories about what Devin in particular was up to by the time he could walk."

He grinned. "Most people blame all three of us."

She handed him an apple. "Most people don't know you very well."

Devin had almost always been the instigator, but he and Matt hadn't been unwilling followers. "We probably would have just found some other kind of trouble without Dev around."

"You go on believing that." Eyes twinkling, she tried to thread the cape under the sewing machine foot. It wasn't the easiest of fits, working around her belly.

He sighed and threw another rock at his bastion of masculinity. "Want me to do it?"

Her eyebrows shot up. "You can sew?"

Sigh. "Yeah. And knit, and braid, and even make a passable friendship bracelet. I draw the line at cross-stitch, though." Nobody sane wanted to work on the same inch of work for three days.

She pulled herself up from the chair and handed over the cape. "My hero. No wonder your nieces love you."

It was his coding skills they loved, and he was sticking to that story. "So you don't think I'm as crazy as Dev, huh?"

Her arms snuck around his shoulders, belly pressing into his back. "Do you?"

Nope. Much as it burnt him to admit it. "He got an extra dose, I guess."

She sat down beside him as he got the cape lined up. "Do you think he's here for a reason? And Sierra?"

Uh, oh. He couldn't sew and be mystical at the same time. "What are you getting at?"

She rubbed slow circles over her belly. "I just wonder if we needed to learn from them. About the different kinds of reckless. So we're smarter when our baby girl arrives."

He grinned at her. "Nothing happens without a reason?" It was one of her favorite themes. And she had a point. He'd grown up with Dev, but they'd still taken a couple of serious wrong turns with Sierra. Maybe he was smarter now.

Or not. He shrugged. "If nothing else, Devin might keep us out of hot water with Nell." His brother had spent several days perfecting the world's best flying broom. Red, shiny, and bat-out-of-hell fast. And that was without Aervyn driving.

He started up the sewing machine. Somewhere to hide might not be such a bad idea.

~ ~ ~

Devin stood, towel in hand, beside a totally mystified Sierra. And grinned as Aervyn came hurtling into the room, wearing his fire-engine-red swim trunks. "Ready to go, superdude?"

"Uh, huh." Aervyn crashed to a halt, breathless. "Mama says not to lose me, or she'll be really mad at you."

Sierra took his hand. "We won't." She looked over at Devin. "Where the heck are we going, anyhow?"

"You'll see." He grinned and activated the Realm transport spell, his eyes on Sierra's face as they materialized at the other end. Joy hit first—and then she shrieked and went racing for the water, Aervyn's hand still firmly in hers, his feet a foot off the ground.

Moira landed just as their shrieks hit maximum volume. "Ah, good. I thought she might enjoy this." She let go of the little girl with her. "Go on in, Lizzie. Just don't go out too far until we join you."

Devin felt Lizzie pulling power. No worries—she was clearly a pretty potent little water witch. He looked over at Moira. "Are you going in?"

Her regal glare had him squirming. Clearly that had been a really stupid question. "Of course I am. What, you think old witches can't swim?"

He wasn't dumb enough to make the same mistake twice. "I'm sure you can." And he'd be sticking close.

"The day I can't swim in warm ocean waters is the day I'm dead, my boy." She grinned at him and dropped her towel on the sand. "Race you!"

It was totally embarrassing that she beat him to the water. Mostly because he was laughing too hard to move, but still. Devin trailed behind as she swam out to where the young ones played, diving under small waves like giggling otters.

Sierra stuck her head up, face radiant. "Thank you so much. This is perfect!"

And it was. The warm water soaked into Devin's bones, the ultimate luxury for a water witch. He'd never admit it, but even he got cold in the blustery weather of December. Sunny rays beat down on whatever body parts momentarily stuck out of the water, and he spied gorgeous colors under the waves—little fish come to tickle their toes.

This was the life. Maybe Lauren was a swimmer. Devin froze as that last stray thought registered—and then spluttered as salt water exploded up his nose. Dammit. Water witches didn't get hit by waves unless they were really, really distracted. He dove down, clearing his nose—and hopefully his head. He had enough to do with four witches to watch without worrying about one who wasn't even here.

When he surfaced, Sierra was showing the two witchlings how to bodysurf. Moira was treading water watching him, a knowing smile on her face. "Something on your mind, my dear boy?"

He scowled, knowing full well that wouldn't disturb her a bit. "Nothing that needs to be."

Moira nodded out toward the threesome zooming on their bellies on the wavetops. "Can you feel what our young Sierra is doing?"

He tapped into power, stretching a finger out toward where they played. "She's making them surfboards." Smart, and safe. "Good. Bodysurfing's tricky. This way they can play and have fun, and nobody gets water up their nose."

"Aye. She's being all kinds of responsible." Moira smiled as Aervyn tumbled off the end of a wave into Sierra's waiting hands. "And having all kinds of fun while she's at it."

Devin nodded. It was very good to see. "It worried me, that she was going to swing too hard away from the fun of magic. Sink too deep into the responsibility."

"It's never one or the other. Every witch needs to find their balance. She'll swing around a bit yet, but she's finding her own way." Moira's eyes held hints of mischief. "It's a lesson we all need to revisit occasionally."

He stared at her, nonplussed—and dodged too late as the second wave of the day sent water up his nose.

She was laughing in delight as he surfaced moments later. "Ah, Devin my love. I should have taken you up on your last marriage proposal. Come. Let's go teach our two littlest ones how to swim in the big swells, shall we?"

He swam behind her, wondering how in the hell this little trip had gotten so out of hand. They were only two-foot waves. Why did he suddenly feel like he was swimming in the Bermuda Triangle?

Heads turned as they approached. Moira simply gestured and angled to swim out to sea. Sierra's eyes widened. "Is that safe?"

Damned if he had any idea what that meant today. "Should be. We might want to give Moira an assist, though." He linked power with Sierra, reaching a gentle current forward to the three ahead of them—and discovered that Lizzie and Aervyn, cavorting like dolphins, had already taken care of it. Punk witchlings. They both had water power to burn.

Putting his head down, he matched Sierra's steady front crawl. Apparently *they* had to get out the hard way.

~ ~ ~

Govin scowled at his computer, at the southeast coastline of Indonesia on his screen, just where it had been for the last two days. "It's getting worse, Teej."

"It's only class two right now." His partner continued to bounce a superball off the wall.

"Smells bad." After ten years, you got a feel for the kind of class-two storm that would eventually fall apart after it drenched a few people. This one wasn't that kind. He knew it in his bones, however unscientific that might sound.

"Yeah." TJ was running models, figuring out if they had any options to intervene. "That area's got good mojo, though."

It was true—big waves hitting that coastline often caused less damage than their models predicted. They liked being that kind of wrong. However, even mojo was only so useful when you were dealing with waves big enough to kill people. "You got anything yet?"

"Working as fast as I can, dude. Go feed us, or something."

The storm was edging past Australia, picking up meanness as it went. "What if we get closer? I think we've got witches in Australia—maybe Jamie can push us there through Realm." Govin winced as TJ growled. "Sorry. You've probably already thought of that."

TJ looked ready to pull out his hair—what little of it was still left. "Do you have any idea how hard it is to make a model that says 'How can I fix this, assuming I can drop a witch pretty much anywhere on the planet we've got Internet?'"

Yeah. Models with a zillion moving parts sucked. And TJ was probably the best mind in the world with them. Govin zoomed in on the storm and tried to imagine how he'd intervene if he was standing on the Australian coast. And realized pretty quickly what the problem was. In general, the best way to help dissipate a storm was to slow its rotation. Australia was exactly the wrong place to do it from.

He held up his hands to triangulate. Shit. The exact right place was middle of nowhere in the Indian Ocean. Not exactly a good place to find witches with Internet access.

Damn. He had a really bad feeling about this.

Chapter 20

Turning five was an uber-major event, at least if you were a Sullivan. Sierra held up one end of a rainbow-colored streamer and tried to turn around without falling off the ladder. "Here?"

The decorating committee conferred. Shay finally looked up. "Yup. Uncle Jamie, your end's gotta go higher. They aren't even."

Sierra tried not to giggle as Jamie glanced around at the off-kilter streamers already up and wisely bit his tongue. The triplets took decorating very seriously. Jamie got his end anchored higher, and they both crawled down their respective ladders.

"We done, girls?" Jamie collapsed to the ground and laid a streamer over his eyes. "It all looks good from here."

Mia surveyed the room. "I think we need more glitter."

"No way!" Jamie sat bolt upright in protest. "This is a boy party, remember?"

"It's red glitter." Mia shrugged. "Besides, Aervyn loves shiny stuff." She squinted. "Hey, can we make it float in the air? Kind of like snow?"

Jamie's eye roll was classic—and clearly giggle-inducing. "I'm a serious witch. I don't do silly spells."

Sierra grinned. "I do." Devin said she was supposed to have more fun. How could glitter snow not be fun? "Do you want it to swirl or anything?"

Mia's look was one of total hero worship. "You can do that?"

Oh, yeah. Sierra thought for a moment and got started. She had an audience to impress. Picking up the huge bowl of red glitter, she ran a quick test on the top layer. Excellent. Enough metal in them to magnetize. It would be a tricky spell on that many individual pieces, though.

They'll love it. Jamie's mental voice sounded resigned. *Want some help?*

I thought you don't do silly spells. Sierra was still getting used to talking inside her head and having other people hear.

He chuckled and stood up, placing his hands on the other side of the bowl. "Who do you think taught them everything they know?"

She felt his incoming power stream and started magnetizing the top layers of red glitter. As they built up charge, tiny pieces started to float up, pushed away by those underneath. She eased off a little—they wanted the glitter floating in the air, not plastered to the walls. The girls were watching with rapt attention.

Ha. Not just them, sent Jamie. *The entire room's watching.*

We are. Lauren sounded highly amused. *Is this a friendly shower or a red-glitter menace you're building?*

Sierra grinned. It was like a whole family inside her head. *The menace is tempting, but the decorating committee might be mad.*

Oh, I think you underestimate my girls, sent Nell dryly.

Not to break up your conversation or anything, but I think you've got most of the glitter floating now. Jamie tried to shoo some away from his face.

Sierra laughed. *Coat yourself in a negative ion charge, and it'll leave you alone.* They'd positively charged the glitter.

Jamie blinked, and then wove a quick spell. *Hot damn. A glitter repeller.* He waved his arm in the air, and glitter flew away. He turned toward his nieces, glee in his eyes. "Behold, the glitter menace." He grabbed a fork, positively charged it, and advanced on them with his tiny, glittery spear.

Only to have Nell jump in front, glitter-covered plate in her hands. "Back off, Sir Forkus. These girls are mine." Jamie's fork flew out of his hands and thunked onto her plate.

The triplets knew a good thing when they saw it and ran to arm themselves. Sierra watched in giggly astonishment as the room broke out in an impromptu glitter fight. It didn't take long for the triplets to be smack in the middle of things. And judging from their weaponry, Ginia's earth magic wasn't having any trouble magnetizing stuff.

Lauren tugged on Sierra's sleeve, tape measure in her hand. "Save us!" Devin grinned from behind her, both of them covered in wet, goopy glitter. "Apparently water magic is no match for floaty red stuff."

Sierra's laughter broke free. "You're not supposed to drown it, silly." She magnetized Lauren's tape measure and winked at Devin. "She's armed. You're hopeless. Stay close."

He snickered as Lauren swept her weapon through the air. "Been in any swordfights lately?" And then grinned as she pulled it out to four feet long. "Never mind. I take it back."

Sierra watched them dive into battle, elbows linked, armed with their long and bendy sword, and marveled. Every person in this room carried big responsibilities. And every person in this room had jumped into an all-out glitter fight, badly armed—just to have some fun. Devin was right—you could be a serious witch *and* a playful one.

Grinning, she reached behind her and grabbed the ladder. There was a lot of glitter in the upper two feet of the room—and it was all hers. The red menace was about to attack from above.

~ ~ ~

Breathe in, breathe out. Nat concentrated on the familiar flow of air and energy, and waited for the quiet of meditation to soak into her soul.

She was afraid.

Afraid of the building energy in her belly, carrying the beat of a very different drummer.

Afraid of the whispers and careful eyes of the witching community and what they meant about the girl nestled beneath her heart.

Afraid of all the faith in Natalia Sullivan's ability to breathe through anything, move with serenity in the midst of a storm.

What if they were wrong?

Because there was a storm coming. She could feel it. And the drummer in her belly reveled in anticipation.

Breathe in. Breathe out.

And then, gently, Nat pushed beyond. Beyond the fear, beyond known and unknown. Beyond herself.

She wasn't alone anymore. The strength of Natalia Sullivan no longer needed to come entirely from inside her own soul. Jamie loved her with a fierceness she was only beginning to comprehend—and he would stand, as man and as witch, for her and for their little girl.

And oh-so-many would stand beside him.

So why was she really afraid?

With the automatic bravery of years of practice, Nat swam toward the roots of fear deep in her soul. And found her mother.

Her mother—faced with a child she didn't understand. Two souls, so very different. And so much damage done trying to mold the child in the mother's image.

Nat let sorrow flow on the waves of her breath. She was not her mother. But she, too, awaited a child who was very different.

And that was okay.

Be who you need to be, child of mine.

She let the words settle into her heart—and trusted that the mindreader in her belly would hear them too. *Be who you need to be, small girl.*

Slowly, the fear ebbed. It usually did, if you could just find the root. Nat released one last breath and opened her eyes.

It was almost time. And her baby girl wasn't going to come easy into this world.

She rubbed her belly. *It's okay, little one. You come any way you have to. We'll be right here waiting.*

~ ~ ~

Devin settled into the new couch in his brother's basement. It wasn't The Monster, but it would have to do. He looked over at Jamie and prepared to start a difficult conversation. "You got room for one more on the Realm team?"

Jamie stopped digging through his snack cupboard. "What?"

"Seems like you're pretty busy right now, so I thought I might stick around for a while and help out. You got any Doritos in there?"

"You want to help with Realm?" Jamie tossed over a bag, grabbed one for himself, and then plopped down in the overstuffed chair next to the couch.

They matched. It was disturbing—man caves weren't supposed to match. "Pretty much."

"Your coding skills are kind of rusty, dude."

Sadly. And they'd never held a candle to Jamie and Nell's anyway. "You've got plenty of coders. Not so many organizers, from what I've seen."

"Devin Sullivan, organizer." Jamie pretended to think for a second, then snorted. "Okay, what's really going on here?"

They'd hit the difficult part faster than he'd hoped. "I have some reasons for wanting to be here. That little girl of yours, for starters. I figured while I was here, I should make myself useful." That sounded weak, even to his own ears.

Jamie stared. Then he busted up laughing. "Damn you, Dev. I owe my wife a whole month of hip-openers classes, thanks to you."

Devin wasn't entirely sure what hip openers were. He didn't plan to find out, either. "What's Nat got to do with this?"

His brother's eyes gleamed. "I bet you'd stick to your itinerant-bachelor ways until the New Year. Figured it was a sure thing."

Crap. *Nothing* got past Nat. Now they were neck-deep in difficult-conversation territory. Devin fought the urge to squirm. "It's no big deal."

"Yeah." Jamie's eyes danced with mirth. "You stick with that story. It might even work, at least until Mom gets here tomorrow."

Damn, damn, damn. Devin tried to look desperate. It wasn't hard. "I was hoping you really could use some help with Realm. Give me a little cover."

"Oh, we totally need the help." Jamie was a hairsbreadth from collapsing in laughter again. "With the new WitchNet stuff and Net magic on the prowl in Realm, there's plenty to do, and I'm gonna be kind of busy for a while." He sobered a little. "What about the clinic?"

That was one of the few easy parts of this decision. "Mom, Dad, and Matt can easily run the place without me. I was useful when we were setting up, but I'm no healer, and Dad does great with all the back-room stuff."

"Well, we'll gladly take you in." Jamie paused a beat. "You know Mom's not going to believe it for one second."

He could always hope. "Leave me with my fantasies, will you?"

His brother grinned. "If you're really lucky, Nat will go into labor and provide a distraction for you."

Devin groaned. Retha Sullivan was about as distractible as a charging elephant.

Jamie reached casually for the TV remote. "How does Lauren feel about this?"

And that would be the next wave of difficult crashing over his head. "She doesn't know yet."

To his relief, Jamie didn't start laughing again. He just nodded. "She's more cautious than you are."

Yeah. "Everyone's more cautious than I am."

"On some things." Jamie was quiet a moment. "But I stood in Lauren's living room and told her she was a witch. Expected her to run like hell or drop-kick me out of her apartment."

Clearly she hadn't done either. And Devin held tight to one other ray of hope. "She channels for Aervyn."

Jamie nodded. "Yeah. She's not reckless. Not even a little. But she knows how to ride a tornado."

Devin hoped he was just a small funnel. Ah, screw that. He'd just have to hope Lauren liked the man he was. "Am I crazy?" He was pretty sure the answer to that was yes.

"Yup." Jamie grinned. "Crazier now than before? Nah. Lauren's about as cool as they come."

And Nat's best friend. "Anybody going to threaten me with a shotgun or ask my intentions?"

"Not me. The woman's a mind witch. If she wants, she could have you down on your knees begging in an instant." Jamie propped his feet on the coffee table. "And I've seen her wield a tape measure."

It was probably bad that one of your favorite "date" memories with someone involved chasing three shrieking girls around with a glittery measuring tool. Devin sighed. "Is this what growing up feels like?"

"Nat says you grew up a long time ago, and everyone but you knows it." Jamie wedged himself more comfortably in the chair. "Basketball or women's beach volleyball?"

Devin stared, disconcerted. "You're sure your wife isn't a witch?"

Jamie grinned. "She also says you'll make a great uncle, and you should come to hip-openers class with me so she can keep an eye on you." He pitched his chip bag into a corner garbage can. "And yeah—that's pretty much my wife with a shotgun. Watch your step."

Devin sighed. That'd be a lot easier to do if he had any idea where the hell he was walking.

~ ~ ~

Her black cohosh supply was running low. Sophie stacked the jar in the small pile of supplies to refill.

"I don't think our Nat will be needing the cohosh," said Moira, rocking in a nearby chair. "Fire witchlings don't usually need any help speeding things up."

"A wise midwife once taught me to be prepared for anything." Sophie smiled, her fingers continuing to sort jars. "And the cohosh is good for hemorrhaging, too."

"Aye. Always a worry when the babe's in a hurry."

Sophie looked at the resupply pile. None of it really needed refilling. She was restless and had hoped checking the contents of her bags would be soothing. "You'd think I'm the one giving birth, with all the nesting I'm doing."

Moira sipped her tea. "You think we're going to have another Solstice babe?"

Aervyn had been born on the Winter Solstice, five years ago tomorrow. Even modern witches took those kinds of portents fairly seriously. "Don't you?"

"Aye. She's got a destiny to follow, this little one."

Sophie went to sit next to Moira. Her instincts had been jangling all day, and apparently she wasn't alone. "Was it like this before Aervyn's birth? Could you feel it?"

Moira grinned. "Oh, my, could we. It wasn't like now, where you can hop into Realm and hop out in California. I'd come to stay with them while we waited, and Nell was two weeks overdue. The energies had been swirling in that house for weeks. I think if Solstice had come and gone without a baby, every witch in ten miles would have gone stark raving mad."

"Well, this babe isn't causing those kinds of disturbances. Maybe she'll arrive more gently." They could always hope.

Moira chortled. "She's just biding her time, this wee one. Don't let her fool you."

"Any other advice?" Witchlings with power before birth were rare—Sophie had only attended the arrival of two others.

"Just the same as always."

The long-familiar words slid easily off Sophie's tongue. "Trust the mother, trust the baby, trust the magic."

"Aye. And this time in particular, trust the circle that holds you safe."

Sophie rubbed her belly. In her current condition, she felt a special empathy for the mama-to-be. "Nat's got no idea what's coming, and I don't know how to prepare her."

"She's heard the stories. It's all you can do." Moira reached out, her fingers warm and comforting. "No woman is truly ready her first time. And Natalia knows how to stay present in the moment as well as anyone I know. As do you."

It would have to be enough. Sophie resisted the urge to get up and check her supplies one more time. "I wonder how Aervyn will feel about sharing his birthday?"

"He's got a generous heart." Moira tilted her head, thinking. "It will be harder for him to share Jamie, I think."

One of Aunt Moira's strengths had always been her ability to see the places a witch might stumble. And then to clear the path, or make a soft landing, as need be. Sophie considered the feelings of a small boy for the very special man in his life—a man about to have a lot more demands on his time. "Well, he'll just have to come visit us if he needs more cuddles."

"Indeed." Moira rocked. "And he'll help out with his young cousin—help her grow to be the witch she's meant to be. It will do him good to have another young one sharing the spotlight."

Sophie heard an undertone in the words. "You don't think she'll be the talent he is?" Aervyn had the kind of power that hadn't been seen in ten generations.

The creak of the rocking chair was all the answer she got for a while. "I don't *know*, my dear girl. But I *feel* it. One day they will stand side by side, and her magic will blaze as brightly as his."

Sophie shivered. Sometimes it was hard to remember precog wasn't one of Aunt Moira's talents. Her "feelings" were almost never wrong.

She got up. Whatever supplies might be needed at the birth of a witchling to equal Aervyn, she planned to have them in her bag.

Chapter 21

The blaring klaxon of emergency alarms yanked Govin out of sleep. Moving quickly, he rolled out of bed, reaching for his phone to page TJ—and nearly got mowed down in the hallway. Damn. Wake up, dude. TJ was temporarily living down the hall.

And he moved fast. Slamming into a desk chair, TJ started banging keys like a frenzied drummer. "Shit. That depression off Indonesia has turned ugly."

Govin waited quietly. He wasn't nearly as fast as TJ, and they needed a definition of "ugly." ASAP. They'd tried some small adjustments to the storm yesterday—low probability—and clearly they hadn't worked.

It was a very bad sign when TJ stopped typing.

Govin steeled himself. After ten years, he still hated this part. The moment before he found out he couldn't do enough.

"It's bad. Really bad." Then TJ's hands slammed down on the keys again. "Get Sierra."

Govin winced. "Teej, she's not ready to watch people die."

"Nobody's ever ready." His partner looked up, eyes fierce. "It's big waves, heading at villages. Fifty thousand people, Gov. With her help, maybe we save some."

Heart hollow, Govin made the call to wake up the girl who had cried a bucket of tears over one dead bird. And then woke up a whole pile of other people. She'd need all the backup they could give her.

~ ~ ~

Nell waited for a Realm shuttle to Govin's place, Sierra at her side. His text had terrified her.

Witches worked very hard to keep their youngest away from life-and-death situations. She knew that one day, Aervyn would be called. But not yet.

Instead, they'd called on the girl who had nestled into all of their hearts. Devin might have been the first Sullivan to adopt Sierra—but he wasn't the last. And dammit, she was too young for this.

Nell felt the tug of a Realm transport spell—and then the odd disorientation as it spit them out the other side.

The vibrating intensity in the room told her what she needed to know, but she asked anyway. *Do you really need her, Gov? This is going to break her into a million pieces if you fail.*

She read the answer in his eyes. And the deep, deep sorrow. He expected them to fail.

The mother in her wanted to grab Sierra and run. The witch knew he would never have asked unless many lives were at stake. Okay, then. Maybe they could change the odds. "How can we help?"

TJ held up a hand. "Give me a couple of minutes to finish running this model, then I'll explain. Devin and Jamie are on the way."

"We're here." Devin held Lauren's hand—and their feet were sandy. Nell blinked. It was 4 a.m.

Jamie landed, still wearing the Spiderman pajamas Aervyn had given him for his birthday. "Lauren. Can you go stay with Nat? I don't want to leave her alone."

That Lauren hesitated at all told Nell volumes about what must be in Govin and TJ's heads. Shit, shit, shit.

Wait. Nell started typing into her phone. "Daniel's monitoring Realm comm channels. It's morning in Nova

Scotia—I'll ask him to fetch Moira and Sophie a bit early. They'll take good care of Nat."

TJ held up his hand again, and the entire room went silent. When he spun his chair around, his face was as pale as Nell had ever seen it. "We had a tropical-storm depression off the coast of Indonesia go off-model. Ran into a warm-water current, spun up some big waves. Forty-footers. Unfortunately, they're headed toward a delta—a valley that's got some of the best fishing in the country. Fifty thousand people living at sea level, mostly in small, rural villages."

No way to warn them. "How long?"

"Less than an hour." He pulled up a map on the big screens behind him. "The waves are coming in here. If we're really lucky, they'll turn a little and run into these hills, here. The hills can handle forty feet."

Jamie moved forward. "How much do they need to turn? Can we push them?"

Govin shook his head. "Not from here. Too far, not enough time." They'd tried last night.

"You might be able to take the edge off the wave speed." TJ pulled up a model. "This is the best option I can find. It shrinks the kill zone some."

Nell watched in horror as 17,163 people still lost their lives.

Sierra's voice was barely a whisper. "I've been there." Moving forward, a walking ghost, she touched an inlet on the screen, right in the middle of the kill zone. "We lived in this village right here for almost a year." She turned, eyes slightly crazed. "We have to help them."

Nell's heart agonized. "We don't know if we can, sweetheart. It's halfway around the world."

Sierra spun to Jamie. "Get us closer. Send us through Realm. If we're closer, we can fix this."

Her brother's eyes were bleak. "There's no Internet in that area. I already checked."

"Internet." TJ whirled back to his computer, a keyboarding maniac. "A satellite signal will pass over that area in about ten minutes." He looked up. "We could get you there. Tricky timing, but we could do it."

Devin stepped in front of Sierra. "I'll go."

"No." Nell couldn't believe she was the only one who had spoken. "We don't drop people in front of killer waves with no exit route until the next satellite pass. That's suicide."

Jamie took her hand. "TJ, can you find us to somewhere close, but with a little elevation?" He squeezed her hand as she gathered breath to protest. "If we take a small group, I can port us closer—and then back to safety."

He'd port them out and leave thousands of people dying on the beach? Not likely. Nell yanked his face toward hers. "You have a baby coming. You can't do this. You'll kill yourself trying to port everyone to safety."

"I won't." Even the possibility left his mind in agony. "I know what I have to live for."

"If we can't stop the wave, maybe we can move the people." Lauren stood staring at the map. "TJ, how wide is the kill zone?"

"Thirty miles, but the worst of it is here at the delta. About four miles. That's where most of the people live, the ones who will be hit first."

Lauren's mind radiated warrior steel. "I can mindproject and reach at least half of those. If they run, some of them will make it to safety." She looked at Sierra. "I need you to teach me how to say 'Big wave. Run!' in Indonesian."

"I'm coming." Sierra's face no longer belonged to a girl. "You might need more words than that. And while you broadcast, I'll see if I can turn the waves."

A RECKLESS WITCH

Dev and Govin closed in, one on each side. She would have help. Nell looked on the faces she loved, anguished. Lives were on the line—theirs, and tens of thousands more.

Jamie handed her his phone. "Work with Daniel. Put us down in the middle of the delta. The closer we can get, the more people Lauren can warn."

Nell squeezed her eyes shut and made the most difficult decision of her life. She handed the phone to TJ. "I'm coming."

Jamie turned whiter. "You have five kids, sister mine."

"Exactly." Someone had to make sure this didn't turn into a witch suicide mission. She looked at the assembled crew. "We're coming back. Every last damn one of us." With everything in her, she willed each one of them to believe it.

~ ~ ~

Devin had never been so terrified in his life. He stood motionless, waiting to beam into the kill zone of a tsunami—with most of the people dearest to him in the world.

Even his risk-loving soul knew this was insane.

And it had been Lauren who had stepped up first.

He'd think later about the fact that she'd nearly made his heart stop.

TJ looked up from his computer. "In five. Four. Three. Two. One. Mark."

And out they spilled, into the village where Sierra had once lived. It was not a quiet arrival—they'd landed in the middle of a group of chattering women preparing the evening meal. Devin blinked. A lot of interested faces turned their way, but no one had moved, no one had panicked. What the hell?

"They know magic." Sierra stepped out of the group, bowing deeply to a very old woman. Then a flow of words, musical and foreign, poured out of her mouth.

Devin watched as the old woman's face shifted from joy, to sorrow, to fear. And then it shifted one more time, and he knew, whoever she was, she had just taken charge.

She turned, spoke six sharp words—and everyone within a hundred feet fled.

Sierra turned, grabbing Lauren's hand. "This is Oma. She asks that you send her words as far as you can. They will listen to her."

Devin stood transfixed, as Lauren, California sand still on her feet, held hands with a tiny brown matriarch. And watched in awe as every person he could see grabbed a child or a basket and ran. In less than a minute, the village was empty except for the old woman and three young women who stood by her side.

"They will carry word as they go." Sierra pointed in the direction of the retreating villagers. "Oma says they will make it to safety—the hills are not far."

The old woman snapped out two more words, and Sierra blushed. "She says we must also go. They are grateful for the warning."

They'd been dismissed. Oma turned and walked toward the sea, the three young women following her.

Devin stepped forward, about to protest—and felt water power stirring. And suddenly he understood. "They're witches. Water witches."

Sierra nodded. "Here they're called water dancers. They keep the village safe. Momma brought me to train with them."

He turned to Jamie. "Take Lauren and port out of here. Govin and Nell too." He and Sierra could survive the landing of a forty-foot wave—nobody else would.

"Like hell." Lauren's look was pure fury.

"You can't help here!"

"I can hook all your minds together so you can work as a unit." She calmly walked after the village women. "You're wasting time."

He'd kill her later. Devin shoved aside the tangled knot in his gut and reached for power. He felt the incoming clink of Lauren's mindlink and the gathering power of each of the water witches. The old woman's power stream already headed out into the ocean, seeking the waves.

Devin tried to overlay TJ's map on the scene in front of him. *The waves are a bit to the left, I think.* He hoped like hell that Lauren's mental links included some kind of translation.

The waves will be to the left, said a voice he didn't know but instantly recognized. Leaders everywhere spoke with the same authority. *But the water we must move will be ahead.*

Devin smiled grimly. *Done this before, have you?*

Since before your mother's mother was born, young one. You have impressive power in you. It is good. We will need it.

He felt her mind stretching to the origin point for the wave stream. And he felt her fear. Then an incomprehensible stream of words—and three minds split off the connection. The young women turned as one—and ran.

It is time for you to go now too. This is mine to face.

Bloody stubborn witches. *Let us help.*

He felt her answer before the words came. *This one is too big. We cannot turn it.*

Then why do you stay?

Her voice was a world of calm, the fear long gone. *Because I can slow it down a little. Enough for my people to get to safety. I was born for this. It is my calling as a water dancer. Go.* And her mind dropped the link.

Like hell. No witch he knew left old women to die. Even heroic ones.

~ ~ ~

Sierra stared at the tiny woman who had once stood in as her grandmother and felt her heart crack. She threw her power streams at the back of Oma's head, screaming as they were rebuffed. It was the tradition of water dancers—they all knew one day a wave too big would come and take them away.

Not today. Please God, not today.

Maybe she could stop the wave herself. Desperately, she gathered energy, looking for a place big enough to ground. And then heard Devin's voice, rock solid, inside her head. *You have a team, Sierra. Use us.*

A team. A team to use. A team to take care of.

Sierra clung tight to the rock of Devin's calm and tried to think. Oma was right—water power wasn't going to stop these waves, even with all three of them working. But Oma had nothing else to use. She did.

Her team. Fire power. Lots and lots of fire power. Rapidly, she mindsketched her idea, praying her team's edge was big enough. It was a humungous spell.

It's time. Lauren's mind voice held insistent command. *Now, or get us out.*

NOW. Sierra held one end of the spell, Devin the other, funneling superheated water into place—an inch of heat to turn a mountain of water. With what little magic she could spare, she reached out and felt the hurtling power of the wave on final approach.

And then suddenly she was on an island, wave coming in behind her as she played with the baby storm, not seeing. *Momma. RUN. MOMMA!*

NO! No. That wasn't real. It wasn't now. Now was a wave, and a wall, and a team. A team. She wasn't alone. They needed her now.

She picked up the shredded ends of the spell she'd dropped, holding on with all the power and love she possessed.

And felt the tsunami smash into their trickling string of warmer water. A feather to turn an elephant.

Power exploded through her channels, white-hot lightning. Then nothing.

Nothing.

And then she felt Oma's hand in hers. "You've done it, child. You turned the waters."

Sierra opened her eyes—and saw the forty-foot swells rushing to land just down the coast. There were hills there—hills to slow down the waves. Please, let the villagers be out of the way. Please.

"We are fishermen." Oma smiled. "No one is foolish enough to stay when the big waves are coming. Now hold my hand, and let's swim in this little one together, shall we?"

The waves roaring in on them now were only fifteen feet high.

~ ~ ~

Lauren squeezed her head, reeling from the power vibrations that had kicked from everyone's channels. Nothing like being mindconnected to a lightning bolt.

But they'd done it. She'd felt the relief hit first the old woman, then Sierra.

Then she opened her eyes—and looked up at a wall of water. Her mind screamed, but all that came out was a squeak.

Devin's hand slid into hers, firm and cool. "Just a little wave left. Time to go swimming."

Oh, holy God. She turned to run. "I can't swim." And nearly dislocated her arm when he didn't let her go.

"I can." His eyes promised everything. "Just hold on."

She held. She prayed. And she believed.

~ ~ ~

Sierra sat in front of a waterlogged hut, her arm around Oma's shoulders as they cuddled under a blanket, watching the village children rushing around finding everyone's belongings. Even small waves could make a pretty big mess if your home was on the front lines.

"You have a big family now, child. I'm glad for you. Your heart is big enough to love many."

The only time she'd ever had a big family before had been the year she and Momma had lived in the village. "They've been really nice to me."

"They love you. That is far different."

They'd come with her. On a reckless, harebrained rescue mission. That was beyond love.

Oma's hand stroked her cheek. "And your mother?"

Tears mixed with the salty ocean water drying on Sierra's cheeks. She remembered now. "I think she went wave dancing. And she didn't come back."

"I'm so sorry, child." Oma was quiet for a minute. "She never quite understood when to dance."

Sierra sat up straight. That was as close as she'd ever heard Oma come to criticism. "What do you mean?"

"The water can be fearsome. A joy, a partner, but also a life-taker. It is why the water dancers of the village are always old. We do not ask the mamas to dance."

"But Momma loved the water dance." Her throat was letting very little air in.

"Yes. But she also loved you." Oma's eyes were dark and sad. "And she danced too often to the edge of life."

Sierra's heart ached. "Didn't we do that today?"

"Yes." The old woman gazed out over her village. "But today we saved many thousands of lives." She smiled. "And you weren't in as much danger as I believed. That nice young man Jamie has powerful magic to be able to move people like that."

He had ported Nell and Govin out of the way of the fifteen-foot wave, trusting the water witches to swim their way through. Well, the water witches and poor Lauren.

Sierra looked over to where a drenched and giddy, but shell-shocked, Lauren sat cuddled in Devin's lap. "I need to teach her how to swim."

Oma smiled. "Bring her for a visit. The young ones will have fun helping her learn, and you and I can chat a little."

Not every piece of her past had disappeared with Momma. Sierra's heart squeezed in gratitude.

Chapter 22

Nell sat in a chair watching Aervyn's birthday party in full swing and marveled yet again at the resiliency of Witch Central. "I can't believe I was on a beach in Indonesia, covered in seaweed, just a few hours ago."

Moira chortled. "Naps and cookies fix most witches up pretty quickly."

Truth. Her cookie stash had been seriously depleted upon their return. She watched her birthday boy chasing one of his sisters around with his new fireman hose and laughed. "I'm pretty sure that hose didn't come with a real water supply."

Sophie giggled as Ginia, soaking wet, turned to retaliate. "Well, it has one now."

The sight of her dripping daughter and laughing son sobered Nell. "Water seems so innocent most of the time."

Moira clasped her hand. "As does magic."

Nell squeezed back, glad her fears were understood. "He's still so little."

"He has time yet." Moira paused, watching Aervyn's giggles. "Time to fully know the joy of his magic before discovering its sadness."

"She didn't get that time." Nell looked over at Sierra, heroine and giddy teenager. "We put her in the path of hell this morning."

"Based on what I heard, she put herself there." Sophie's voice was quiet, but firm. "You saved twenty thousand people this morning, maybe more. That's a miracle, Nell."

It was. But her heart iced over with the knowledge that it probably wouldn't be the only miracle asked for in her lifetime. Or that of her son.

And then thawed again, knowing how many witches stood between her son and that day. Sierra just added one to their number. "She was amazing. We've shaken her hard these last couple of weeks, and she just stood there in the face of a forty-foot catastrophe and figured out how to do the impossible." It would be a long time before Nell erased the mental picture of the wall of water that had crashed down on the four witches Jamie hadn't been able to port out of the way in time—and that had been a baby wave compared to what had originally threatened.

"As did every one of you." Moira's eyes looked off in the distance. "It is the calling of witches, the weight that comes with the gift of power. We must stand for others—and we must choose wisely when and where to take our stands." Her words got very quiet. "It's the second that is the far more difficult lesson to learn."

Nell breathed deeply. "I think I'm still working on that one."

Sophie laughed as Devin and Jamie intercepted Aervyn's fire hose, getting thoroughly wet in the process. "Aren't we all." She threw up a shielding spell as water started to spray everywhere.

Nell just shook her head. All the furniture had long since been protected with waterproofing spells. And she had two brothers who were going to be heading up the clean-up crew. After the fun was over, of course. She grinned. "I have a spare hose."

Moira chortled. "You might want to wait on that a moment, dear."

Nell turned to see what Moira was looking at—and winced as a hose blast hit Retha Sullivan square between the eyes. Nell watched as the cascade of water poured down her mom's face—

and gave many thanks she wasn't the one standing with a hose in her hand. Two minutes more, and she might have been.

Retha stood regally still, blinked three times—and then lasered in on the culprit. "Devin Theodore Roosevelt Sullivan. How many times have I told you that innocent bystanders aren't fair targets in a water fight?"

"Hi, Mom." Dev rolled his eyes and kissed her cheek. "I didn't know you were there. Besides, how come you're blaming me? I didn't start this. Honest."

"You're holding the hose, my boy." Retha grinned as her grandchildren started to giggle. "And you know the penalty for watering the innocent."

The triplets scrambled. "We're on Gramma's team!"

Nell snorted with laughter as all the smart people in the room lined up behind them. Sullivan rules said that if you fired on innocent bystanders, you got to play against Retha. Without magic.

That left her two brothers standing alone. Jamie threw an arm around Devin's shoulders. "Way to go, bro. We're going to get soaked twice in one day. Matt, come on out."

Her third brother emerged from the hallway, shaking his head. "Only you guys could get me in trouble before I even make it into the room."

Devin grinned. "It's a talent."

Aervyn stepped out of the crowd, wearing his full firefighter gear. "I'll be on your team. I'm getting big now, so I'm probably a Sullivan troublemaker too."

Nell shook her head, laughing. Only in her weird and wacky family could a water fight on the sure-to-be-losing team be considered a proud rite of passage.

Devin hoisted her son up. "Excellent. Your job is to keep Gramma distracted with your cuteness while we steal the hose."

Aervyn giggled. "You're not a'posed to tell her your plan, silly."

"Troops!" Retha held up one arm, pointed the other at the door. "Battle stations!"

Moira rubbed her hands together as the hordes stampeded out of the house. "How about we find that extra hose and go provide Devin with the distraction he needs?"

Nat wiggled out of a chair in the corner, grinning. "I could pretend to go into labor. That would probably work."

That did it. Nell busted up laughing, and then lurched to her feet, headed into battle with a seventy-six-year-old witch and a woman about to go into labor at her side. They were going to get so wet.

~ ~ ~

Sierra looked up in gratitude as Govin finished the quick-dry spell on her clothes. "Thanks. I wasn't getting very far myself." Her fire talents were pretty miniscule. And she'd gotten seriously drenched in the water fight.

He smiled. "Even teenagers don't have unlimited magic. You've been kind of busy today."

Yeah. What a totally weird day. "How do you do it?"

He looked up from drying her shoes. "Do what? The quick-dry spell? It's pretty simple."

She shook her head. "No. How do you do the work you do?"

"The weather work?" He sat down on the grass beside her, eyes serious. "I don't know. It's what I'm meant to do, I guess."

Just like Oma had been born to water dance—to keep her village safe from the ravaging waters, and to someday give her life to the waves.

Like Momma had done. She'd felt the truth in the water—Momma had danced and lost.

Sierra didn't want to die. "Does it scare you?"

Setting his chin on his knees, Govin picked up a couple of small stones and rolled them around in his hands. His smile was sad. "I'm not brave like you, Sierra. I'm a very cautious witch and a math geek. I only do magic when the models say it's probably going to work. Mostly that keeps me safe."

She knew that wasn't true. "You came today. The models said everybody was going to die."

Now his eyes were sad. "The models are based on my magic—on what I can do. We've never had a witch with your skills. Or the ability to travel through Realm to get close."

Those should be good things. "Won't that help you save more people?"

He nodded. "It will."

There was a weight in his eyes. She frowned, puzzled. And then the dead baby bird flashed into her mind, and she understood. "But not all the people."

"Never all the people. And it will be more dangerous for the witches on the front lines." His head bowed under the weight of the magic he carried. "Today we won. We don't always."

"You'll win more if I help."

It was a long, long moment before he nodded.

Sierra sat quietly, thinking. Of Oma, and the waves that would come next year. Of Momma, and the waves she would never see. "You *are* brave. You stay alive. So you can help the next time." She met his eyes, and for the first time, appreciated the strength in them. "You stay alive. Teach me how to be that kind of brave."

~ ~ ~

Retha watched her two sons sitting nonchalantly in their still-wet clothes. Such different men—and right now, their minds tangling with exactly the same worry.

How to love in a world that wasn't always safe.

She sat down on the couch between them and started with what she hoped was the easier tangle. "It won't be long now."

Jamie looked over at his wife, cuddled under a blanket and pampered by three nine-year-old waitresses. "Is that mom intuition, or something more?"

He'd learn more respect for parent intuition soon enough. "Your little girl's a Sullivan. Do you really think she's going to arrive the day after Winter Solstice and miss her grand entrance?"

He chuckled. "Nat thinks it will be today. She's ready."

As always, she heard the words he didn't quite say. "You're more ready than you think."

He blew out a breath. "What's that you used to say? That you wished sometimes you'd stood in the line for nice, normal, boring babies?"

"Never did find it." Her lips twitched. "I had hopes for Nat, but apparently she found the same line Nell and I did." She grinned. "You'll survive. Probably."

Devin snorted. "Way to make him feel better, Mom."

Retha smiled, well aware she already had. "And how about you? Other than watering your mother, adopting a new sister, and falling in love, gotten into any trouble lately?"

He just gaped.

She grinned. "Mom intuition. Never underestimate it." And then took pity on him. "Sierra's a lovely girl." They'd get to the other girl in his life in a moment.

"Scared me spitless today." He scowled. "Standing out there in front of a killer mountain of water, waving her magic wand."

She didn't bother to point out that he'd been standing right beside Sierra. Or how knowing that would haunt her dreams for a while. "She shares some of your adventurous heart." And his huge need to rescue others.

"Her magic's a lot stronger than mine. She'll be more at risk."

Again she heard what he didn't say. "The burdens of power can be heavy, and they don't always wait for the witch to be ready." She took his hand. "The world needs those willing to live on the front lines." And those able to watch as the ones they loved stood in the way of danger.

Both her sons would learn soon enough that watching and loving was its own act of bravery.

And that was more than enough seriousness. She patted Jamie's hand, looking at Devin. "He's finally given me a grandbaby. How does Lauren feel about children?"

Jamie cracked up laughing as his brother swallowed his tongue. "Told you, dude."

"She's... I... We're..." Dev just spluttered, much to his mother's delight. Not much tongue-tied her wild boy. He turned a lovely shade of pink, and then stomped off. "I need cookies."

Retha nestled deeper into the couch, well pleased. "I didn't expect it to happen so quickly."

Jamie's voice held a note of warning. "It's not a done deal yet, Mom."

Oh, she knew that. But she also knew her son. He never walked when he could run. He never took the path of least resistance. And Sierra had not been the only witch who had scared Dev senseless with her bravery today.

If she knew her son, he would find that irresistible.

~ ~ ~

Sierra stuffed in more cookies. It was time to give Aervyn his birthday presents, and she was still kind of low on energy. But no way was she going to miss out on the arrival of the Red Rocket. She'd helped Devin with the magical paint job.

It was the coolest flying broom ever. And fast, probably because it was designed with flying in mind instead of sweeping. Sweepers didn't care so much about all that aerodynamic stuff.

She watched as Aervyn tore into his first gifts, totally in love with each one. A set of Harry Potter books from his grandparents—bespelled to read with their voices. The invisibility cloak from Jamie and Nat—he looked totally goofy with only his sneakers sticking out. Hide and Seek had just changed forever.

From his parents—Harry Potter pajamas and his very own laptop. "This one isn't for taking apart," Nell said sternly. Sierra giggled. Nell's whole strict-mama thing wasn't very convincing.

A pointy hat from Sophie—she and Mike had built in a ton of head protection. With two earth witches behind those spells, not much was likely to dent Aervyn's head. Even big rocks.

Nell listened to Sophie's careful explanation and snorted. "I'm guessing one of the other presents will explain why my son needs the best-protected head in the universe?"

Sophie held up her hands, laughing. "That one's not on me. I'm just averting head injuries."

Sierra figured Nell probably didn't feel any better as Aervyn opened his next gift—a bunch of healing salves from Ginia and Moira, and hand-drawn dragon Band-Aids from Mia and Shay. Aervyn bounced up and down. "Do I have to wait 'til I get a boo-boo to wear one?"

Mia giggled. "Nuh, uh. We can make more if you run out."

And then Aervyn got to the last gift, his eyes widening in glee as he tore the paper off the Red Rocket. "Uncle Dev, is it the fastest broom ever? In the whole wide world?"

Nell grabbed the broom as he swung a leg over. "Nice try, superboy." She pinned her brothers with a look. "And exactly who's going to keep up with him and dig him out of trouble?"

Devin's grin was pure mischief. "We've got that covered, actually." He waved a hand at Matt, who stood holding another broom. This one was purple and shiny. "Sierra gets to be his wingman."

For her?

Sierra's insides melted. And every inch of her itched to fly.

Nell looked out the window at the darkening night, looked back at her quivering son, and popped up two fireglobes on her hands. She set one on the end of the Red Rocket and the other on the end of Sierra's new ride. Headlights. "Go for a ride, superboy."

Sierra giggled as everyone in the house dashed for a window, a camera—or a broom.

~ ~ ~

"Remind me that I want to get more sleep before his sixth birthday party." Jamie plopped down beside his wife, feeling the seeping tiredness in his bones. Broom riding was for the young, especially at the supersonic speeds of the Red Rocket. He put his hand on Nat's belly. "Gramma's here, so you can come on out any time you like now." He yawned. "I wouldn't mind a nap first, though."

His wife grinned. "You guys keep having this much fun and she's not going to be content to stay in here much longer."

He lit a small fireglobe up on his palm, delighted when an answering ball of light formed over Nat's belly. They'd played this game for days now. It was pretty much the coolest thing ever, and made his actions of the morning feel even more insane.

He'd been wrestling with that decision all day. "I shouldn't have gone this morning."

"I was alone for all of three-and-a-half minutes." Nat's eyes sharpened. "That's not what you mean, though."

It wasn't. "Being a witch is about balance. Power and life. Responsibility and fun. Possible and not." And just as he'd almost gotten it figured out, the rules were changing. "It's different now. I wasn't thinking like a parent this morning. Nell was—she only went to drag me and Dev back home in one piece."

"You underestimate your sister." She paused, rubbing her belly again. "And going was the right thing."

She sounded so sure. "We could have died, Nat."

"I know that." Her eyes never wavered. "But you didn't. I don't think I really understood the line you have to walk until today."

He studied her, bewildered. "And that sits okay for you?"

She smiled, and the look in her eyes made him swallow. "One of the things I've always loved most about you is your capacity for joy. But I've never really understood why it was there." She took his hands, tears in her eyes. "Until today. Teach your daughter, Jamie. Help her find that joy so she's able to carry the load that comes with her magic."

Whatever he'd done to deserve her wasn't nearly enough. "I'll do my best." His grin was a bit wobbly. "Assuming she ever comes out."

Nat grimaced. "Oh, I think she's on her way."

His brain shattered. "Now? Right now?"

Every head in the room turned. Nat giggled even as she bent over, blowing out strongly. "Yup. Pretty sure this is what labor feels like."

Chapter 23

Sophie grinned at Moira. "I wondered how long she was going to wait to tell him she was in labor."

"She did well for a first-timer. Those warm-up contractions have been coming for quite a while now. She's done well to give everyone this much of a chance to regroup." Moira studied Nat's face. "But this babe is coming fast now. You'd best be getting your things ready. I'll go chat with Devin and Lauren and get them moving."

Sophie stood up and walked over toward Nat. Moira was never wrong about these things. She tried to gauge how much the excitement in the room needed to tamp down for Nat's comfort. Some laboring mamas needed absolute quiet. Others welcomed a circus in the early stages. Currently, the room leaned more toward the latter.

"She's okay for now," Lauren said quietly, touching Sophie's shoulder. "Jamie's about to hyperventilate, though."

Sophie laughed. Generally a midwife's first assignment was the father-to-be. "Do me a favor—find the calm minds and start gently clearing the room. No rush just yet."

Lauren eyed her. "You're expecting one though, aren't you." It wasn't a question.

"Yes." If you had a handy mind witch, you might as well put her to work. "How's the baby's mental state?"

"Intent." Lauren closed her eyes for a moment. Her breath caught. "She has a lot in common with several witches facing down a tsunami this morning." Her eyes popped back open. "She's scared, Soph. And ready to charge a mountain headfirst."

Sophie tried not to giggle. When you were talking about babies birthing, headfirst was a good thing. She met Lauren's worried gaze. "She's about to be born. That's a force of nature bearing some resemblance to a forty-foot wave."

Lauren paled. "Is Nat ready for that?"

"Not yet." It would come. It always did. "But she will be. And your job is to believe it, even when she doesn't." Because that, too, would likely come. Birthing mamas had discovered "hitting the wall" long before marathon runners. She heard another contraction arriving for Nat and glanced at her watch. Three minutes. Damn. Moira was right. This one was going to move fast.

She looked at Lauren. "Never mind. Go get Devin."

Judging from the speed Devin flew out of the crowd, Lauren had paged him with some impressive volume. "What? What's wrong?"

Sophie tried to project a sense of calm. Insanity would come soon enough, and ideally not from the birthing team. "Get your circle ready."

His eyes bugged. "Now?"

"Now."

Shifting into high gear, Sophie parted the crowd, catching Retha's eye. It was time to clear the room. And then they all stopped dead as Aervyn's mental voice boomed. *Everybody outta here. Nat's gotta have a baby, and we're too dis-trac-ting. We can all wait in the back yard and stuff.*

Caro patted his head. "First babies take a long time, wonderboy. Maybe we should go wait at my house."

"Nope." Aervyn grinned. "She wants to share my birthday, so she's coming really soon." He patted Nat's belly, then hopped off the arm of her chair. "We'll go make a circle now, and I'll save her some cake."

The room cleared out just in time for Nat's next contraction. Sophie knelt down by her patient, scanning quickly. Good oxygen, strong heartbeat, and a body readying for the opening necessary to birth a baby. Excellent. She looked up at Nat, reassurance in her eyes. "She's doing beautifully in there. How are you?"

Nat blew out air. "A little scared. I didn't expect the early contractions to be quite this wild."

Sophie's scan had shown what Moira already knew. "These aren't the early ones, love. You've jumped straight into the thick of things." Time for a little truth-telling. "It's looking like this little girl's coming fast and fierce. We just need to stay with her. It'll be pretty intense, but I don't think it's going to take very long."

Nat nodded, still breathing. "Stay in the moment."

"Exactly." Sophie nodded at Jamie. "Let's get her into the birthing room after this next contraction, into the water tub." They had a huge and lovely pool for Nat to labor and birth in, if she wished. Most mamas wished—the water was blissful.

Jamie looked panicked. "We didn't put the water in or heat it up yet."

Sophie tried not to laugh. "You have a house full of witches, Jamie."

"Oh. Right." He looked around. "Mom? Can you get the tub ready?"

Retha's eyes crinkled from the doorway. "Matt's got it covered. Get your swim trunks on. We're ready whenever you are."

Jamie crouched down in front of his wife. "How do you want to get there, sweetheart? Walking, or I can carry you, or we can port."

Nat tried to smile, even as the next contraction ramped up. She grabbed his shoulders and moaned as her belly shuddered. "I'll walk. I think."

Sophie scanned again as they walked down the hall. Nat was clearing tension from the contractions as well as anyone she'd ever attended. Good. They weren't all that far from transition.

Otherwise known as the moment when all hell breaks loose.

~ ~ ~

Lauren looked at Devin as they followed Nat down the hall, glad she was a mind witch. Otherwise she might have believed he was as calm as his exterior suggested. "Now what?"

"We let Nat and Jamie get in the pool." He squeezed her hand. "Relax. You need to go link with Nat next, and you want to send her some of that serenity she drinks like water."

She frowned, trying to figure out the logistics. "How do we link up with the rest of the circle?" And then felt Caro and Retha's inbound mindlinks. "Never mind."

Devin grinned. "They're always on point for the birthing circles. They'll feed to us, and we'll feed to Nat and Jamie."

Lauren barely heard him. The rising tide in her head was one of the most amazing things she'd ever felt. She paused, soaking in the vibrations. "How many people are out there?"

"Everybody." His simple answer rocked her. "The ones with magic send power. They all send love."

Lauren breathed, flooded by the magic—and added every ounce of love for her best friend and the man Nat had chosen. Then she took Devin's hand and prepared to be a conduit for the immense welcome waiting to greet one small girl.

Sophie and Ginia looked up as they knelt by the pool. Nat was deep in another contraction, Jamie spooned behind her in the birthing pool. Panic was gone. Now there was just focus.

Lauren watched—awed, but not at all surprised, by her friend's courage.

"Not long now," said Sophie, whisper quiet.

Nat's eyes opened as the contraction eased off, and she gulped from the water Ginia held out. Jamie murmured wordless gratitude and pride.

Devin took Lauren's hand again. It was time to link. She could already feel his connection with Jamie, the rock solid bond of brotherhood.

Lauren reached out, extending a gentle link to her best friend. *Feel this, Nat. Feel how much they love you.* She let the flood in her mind flow out and around Nat and the girl in her belly.

And reveled in the joy of sharing magic with her best friend for the first time. Nat's eyes shone with stunned awe, and Jamie's eyes glistened as he wrapped careful arms around his wife.

Soaked in magic, Nat rode the next contraction, body straining, and heart clear. Sophie touched Lauren's arm. "Loop in the baby. It's time."

Steeped in communal joy, Lauren reached the gentlest of connections toward the baby—and stopped breathing as a questing mindlink reached for hers. *We love you, sweet girl.*

Love surged through the birthing circle, the fourteen strong in the inner circle, and dozens more surrounding them. Time stood still as hearts called to the witching community's newest member.

For a moment, she only listened, cradled in endless love.

And then power flared, surging for freedom. The baby's mind held only one focus. She was coming. *Now.*

Nat sprang halfway out of the birthing pool, primal roar sounding as the desperate need to *push!* slammed into her body.

Lauren yanked down enough barriers to resist the screaming need to join Nat on hands and knees. Barely. Holy hell. Wasn't there supposed to be some kind of warning before this part?

Dazed and gasping for air, she watched as Nat's body finally relaxed—and then immediately surged again. Jamie held on, anguish all over his face, as the intensity overwhelmed his wife. Her voice was tortured. "I... can't. I can't." Focus shattered, her mind and body ran, looking for a place to hide.

And got hit by the third contraction in a row. God. Lauren had never felt so totally helpless.

Sophie grabbed her hand. "Pipe me in. Into Nat's head. *Now.*"

Lauren piped, throat closed in fear.

Still connected, she felt the weight of Sophie's absolute trust and love land in the middle of chaos. *You can do this, Natalia Sullivan. It's time to push, sweetheart. Your girl's on her way, and she needs your help.*

The world stopped for a moment—and then Nat drank in the hope Sophie offered. From some impossible well deep inside, she pulled out more strength. And this time, when the contraction hit, every cell in her body bore down.

And to Lauren's utter shock, Nat's fear vanished, replaced by utter commitment.

Sophie smiled in deep approval. "Good." She looked over at Lauren, command in her eyes. "She's going to get her part done. You get ready for our baby girl's magic."

Lauren clutched Devin's hand. She'd heard the stories. Until this moment, she hadn't really believed them.

She believed now.

Leaving Nat in Sophie's abundantly capable hands, Lauren focused on her connection with Devin. They felt the steady support of the circle, waiting and ready.

She held her breath as Nat quieted for a moment.

And then hung on for dear life as the dynamite lit.

~ ~ ~

Sierra was the first to feel the enormous storm blasting out of the room where Nat gave birth, every channel inside her tuned to the massive energies. She held tight to Mia on one side, Aervyn on the other. Birthday-boy's eyes were big as plates. "It's just like me. Just like when I was born."

The nine witches of the inner circle, led by Caro and Retha, turned as one, facing the torrent of power streaming out of the bedroom.

Sierra watched in awe as witch after witch behind them stood up. Dozens of them, inside the house and out, all doing the same thing. Taking whatever power they could handle and grounding it. Safety for the baby witchling.

One small boy with purple hair quietly scooped and grounded, never touching more power than she might use to light a candle. His steady effort of love nearly brought her to her knees.

Standing up, she joined in. Scoop and ground. Keep the baby safe.

Nell looked up as thunder crashed overhead and wind screamed around the house. "Damn. I guess she's an air witch too."

"No." Sierra gulped and tried to read the lines as power beat against all of them. "She's doing all this with fire. I think."

Aervyn nodded, eyes even bigger. "She's really scared, Mama."

Nell held his hand more tightly. "We need to hold on for her. Hold her and take all this power of hers and put it somewhere safe."

Sierra kept collecting and grounding, speechless that one small baby could handle this much power.

And then she felt the lightning bolt coming.

Magic from the circle instantly rose up to meet it. A shield. Soft. Absorb the lightning.

NO! Sierra jumped forward. Too late. She yanked for power as lightning hit the shield and sprayed off in a hundred directions, witches scrambling to clean it up.

Sierra shook her head at the mess as the energies coming from the birthing room eased off momentarily. Dammit, had none of them ever caught lightning before?

No. Devin's voice held a trace of humor. *And I think there's more coming. You're in charge of lightning patrol. Take Aervyn.*

She grabbed wonderboy's hand. "Time to go be superheroes. Can you get us up on the roof? With the brooms?"

Aervyn looked scorched by joy.

"Hang on." Nell grabbed his other hand just as they ported.

Sierra swung around, agitated. They had to hurry. "I can keep him safe!"

"Of course you can." Nell added fireglobes back to their brooms. "Now you'll be able to see him. Go!"

A quick landing on the roof ridge, energies sizzling all around them, and then they were on their broomsticks, capes flying. Sierra had a hard, dish-shaped shield up just as the next lightning bolt crackled. She shot left, clinging to the broom with her knees, and snagged it with the very edge of the shield. Victory. Barely.

Hard and fast now, lightning flung itself down from the sky, streaks of searing fire slicing the black of the darkest night. Wind buffeted their brooms, tossing them around as they flew the shield, storm-riders bouncing lightning back up into the sky.

Sierra ducked under a streak of fire just as it branched—and heard Aervyn laughing like a maniac, even as he blazed power. No birthday present on earth was ever going to beat this.

Except possibly a new cousin.

~ ~ ~

Devin could feel Lauren trying to soothe the baby. It was kind of like trying to pet a tiger. A really mad, scared one.

At least the house hadn't gone up in flames yet, thanks to a seriously busy magic bucket brigade.

He saw Sophie, head down beside Nat's, encouraging her through yet another round of pushing, Jamie glued to her back. Maybe someday the terror would fade, and he'd only remember the fierce beauty of it.

Right now, he was too busy trying to manage all the totally reckless magic his niece-to-be was throwing at the world on her way into it. They had a broomstick lightning patrol, every water witch in the place putting out fires, and he was pretty sure this half of Berkeley mistakenly thought it was morning, courtesy of the fire globe as big as a small planet that currently hung over the house.

Quite the way to light up the darkest night of the year.

With what little energy he could spare, Devin reached out for his mother's mind. *Everyone holding on out there?*

Of course. Her calm unfrayed some of his nerves. *What else would we be doing?*

I can't believe you did this three times.

Her laughter bubbled. *You can thank me later.*

He reached for yet another blazing power stream. Little punk was trying to heat up the water in the birthing pool. *That'll boil both you and your mama, silly girl.*

Lauren slid back into contact, her mind lurching. *Toughest damn negotiation of my life.*

She throw you out again?

Yeah.

His niece needed some work on her manners. He grinned. She was such a Sullivan.

He scanned, watching for her next trick—and then in a whoosh, the storm of power vanished.

His eyes snapped open.

And saw Lauren's, gooey with joy, peering over his shoulder into the birthing pool.

Slowly, he turned around—and saw the latest baby Sullivan floating in the water, absolutely calm, big brown eyes looking up at her parents.

He was almost prepared for the wallop of love that hit his heart—Aervyn's birth hadn't been that long ago.

He was totally unprepared for the hammer stroke of longing. He looked at the gorgeous naked baby curled up in her parents' arms. And wanted. Yearned. Then he looked over at Lauren— and knew who he wanted it with.

He cursed. Mightily. He pleaded with whoever might be listening.

Then he gave up and let the third tidal wave of the day knock over his heart.

Reaching out, he wrapped an arm around Lauren's shoulders, pulling her into his chest. Taking one last moment, he breathed in the still-salty smell of her hair. And dove in. "Marry me."

Her eyes, snapping up to his, looked exactly the way they had before the fifteen-foot wall of water had engulfed them earlier in the day. "What?"

He'd spent a lifetime with mind witches. He said nothing. Just opened.

He watched the waves crashing in her eyes. Disbelief. Desire. Fear. Love. And then, finally, the one he really needed to see. Lauren found her inner sense of adventure.

He spun her around, grinning, as she crushed her lips to his. She might want to take swimming lessons.

Chapter 24

Moira sat in the big rocking chair in Jamie and Nat's living room and waited for the guest of honor to make an appearance. It had always been a joy to be present at the birth of a babe—but these days, she treasured each one even more.

Perhaps she would get to rock a wee one today. And if not today, then with the magic of Realm, there was always tomorrow.

She looked across at the faces sitting on the couch. Devin—a man who had finally grown up. The lovely Lauren sitting beside him, looking utterly shell-shocked. Ah, she'd just signed on for a wild ride, that one. The most reckless Sullivan in the bunch, and at least a couple of babes with talent in their future, if her scrying bowl wasn't mistaken.

Sierra, draped in the wonder of her first witchling birth.

Nell and Daniel, remembering the not-so-long-ago arrival of their small boy.

It was Moira's old ears that heard the steps on the stairs first. She got her arms ready—and then, as Jamie stepped into the room, his girl cuddled in his arms, knew the little one had a stop or two to make first.

Kenna. *Born in fire.* A seeker, this beautiful little one would be. Her eyes were open, dark, and shining—such an alert little thing.

Moira watched. Instinct tugged at her. A small bit of Kenna's destiny waited in the room.

Sierra reached out her arms, and then dropped them back, eyes apologetic. "Sorry. I'm sure other people want to hold her first."

Moira was watching Sierra's eyes—and she knew the magic of the night was not quite yet done. "We'll have our turn, dear girl."

Jamie looked at Moira and raised an eyebrow, puzzled. Seniority usually earned her the first cuddle. She simply smiled.

He handed Kenna into Sierra's waiting arms and took a seat beside Moira. "What are you up to?" he murmured.

"Just watch."

Sierra nestled the gorgeous girl in her lap—and began to sing. A beautiful lullaby, old and deep, the melody floating into all their souls. Moira's heart welled—it was the same song she'd sung to Amelia and every babe she'd ever rocked.

Ever so gently, Sierra pulled magic as she sang, wrapping Kenna in a shimmer of watery light. The small girl stared, with the knowing eyes of one newly born.

Jamie grinned and kept his voice low. "Hot damn. We have a babysitter."

"You have much more than that, my boy." Moira lifted her voice as the lullaby ended. "I see she's picked her guardian angel, then."

Sierra looked up, a dopey smile on her face. "What's that?"

"There's an old Irish legend, child." Moira's eyes misted as Sierra's gaze was pulled back to the sweet, tiny girl nestled in her lap. "When a baby is born, the first face they favor, besides their mama and papa—that's the person meant to be their guardian angel. Someone to watch over them and help keep them safe."

Sierra looked up in awe. "And how do I do that?"

"Just love her, child." Moira felt the truth of what she was about to say flowing in her blood. And this time, she was saying it about the right child. "It has been, and always will be, love that keeps a reckless soul safe."

Kenna stirred—and the same dancing lights Sierra had made during the lullaby started to shimmer. Sierra giggled softly, enthralled by the baby's magic, and reached out to touch her cheek. "Well then, smart girl, your first lesson is about groundlines." She moved her fingers slightly. "See? You just take this little bit here, and tie it over there…"

Nell leaned over quietly as Sierra and Kenna gazed on each other in mutual adoration. "I've never heard that story before."

Moira just smiled. Irish legends were very flexible things.

Thank you!

I hope A Reckless Witch was a good read. Please feel free to share it with a friend.

Want the next book in the series? Visit www.deborageary.com to sign up for my New Releases email list. The series so far:

A *Hidden Witch* (book 2)

A *Reckless Witch* (book 3)

A *Nomadic Witch* (coming late spring 2012)

And five more in the planning stages!

Made in the USA
San Bernardino, CA
22 February 2014